MADELINE MARTIN

DIVERSIONBOOKS

Also by Madeline Martin

Deception of a Highlander

Diversion Books
A Division of Diversion Publishing Corp.
443 Park Avenue South, Suite 1008
New York, New York 10016
www.DiversionBooks.com

Copyright © 2015 by Madeline Martin
All rights reserved, including the right to reproduce this book or portions thereof in any form whatsoever.

This is a work of fiction. Names, characters, places and incidents either are the product of the author's imagination or are used fictitiously. Any resemblance to actual persons, living or dead, events or locales is entirely coincidental.

For more information, email info@diversionbooks.com

First Diversion Books edition August 2015.
Print ISBN: 978-1-62681-709-8
eBook ISBN: 978-1-62681-708-1

To the minions.
You keep my life full of laughter,
inspiration and love.

Chapter One

Angus, Scotland - June 1606

Brianna Lindsay's time had run out.

Soil caked the undersides of her rounded fingernails and creased her palms like black sin. There was still much to do.

The sun burned high overhead, baring her deeds to all. Reminding her she could be discovered at any moment.

She plunged her hands into the cool, moist earth. But she mustn't delve too far.

She didn't know how deeply they'd buried him.

Her body clenched around another dry retch. There was nothing left for her stomach to give.

She could go no further. The gouged hole would have to do.

The rosebush at her side stretched away with twisted limbs, and its leaves quivered in the wind. Did it seek another way out as she did? Did it feel the looming threat?

"We all must make our sacrifices." She spoke under her breath in a soothing tone that would fall deaf upon wicked thorns.

It mattered not.

She had no other options. None, except this or surrender.

And there were too many lives at stake.

A pearl of sweat tickled a path from her brow to her chin. She swiped it away with a dirty fist.

The moisture upon her cheeks should be tears.

Edzell Castle had lost its earl the day before. No one could find out, most especially her uncle. Not until she figured out an alternative.

Bernard, her Captain of the Guard, had left hours before with a letter tucked safely in his vest.

This would all be over when he returned from Edinburgh. She hoped.

She grasped the hearty base of the rosebush and cradled its roots. With reverent care, she transplanted it into the freshly turned earth, beside the other three. Only two more remained to be sown into the ground.

Together, they would cover the makeshift grave in a tangle of fragrant blooms and barbed vines.

At least he lay in consecrated ground.

For the countless time, she willed the tears to come. For the countless time, still, they did not.

She winced beneath a slice of regret.

No matter how callous he had been, no matter how cruel a position he had left her in, surely Brianna should mourn the death of her own father.

* * *

Colin MacKinnon quickened his pace through the maze of curling ferns. Sunlight cut through the trees overhead and flickered around him, hastening his sense of urgency. The rich scent of soil rose from underfoot and mingled with the copper odor of blood.

He locked his arms beneath the battered old man he carried. As it was, the man's breath grew shallower by the moment. He would not last long.

"Do ye see the castle, Alec? Are we close?" Colin asked. He would run if necessary.

Alec strode several paces ahead, his large body clearing the forest's heavy growth from their path. "Aye, I see it just ahead."

"We're almost there," Colin said through gritted teeth. "Ye're almost home."

The man's mouth moved, and a weak exhale gasped through thin, bloodied lips.

Colin ducked beneath a veil of thin branches and found

himself bathed in the warmth of dazzling sunlight. Lush grass stretched before him, lining his path. Beckoning.

Edzell Castle rose at its center, nestled like a rare pearl behind walls tinged pink with precious sandstone.

Colin glanced over his shoulder to where a small white building sat against the forest. A servant knelt in the dirt beside a row of rosebushes, her long brown braid thrown over her shoulder.

Before either he or Alec could call out, her head snapped up. She tensed. The narrowed look on her comely face was not one of welcome.

"Who are you?" she demanded, her voice sharp. Suspicious.

Colin turned, and her gaze dropped to the man in his arms. "We seek Lady Lindsay."

All hostility drained from her widened eyes. She lurched to her feet and staggered toward them in a frantic run.

"What have you done?" Accusation screamed from her wild gaze. Soil smudged one flushed cheek.

"I seek Lady Lindsay," Colin said again.

The man stirred, and a low moan croaked from his throat.

"He's alive," she gasped. "What's happened? Who has done this?"

His patience waned. The dying man did not have time for the servant's lamentations. "Damn it, lass, listen to me. He is badly wounded and requests Lady Lindsay. All questions will be answered later. For now, I demand to see the lady of the castle."

Her generous lips fell open, but no words emerged. She dropped her gaze to the man, and her brows knit together. "This way." She motioned toward the white building and sprinted ahead, her thick braid bouncing against her back with each hastened step.

The structure was cool inside, a reprieve from the heat of the noonday sun. Costly stained glass windows lined either side of the walls and shot streaks of reds, yellows, and golds across the rows of wooden benches. A church. The location was fitting for a man soon dead.

Colin glanced down at the man, Bernard, in his arms, and

found his face had gone white beneath the streaks of blood. A bad sign.

The lass pulled a length of embroidered white silk from the altar and spread it on the ground. "Lay him here," she said.

Colin hesitated. The workmanship on the fabric was incredibly detailed in its depiction of the Garden of Eden, each leaf and flower crafted with obvious care. He glanced up at the servant. She would be whipped for using so costly a cloth for a dying man.

"Lay him here," she repeated, her voice strained with desperation.

Colin sank to his knees. "He is bleeding heavily."

"I understand." Her tone had lost its edge and was soft, somber. "Please." She motioned to the altar cloth once more with trembling fingers tinged black and dirty.

Colin eased Bernard to the silk-covered ground. The old man was finally home.

The furrows of pain on the man's weathered face smoothed into a smile. "Thank you." The words rasped from within his chest. He was still alive. There was still time.

The woman fell to the ground, her head bent over him. "What's happened to you?" Her voice broke in a way that would tug at any man's chest. Colin was no exception.

"Brianna?" The dying man squinted up at the servant.

"Yes," she whispered. "I'm here."

Colin cleared his throat, an inadvertently loud interruption in the silence of the church. "He needs Lady Lindsay," he said one final time.

"What?" The woman looked up at him from where she sat with her rough skirts tucked under her legs. "You don't understand." She pressed her dirty hand to her chest. "I *am* Lady Lindsay."

Chapter Two

Blood stained Brianna's fingers and smeared the floors of the church. Sunlight poured in through the stained glass windows and filled the room with a frantic splash of colors.

This couldn't be happening.

The auburn-haired Highlander who'd carried Bernard into the church stood in front of her. "We'll be outside if ye need us, my lady."

She gave a nod, a feat difficult to do when her throat swelled with such anguish, and barely registered the sound of two sets of heavy feet leaving the building.

Her gaze was fixed on Bernard, on the free-flowing wounds peppering his body, on the unnatural gray of his face. Realization sliced through her heart like a sharpened blade.

Bernard would soon be dead.

She caught his thin hand in hers and tried to swallow away the tightness of her throat.

"I failed you." His words were almost inaudible. From the grimace on his face, they had cost him dearly.

She blinked rapidly, and yet tears still welled in her eyes and rolled down her cheeks. "You don't need to speak."

He shook his head, a subtle rocking of the back of his skull side to side against the ground. Blood streaked brilliant crimson through his thin, white hair. "The letter was not deliv—"

"Please do not worry yourself." Her voice shook. The letter to Parliament could be addressed later.

His soft blue eyes watered with despair. "They took it."

The air quit her lungs.

No.

"Who?" She kept her voice low, free of the anxiety clawing inside of her.

"No livery." Deep lines of pain etched his face. "Highlanders tried to help."

His fingers curled around her hand. Even on his deathbed, he sought to offer her comfort. A sob burst from within her and echoed off the empty walls.

The sigh exhaled from deep in his chest, and his body went still.

"No," she mouthed. "Please."

His face relaxed, and all the decades of laughter and earnest joy remained creased around the aged skin of his eyes and mouth. A burning ache exploded within her. Disbelief. Desperation. Despair.

She bent beneath its weight. Choking cries ripped through the silence, and grief trailed hot down her face.

She would not think of the letter now, nor what its loss meant. How could she when Bernard lay dead on the floor of her chapel?

Bernard hadn't only been Edzell's Captain of the Guard, he was the only surviving member of the household who could vouch for her legitimacy, the only one of sound mind who had been at her mother's side and could verify she had been faithful. Bernard had been the father the earl had never sought to be.

Now he was gone, and Brianna had lost two fathers in as many days.

* * *

Colin glanced toward the white building from where Lady Lindsay had still not emerged. Brianna. The dying man had called her Brianna.

Regret lashed through Colin. He should have been able to stop the band of men attacking the old man, but he and Alec had been a distance away when the first blow landed. The aggressors had moved quickly. Too quickly.

Their work was that of paid men, not bandits or rogues. The attack had not been a random act of violence.

He paced in the shade along the edge of the forest, his steps silent except for the whisper of grass against his boots. This was not how he'd wanted to make his appearance at Edzell Castle. Certainly not how he had wanted to meet Lady Lindsay.

Alec stood immobile beside him, lacking the restlessness plaguing Colin. "No a bad place to live, aye?"

Colin stopped and stared up at the rose-hued castle. His gaze skimmed the familiar rectangular block-shaped layout common among Lowland nobles. A second building rose lower than the first, the worn stone edges of an older structure never torn down.

"No a bad place to live at all," Colin said.

Alec shrugged beside him. "I've slept in worse places."

Colin shoved Alec's shoulder. "Damn right ye've slept in worse places." He glanced to where the entrance to the little white church still stood tightly shut. "Mark my words, Alec. This will be my land."

The Lindsay seal marked the arching entrance, declaring the castle's ownership. A sign meant to ward away outsiders. The MacKinnon seal would grace the delicate stone beside it someday and boldly declare the opulent castle his.

Thus far, Edzell had proved true every rumor he'd heard of the Lindsay fortune. His chest swelled with resolve.

He would prove to his father that he was worthy of the family land. He would win the title wrongfully denied the firstborn son of Laird MacKinnon.

First though, he'd have to woo Lady Lindsay into marriage.

* * *

Brianna cracked open the wooden door of the chapel and peered out to where the copper-haired Highlander paced. He waited for her as he said he would. For her protection or did he want coin for his deed?

The leather of his boots shone with quality, and intricate

carvings etched the hilt of the sword slung between his shoulder blades. The man had money.

His dark-haired friend lurked nearby, scanning her home with a look that could only be described as mistrust.

Both wore the garb of the Highlands, with loose-flowing white leines on their torsos and plaids slung around their hips.

She didn't want to face them—she wanted to curl into a ball on the ground and give in to a fresh bout of grief. But Bernard would not have let her do that. He would have gently reminded her she was the lady of the keep and encouraged her to be strong.

She brushed a strand of hair from her slick forehead and tucked it back into her braid. Tempting though it was, she could not hide in the chapel forever.

She pushed the door open and stepped outside. Shards of sunlight splintered in her brain, blazing against the ache of her tears. She ground her teeth against the pain and forced herself forward. The sooner she paid the men for their assistance, the sooner they would leave.

Highlanders could not be trusted.

The one who'd carried Bernard stopped pacing and turned toward her. Blood stained the front of his leine. Bernard's blood.

The sight gripped her heart in a fresh clutch of pain. She pushed her gaze to his face instead and found it lined with sympathy.

"I'm sorry we couldna do more." His eyes searched her face with more scrutiny than she cared for. "Are ye well, lass?"

"I am, thank you." She hoped her forced smile would diminish the terseness of her tone and rush his plea for compensation.

His slow nod indicated he did not believe her words any more than he did her smile.

She resisted the urge to press her fingertips to her aching temples and tried again. "I am grateful for the assistance you both offered. Is there anything I can do to show my appreciation? Some coin perhaps?"

"I'd like to speak with yer Captain of the Guard." His

steady gaze did not waver from her face.

The muscles of her back tightened. Perhaps she should not be honest, but had they meant her harm, they would already have taken advantage of the situation. "My Captain of the Guard lies upon the floor of the church." Her gaze flicked to his bloody leine once more. "His blood now stains your clothes." A harsh edge grated in her tone.

The man crossed his arms over his large chest. "I will need to speak with his replacement then."

Brianna stared up at the man in shock.

Replacement?

As if she were so cruel as to have a man at the ready in case Bernard were to die.

She shook her head, unwilling to speak lest her voice tremble. She would not appear weak before such stoic men.

He tilted his head with measured patience. "The laird then. May I speak with him?"

Her pulse spiked. This man asked too many questions, sought too many answers. "He is detained presently."

The Highlanders needed to leave.

"Ach, in that case, we will wait." He relaxed his posture and glanced toward the sky in a way that suggested he had more time than sense.

"You can't." Brianna drew a deep breath and fought for composure. "He's ill and will not be able to meet with you." It was not wholly a lie. The Earl of Edzell had been ill for over a year before he'd succumbed.

"Countess Lindsay perhaps?" the Highlander asked.

Brianna's heart squeezed with an ache that never seemed to heal. "She has been dead some years. I am the lady of the castle now."

His eyebrows rose. "I see." He narrowed his gaze at her, studying her for a moment.

She had been incorrect—the man had sense. Far too much for her comfort, in fact. And she was pinned beneath his scrutiny.

She concentrated on every part of her body, forcing herself to be still beneath his assessment. No straightening her back, no clutching her skirt with her hands or folding her arms in front of her. Such stillness made her feel more exposed than the concealing gestures she longed for.

His arms opened in surrender, as if demonstrating his lack of threat. "I'm Colin MacKinnon." He nodded toward the dark-haired Highlander. "And that's Alec MacLean. I promised yer man we would see ye to safety and that is what I intend." His eyes locked with hers, and his head lowered as he spoke. "That said, we wish to stay the night in yer castle."

Stay within the castle? Her gaze trailed over his broad shoulders, the corded muscle of his exposed forearms, and the powerful expanse of his chest. She craned her neck, taking in his imposing height. He could crush her skull beneath those large hands if he were so inclined.

The Highlander thought her father feeble and knew her Captain of the Guard lay dead.

She'd revealed too much and now regretted what she'd so willingly, so foolishly, volunteered.

He stepped toward her, his face softening. "I believe ye may be in considerable danger."

Chapter Three

"I dinna mean to frighten ye." Though he kept his voice soft when he spoke, it did not ease the wide-eyed stare from her face.

"You tell me my life is in danger, and then you say you didn't mean to frighten me?" Her words pitched high at the end of her question.

He took a step toward her and tried to ignore the way her body flinched before going stiff-still once more. "The men who attacked your Captain of the Guard may come back to ensure he is dead. I've seen it before."

Especially men like those who assaulted the old man, but Colin tempered his tongue. Such information was meant for the ears of men, not the fairer sex.

Brianna's chin rose a notch. "I am not unprotected."

Alec snorted beside him. Her gaze shot to him before settling on Colin once more, her eyes bright with indignation.

Colin frowned. "While we waited, I glanced at yer castle entrance and saw but one guard. If the band of men who attacked yer Captain of the Guard come here, they would be inside yer walls within moments."

Her gaze slid toward the entrance of the castle. "One guard?"

Colin nodded slowly. "Aye, my lady. If ye allow us to stay tonight, we will keep watch to ensure ye're safe."

She lowered her head, and her fingertips rested on the center of her brow. "Very well." She looked up. "You may stay, but only until morning." The delicate muscles of her neck tightened. "However, you will not be permitted in the main part of the castle. Those doors will be locked."

Ah, the famed Lowland hospitality. Though perhaps

the lass was not as naïve as she appeared if she exacted such caution with strange men. "Of course, my lady. We will leave after we help ye find a suitable replacement for yer Captain of the Guard."

Her smile was brittle. "That will not be necessary."

"It is more necessary than ye realize."

Her suspicious glare turned frosty. "I am perfectly capable of selecting my own Captain of the Guard."

He closed the distance between them with one step, but this time she did not back away. This time her head lifted in challenge.

"Do ye know when a man is brave?" he asked. "When he willna run, when he will stay and fight?"

"I know of bravery." She crossed her arms tightly over her chest, that indignant look flashing in her large brown eyes once more.

"Bravery off the battlefield is easily feigned. Ye want a man whose eyes glint with power, whose confident words are backed by confident actions, one who will be looked up to by other men. One whose body bears the scars of battle." Her fair skin appeared flawless in the bright sunlight. Smooth and creamy beneath the smears of dirt, unscathed by the foul effects of war.

He lowered his voice. "Do ye know a man so intimately that ye can detect how brave he truly is?"

She drew a sharp breath and her eyebrows furrowed. "How dare you ask such a question?"

He held his position and reveled in the clean lavender scent wafting from her glossy hair. It'd been too long since he'd smelled anything but sweat and dirt. "I ask only what ye should know if ye intend to select yer own Captain of the Guard, aye?"

A bonny flush colored her cheeks.

"Or ye can at least accept my advice tomorrow morning before we leave." He eased back and left her to make her own decision. He'd made his point.

Her lips pursed and lent her young face a shrewd appearance. "I will allow you to offer your advice."

He truly did not wish to leave her unprotected. He'd been

entirely honest about that. The few guards Colin had seen would easily prove the need for his continued presence within Edzell.

He glanced at Lady Lindsay's clenched jaw.

First though, he would have to convince her.

* * *

Brianna's shoes rang sharp against the stone floor of the hall, a harsh accompaniment to the steady swish of her fine skirts. She'd worn her blue silk gown with the silver buttons and delicately embroidered sleeves. Yesterday she'd appeared before the Highlanders as a servant. Today she would leave no question in their minds that she was lady of the castle.

She paused before the main door and pulled the heavy iron key from her pocket. They would be waiting on the other side. Her hand skimmed the slick fabric of her left pocket, fingering the comforting shape of her dagger. In case they decided to do more than assist in the selection of the next Captain of the Guard.

Not that she intended to listen to their opinions, regardless. She would placate them by feigning interest in their choice, and then they would leave.

Finally.

There were too many questions she could not answer and too many secrets that could be unearthed, especially by men she did not trust.

The key slid into the greased lock with ease. She paused and mentally combed through plausible questions they might ask, filtering through her own plausible answers. One loose reply and the truth of the earl's hidden death and her illegitimacy could come unraveled.

Bernard's signature on the letter to Parliament was supposed to secure her legitimacy and tie Edzell to her forever. Her throat tightened at the thought of the old man.

Bernard.

The stress of her situation gave way to a peel of hurt. He had been so battered, so wounded before his death.

He'd died trying to help her.

She turned her head to the side, but the physical movement could not knock the painful thought from her mind. She could not dwell on such things. Not when there were other matters to think on. Like what she could use to prove herself the rightful heir to the Lindsay estate. She had pored over the earl's documents through the night and into the gentle grays of morning. Her efforts had been in vain. Not one document mentioned her as his daughter.

An old wound that would never cease to sting.

The key twisted easily until she heard the subtle click of the lock giving way. She pushed through the door and stepped from the shadows of the heavy stone walls into the blinding morning sunlight, a radiance grating to her dark mood.

Her unwelcome guests leaned against the shaded wall of the castle with an ease that rattled her all the more. Resentment flared through her. She would have preferred Bernard's replacement wait until he was at least buried.

The dark-haired Highlander watched her cross the courtyard, his gaze steady, his face unreadable. The other man, the one who had spoken to her yesterday, nodded in greeting and gave her a grin so wide she had to fight the urge to roll her eyes.

"I dinna expect ye so early, Lady Lindsay," he said.

She surveyed the empty courtyard, and her back straightened with awareness. Other guards should be present. "Nor did I expect you to be so full of compliments so early," she said with a smile. It was meant to remind him of his place, to check his carefree humor.

"Ach, if I were complimenting ye, ye'd know." He winked at her, completely nonplussed.

Did he think he was being charming?

Impatience nibbled at her fortitude.

"Before we begin," he said. "I'd like to give ye my suggestions on yer next Captain of the Guard."

"Oh?" Another sweeping glance confirmed they were the only people in the courtyard. The weight of the dagger along her thigh offered security where her own men failed. "You know my men well enough to select the one best suited for the position?"

"Aye, I do." An arrogant smile lifted his lips. "Me."

Brianna's eyebrows raised at his audacity. "You?"

"Aye. Let me be yer Captain of the Guard. Alec will, of course, stay on to help me as well."

The linen of his leine was made of exceptional quality. Expensive, like the sword on his back. "You don't need the funds. Why do you seek this position?"

His gaze met hers, soft and coaxing. "Sometimes there is more to life than coin," he said in his gentle burr.

She narrowed her eyes in an effort to further shield herself from him. "What do you imply?"

"I mean that sometimes a wandering warrior longs for a place to call home, and Edzell Castle is verra lovely." The heat of his stare remained fixed on her face. "Sometimes a man canna turn away from the lure of beauty."

* * *

Colin's true meaning was not lost on Brianna, based on the nervous press of her tongue between her full lips. She understood his words whether she cared to admit it or not. "What qualifies you to be my Captain of the Guard?"

"I was under the lead of Keiran MacDonald for the last five years and saw much war and fighting."

Not that Colin's father had been impressed.

She tilted her head in a way that demonstrated her thinning patience. "Of course you saw much war and fighting. He is, after all, a MacDonald."

If she was trying to get a rise out of him, she would be disappointed. "All the better to keep me on yer side," Colin said with a good-natured wink. "If ye dinna believe me, put me against five of yer best guards and ye'll see for yerself."

"Five?" Her eyebrow arched in disbelief.

"Aye, ye're right," he conceded. "Ye better make it ten."

The corner of her mouth tightened. "Are you trying to

impress me?"

Colin laughed, knowing his mirth would goad her further. "Dinna act as though ye dinna want to see it."

"Actually, I think I do." A slow, cunning smile slid over her lips. "I'll have my ten best guards assembled for you to fight. If you lose, you will be removed from my lands, never to return."

He shrugged off the sheathed blade he wore strapped to his back and reached for one of Edzell's unmarked practice swords. "Dinna worry." He swung the dulled weapon. "I never disappoint."

Certainly not when so much balanced on his victory.

Chapter Four

Assembling the guards had taken as long as Colin had anticipated, and longer than Brianna had expected, if her red cheeks were any indication.

Her ten best soldiers surrounded him, their expressions glowing with unwarranted confidence. Too late would they realize what a mistake that was.

Colin focused on his surroundings, marking the direction the gentle breeze shifted, his feet easily adjusting to the subtle swells and dips of the cobblestones beneath him. The borrowed practice blade in his hand was slightly off-balance. He would compensate for that with his swing.

His prize stood tersely to the side of the courtyard. She pinched her lower lip between anxious fingers, all pretense of nonchalance abandoned. Her gaze was sharp like a hawk seeking prey, seeking any show of weakness.

Colin was confident she would find none.

There was no discussion among the men to plan an attack. Instead, the first man lunged, young and overeager to prove himself, based on the wild swipe of his sword. He was careless and left his abdomen exposed when he raised his blade for a blow that would never land.

Colin stepped into the attack and ducked low. The blunted edge of his practice sword caught the lad in the stomach, knocking the wind from him. Had the battle been real, Colin's opponent would have paid for the error with his life.

Another man darted from the group and charged with the Lindsay roar in his throat. His sweat tinged the air with a musky scent. The sharp clang of their blades clashing split the air and tingled deep within Colin's ears. Three additional guards leapt into the fray.

Finally, a semblance of a team.

Colin's arms burned with the surge of a challenge. His vision sharpened, his senses in tune with every action each man made.

The battle was about to get fun.

Of the remaining five men not engaged in battle, one in particular, the one with white-blond hair, watched Colin's movements with a calculated intent. Perhaps there was a worthy opponent among Edzell's soldiers after all.

Colin dispatched the four men with ease, and another four took their place. Each jab and thrust of their dull blades was done without finesse. Brute force powered their moves—and poorly.

Their labored breathing suggested a lack of regular exercise. Colin would see that oversight corrected.

The glare of the sun shone down upon him, but he did not feel its heat against his back, nor was he blinded by its glint. He was a warrior, a man trained to block out the elements and focus on his opponent. Something these men would learn in good time.

One of the guards ran haphazardly toward him, face flushed and arms lax with exhaustion. Colin almost felt bad about knocking him from the fight. He caught the man's foot with his boot and sent him sprawling toward the dark cobblestones. Colin drew the flat of his blade across the man's slick neck, implying death.

Training was difficult. Colin knew all too well exactly how difficult. He also knew the importance of weapons mastery, and how many times such knowledge had saved his life.

A sharp thrust of his blade behind him caught another guard in the gut and left the man grunting in pain before walking the same defeated path as his comrades. The two remaining men lunged at Colin together, and together they were defeated with the same swipe of Colin's blade.

Only the blond man remained. He did not charge as the others, but calmly approached and lifted his sword between them with measured composure. The silent challenge grew tense in the still air.

He feinted left and thrust to the right with a grace even Colin could not teach. Colin parried the blow and whipped his blade toward the man, only to have the attack stopped with a well-executed block. There was confidence behind his opponent's moves, a natural skill.

Colin was tempted to let the fight go on longer than necessary, but there would be ample time to spar with the man in the future. Instead, Colin swung his blade toward him, stopping just before the steel connected with his opponent's neck.

Surprise flickered in the man's dark eyes. Before hard feelings could set, Colin clasped his arm in a solid grip. "Ye did verra well, lad."

The guard gave a single nod before turning to join the rest of the bested soldiers.

Colin set the borrowed practice sword in the pile he'd drawn it from. Taking on ten men was no easy feat, yet this battle had taken mere minutes. He hadn't even begun to sweat.

Brianna's men were out of shape and lacked proper training. Edzell was weak. That would all change when he became Captain of the Guard.

The same raw stare that had lingered on him as he fought now burned into his back. The lass was fascinated by him. He planned to wield that fascination to his advantage.

After all, he knew women well. Every soft, supple curve of their bodies, every sensitive bud and inviting valley. He knew when to stroke, when to tease, when to taste.

Aye, he knew women very well.

Brianna Lindsay would be no different. She may be naïve and innocent, but she was ready to fall in love.

What woman was not?

All would come with time, and Colin was a patient man. For now, he was satisfied with collecting his winnings.

• • •

A merciful breeze blew through the courtyard and fluttered the skirt of Brianna's light silk gown. Her men sagged in the shade of the chapel, their faces red and sweaty from their efforts. The Highlander turned toward her. His arms were crossed over his chest and a smile hovered on his lips.

"Well?" he inquired in a low voice. "Did I impress ye?"

Brianna nipped the tip of her tongue. He had just taken down her best men with hardly any effort. Did he not understand the insult of his actions? His rapid victory had shown how poorly trained her men were, how poorly she managed her estate to leave it so ineffectively protected. His conquest wasn't a victory to be commended—it was a slap.

Unfortunately, the speed with which he defeated her men proved his instruction necessary. Brianna knew enough about fighting and warfare to understand the Highlander's skills of fluid motions and lethal accuracy.

He stood at least one head taller than any of her men, his height and strength carried with relaxed ease. His leine fell open at the neck during the mock battle, and she could glimpse the smooth muscular flesh beneath—if she wanted to.

He uncrossed his arms and hung his thumbs from the sides of his belt. "Six months with me and ye wouldna see yer men so easily defeated."

The weight of the sun's heat was almost as unbearable as the unpalatable decision that lay before her. She scanned his well-made clothing in a most obvious manner. "I still don't understand why you are so insistent on taking Bernard's position when you so obviously do not need the funds."

That carefree smile touched his face again. "I told ye, lass, I gave my word to your servant that I would see ye safe. I dinna take my promises to the dying lightly, aye?"

She eyed him, taking in his earnest expression and stubborn wide-legged stance that declared he wouldn't give up. Part of her wished he would, yet the pragmatic part of her realized the importance of his presence, of his tutelage.

But there was another reason he wanted to stay on. Perhaps he was out of money to buy such fine things, perhaps he had nowhere to go. Perhaps there was a far more sinister reason.

Whatever it was, she would unveil the truth. In the meantime, she would take advantage of his offer to strengthen her guards.

"Very well," she said decisively. "You have six months. I'll have someone bring you to my solar after supper, and we'll arrange the details of your stay." She turned her head toward the dark-haired Highlander. "If you're half as good as your companion, I'll ensure you have a room and pay as well."

The man regarded her with icy blue eyes and gave a sound akin to a grunt. She paused, debating if he indicated agreement or not.

The Highlander with the reddish-brown hair gave her a broad grin, displaying a flash of white, straight teeth. "I'm grateful for the opportunity."

She averted her gaze, unsure of what to say, and turned toward the castle, eager to leave the overwhelming presence of the man and his rude companion. There was much to secure in preparation for the men's stay, and it had little to do with their quarters. Avoiding the uncouth Highlanders for six months would be possible, but keeping them from asking questions could prove difficult.

She needed to come up with a plan, and soon.

Chapter Five

The rush nips burned bright in the polished sconces lining the luxurious red walls of Brianna's solar. Her palm skimmed the slick front of her gown, smoothing the dark blue fabric for the countless time. Her impending meeting with the Highlander left her more disconcerted than she cared to admit.

Of course, her agitation could have something to do with the way he'd continued to glance at her through dinner. Men had watched her thus before, with a mixture of ardor and interest, but never had their gazes left her so self-conscious.

A knock at the door caused her to jump, and her fingers instinctively went to her bodice. With an irritated sigh, she dropped her hand. She refused to primp for her meeting with him. No matter how much he rattled her.

Brianna clasped the thick iron handle and tugged the door open. The Highlander gave her that infuriating grin and strode into the room with a swagger too cocky for her liking.

Magda, her aging nurse who sat in on her meetings, had not yet arrived. Surely she would arrive soon though. Brianna never left the door to her solar open, but in this rare instance, she felt it prudent to do so. She pulled the door open even wider, but the handle slipped from her grasp and the door slammed closed, sealing them in her solar.

Every muscle in her body locked in place where she stood, her hand still outstretched toward the door handle, her back still facing him. The whisper of his breathing was loud in the oppressive silence, making her all the more aware it was just the two of them.

Alone.

It was indecent.

Brianna could either open the door and acknowledge her mistake in front of the Highlander, allowing him to see she was not entirely comfortable with him, or leave herself closed in a private room with him. Too stubborn to admit fault in his presence, she left the door shut and prayed silently for Magda's swift arrival.

She turned and looked at him. His Highland garb was primitive, despite the fine material, and his shoulder-length auburn hair had been tied back with a leather thong. He still looked every bit a barbarian.

Perhaps it was best she open the door.

"Ye looked verra lovely today." His voice was surprisingly gentle. "No that ye're the kind of woman who needs a fine gown to be bonny, but it suits ye well."

The compliment disarmed her, and an unexpected heat rose to her cheeks. Immediately she felt guilty for her own thoughts of his attire. "Er-thank you," she stammered and turned from the closed door.

Men had always praised her beauty, as was deserving of her station, but their eyes never reflected their sincerity. Not like his did now.

She almost believed him.

"You and your companion will take lodging in the older part of the house." Her hands remained clasped in front of her where she couldn't tug at her bodice again. "Your private rooms are being prepared as we speak."

"Thank ye." He didn't look around the room as he spoke to her. Not once had he even glanced at its opulence, not toward the piles of ledgers, the rich wall hangings, or even the small locked chest on her desk.

His presence filled the room, and it had little to do with the way his head almost touched the painted ceiling. Awareness tingled across Brianna's flesh.

He stood close to her.

Too close. The heat of his powerful body cast a warmth upon her skin and made her want to stagger away.

Where in God's toes was Magda?

* * *

The solar had not been designed with Brianna in mind. Colin knew that the moment he stepped into the room. The lines of the desk were too sharp, the walls too savage red, the seat too large for her feminine body. But it was hers. The room was cast in a sweet, heady lavender scent, her scent, and it softened the hard masculinity of the room.

She strode stiffly past him and crossed the floor with the comfort of ownership before pulling a weathered book from the depths of an alcove. Her fingers pinched a faded blue ribbon and slid the book open with its marker.

He caught her glance toward the door again. The slight movement confirmed what he already knew. For all the strength and authority she attempted to convey, she was uncomfortable around him, if not afraid.

She started to smooth down her bodice, but stopped midway and balled her hand into a fist. "My nurse should be arriving soon. She is usually present for all my appointments."

For all her appointments. Her mother was dead, her father ill, and there was no steward per what Colin had assessed with subtle questioning earlier that day.

The lass was clearly running the estate.

It was an unusual thing for a girl, especially one with a dowry and of marriageable age, but she appeared to wear the responsibility like a mantle.

She strode past him once more, settled into the chair, and craned her neck over the ledger. She looked almost lost in the slick leather upholstery.

Colin settled into the chair opposite the desk. As much as her chair was too large for her, his chair was too small for him. One shift in the wrong direction would send the wobbly legs crushing beneath him. "If ye canna feel safe with yer Captain of the Guard, who can ye feel safe with?"

Her eyebrows lifted in surprise, then knit together as if she was mulling the concept over.

Rather than reply, she pulled a quill from the pewter inkpot and regarded him from across the wide expanse of the desktop. The feather trembled where it perched in her hand. Her fingers were still stained from the dark, rich earth. She gave him a pointed look, drawing his attention to the warm honey-brown of her eyes once more. "You will receive lodging and food for your services, as well as a stipend."

The quill scratched against the parchment before she slid the book in his direction.

Colin glanced at the number written on the ledger.

"Does this seem fair?" she asked.

"Aye, verra much so," he answered. The funds were generous, even for the role of Captain of the Guard. Still, the amount was insignificant next to the wealth he'd amassed while in the employ of Kieran MacDonald. But guards did not work for free, and he wasn't eager to arouse suspicion of his true purpose.

She nodded once and pulled the book toward her. Her lips pursed together, thinning her generous pout.

Colin leaned forward and watched her write in the journal with long, looping letters. "I dinna mean offense, but I've no ever heard of a woman handling an estate's accounts." He knew her father was ill, but he could not imagine a laird allowing his daughter to run the estate.

"And I've not ever heard of a Highlander being in charge of a Lowland army." She lifted her head in a silent challenge before she shook a pewter cup over the ledger. Fine sand sifted through the dotted top onto the glistening ink of freshly printed words. "I suppose we are both anomalies who should be grateful for our positions and not question them lest they be revoked." She turned to the side and blew the drying powder off the page.

"I need to know who I should speak with regarding the castle's defenses," Colin said.

She lifted her chin. "That would be me."

Oh, Alec was going to love that. The thought of him taking orders from a lass dwarfed by her seat of authority was almost more than Colin could bear. He choked down his mirth. "But ye're a woman."

Brianna snapped her book of accounts shut in a cloud of dust. "And I am the one who will answer your questions." She stood so abruptly that her chair screamed in protest against the stone floor.

She eased around her desk with a graceful sway of her hips and returned to the alcove, book in hand.

He turned in his seat, watching her walk. There was slow sensuality to the way her round bottom swished the fine silk of her dress, even more so when he knew the act was unintentional. "What do ye know of battle?" he asked.

She slid the ledger back into the alcove before turning to him with a proud tilt to her jaw. "I have read many books on war, and I've studied Di Grassi's manuals extensively. In Italian." Her chin tipped higher with pride, as if daring him to be impressed with her feat.

Knowing Italian didn't win battles, but considering he'd already offended her at least twice, probably more, he swallowed his reply and rose from his chair. Assaulting her with inquiries was hardly the way to begin wooing.

He approached her with a slow intent he hoped would not frighten her. She did not move, not until he was directly in front of her, then she took a step back and bumped into the wall.

Her brow furrowed slightly and her cheeks pinked. Her mouth was heart-shaped, soft pink against her alabaster smooth skin, her lower lip slightly larger than the top. Perfect for teasing with his tongue.

He leaned toward her, lured by the temptation of her innocent mouth.

Wooing Brianna Lindsay was going to be enjoyable.

He took her small hand in his and looked down upon it. Her palm was slick with sweat beneath his thumb, confirmation that he did indeed make her nervous. As if the quickened rise and fall of her bosom did not suggest as much already.

Black smears stained her fingers, though now upon closer inspection, it was evidently ink and not soil as he'd assumed. Some stains were fresh, some set in the grooves of her fingertips. The lass wrote often, if her hands were any indication.

"What are you doing?" she demanded.

"Checking for calluses from handling a battle axe." He gave her a teasing wink and was rewarded with a tentative smile.

He shifted closer, so the fabric of her gown whispered against his body, the nervous flush along the top of her bosom was visible. Her sensual lips appeared petal-soft in the low, golden light and sparked a deep pull of desire in his loins.

His thumb skimmed the graceful point of her chin, and he felt more than heard her soft intake of breath, a gentle whisper of air across the back of his hand. Her face tilted up, her mouth parted.

He had to kiss her, to taste what he knew would be sweet and intoxicating. Just enough to lure her in.

Or so he told himself.

Colin bent over her, and while she did not pull away, he could sense her uncertainty. Her stare dropped to his mouth, and her tongue darted nervously between her lips, wetting them, tempting him beyond what she could possibly comprehend.

The solar door slammed open then with an abrupt smack, snapping their delicate thread of intimacy and leaving them exposed to the intruder.

Chapter Six

Brianna remained frozen where she was with her bottom pressed against the plaster behind her and the wall of Colin's body before her, massive and filling all the space around her. Someone was in the room. A flutter of panic scrambled in her chest. Someone had entered the room.

They could not be caught thus.

She tried to move away, succeeding only in slamming the back of her head against the wall in a righteous thwack of pain. Stars danced in front of her eyes and the Highlanders grip tightened on her palm. "Yer head."

When had he held her hand?

She pulled herself from his grasp and gingerly brushed the back of her head. Her fingertips met the swell of a large bump but returned dry. No blood.

Magda sauntered into Brianna's line of vision with a nonchalant smile on her lips, as if she was not over half an hour late.

Brianna's chest squeezed. Her old nurse was having one of her bad days.

Magda's gaze settled on Brianna, and one smooth gray eyebrow arched in an austere manner.

"Did you begin the meeting early?" Magda asked. Her kind, blue eyes narrowed with as much of a threatening look as she was ever able to muster.

The Highlander had the decency to step back before turning to address Magda. "Ach, ye must be the nurse Lady Lindsay spoke of. What a lucky man I am to be in a room with two beauties."

Magda was not swayed. "May I ask what you were doing with my ward?"

"Aye," the Highlander said readily. "I was checking her hands for callouses from a battle axe."

"A battle axe?"

"I imagine two ladies as bonny as ye dinna need a battle axe." He winked. "I imagine men are always verra ready to help."

Magda ran a hand over her hair, smoothing the graying gold of her perfect coif. Color warmed her withered cheeks. "A flatterer. You, sir, are the worst kind."

Was that a smile on Magda's face? Brianna stared. Had the Highlander won over her nurse so quickly?

"He was just leaving," Brianna said sharply. She edged away from her cornered position and crossed the room toward the open door.

Magda tilted her head in light chastisement. "I don't believe I've been introduced to this man yet."

Before Brianna could open her mouth, the barbarian bowed with all the grace of a courtier. "Colin MacKinnon, my lady."

"A strong name for a Highland lad." Magda nodded to herself. "You come from good stock."

He inclined his head. "Thank ye, madam."

Brianna watched the exchange with trepidation. The conversation couldn't last much longer—they seldom ever lasted this long on bad days.

Brianna had to stop this. Now. "I'll have someone show you and your companion to your rooms."

She caught Magda's furrowed brow and noted the look of confusion flutter across the woman's face. Brianna's heart slid into her belly.

She tried again. "Please, if we can just leave—"

"Greetings, sir. I don't think I've met you yet." Magda looked pointedly toward the Highlander.

Brianna cast a wary glance at him, waiting for the cruel laughter she was certain would follow.

"My name is Colin MacKinnon, madam." He bowed low once more.

"A strong name for a Highland lad. Ye come from good stock." Magda nodded, and appreciation lit her rheumy blue gaze.

Everything inside Brianna winced. If forgetting the man were not enough for him to mock the old woman, surely the repeat of the exact phrase she'd uttered before would earn his mirth. Any other outsider would be slapping his knee by this point.

But the smile on the man's face was not malicious. It was as genuine as it had been before. "Thank ye, madam."

Brianna watched him carefully, waiting for a sign of cruel mockery. None came.

"Shall we?" He motioned politely toward the door.

Brianna gave a slow nod, but could not bring herself to move forward. Aside from Bernard, no man had ever been so gracious toward Magda on her bad days.

"After ye, lass." He motioned with his palm for Magda to proceed ahead of him.

"Ach! I haven't been called a lass in years." A deep blush stained the old woman's cheeks once more, and Brianna felt a carefree smile touch her own lips.

The Highlander extended his hand toward her in silent invitation for her to walk ahead of him. She stepped into the hall with automatic movements, her mind reeling. Perhaps the stranger was not as bad as she had initially assumed. She glanced at him from beneath her lashes.

Certainly she had never seen eyes so green as those belonging to Colin MacKinnon.

・ ・ ・

Sweat ran down Colin's temple, and the sun burned against his bare back. It was the hottest damn day of the year, and not a semblance of a breeze passed through the still courtyard.

"Again," he ordered.

The men did not complain at being told to perform the action for the tenth time. They lined up with their practice swords pulled from their scabbards and dutifully lunged at one another in mock battle. Heat flushed their faces and dampened their hair. If they felt tired, they did not let it show.

The soldier with pale blond hair stepped out of line. "I feel like I don't have enough control over the blade when I parry in this position, Captain. Am I doing it wrong?" He demonstrated the maneuver, and Colin noticed the tip of his sword dip low.

"Try it like this, Jonathan." Colin stepped forward and parried, keeping the blade of his sword level.

Jonathan adjusted his weapon and lunged at Colin with a playful smirk. It connected with Colin's own sword in a solid clang.

"Think ye can take on yer Captain, eh?" Colin waggled his brows. He feinted to the right and stuck his foot out, catching Jonathan off-guard and sending him to the ground.

With a hearty laugh, Colin bent down and helped him to his feet. "Ye're getting better. Ye'll be besting me before the month is out."

A husky, feminine voice sounded behind him. "And here I thought you were training my men, yet I find you playing."

Brianna.

Colin turned toward his visitor like a plant turns toward the heat of the sun.

Almost a week had passed since they last spoke in the solar. She had avoided him since. Or at least that's what he could assume, considering he'd only ever seen the hem of her skirts whipping around corners since he arrived.

She was no longer pretending he didn't exist. Her amber eyes were on his naked torso, wide with surprise. A blush stained her cheeks, matching the luscious red of her velvet gown and making her lips stand out like a freshly picked cherry.

No doubt she wished she'd continued her evasion.

"Is it necessary to practice so obscenely naked?" She glanced toward the castle.

"Did yer men no practice without their leines prior to my arrival?" He motioned to the small army of red-faced, bare-chested soldiers.

Brianna glanced to the men, and the flush of her cheeks deepened. She lifted her head haughtily. "I have more important things to do with my time than watch the men practice."

"So I can presume it's my charming disposition that brings ye out in this heat?" He grinned down at her.

Brianna locked his stare. "You can presume I am monitoring my investment. You promised me six months, and it's been a week. I want to ensure you aren't wasting my time."

Colin held his arms out, palm up. "Are ye happy with what ye see?"

Her gaze trickled down his naked chest, and her cheeks darkened further still, a feat he had not realized possible.

"That question is highly inappropriate," she said in a breathy voice and angled herself away from him.

"I meant the men." He added a wink.

She spun back around toward him, her lips parted with a stammering explanation. "I knew what you meant—rather, it was not appropriate for you to ask so precipitously."

Her chin lifted another inch, haughty and indignant. Brianna Lindsay apparently did not like being wrong.

A carriage rattled in through the gates behind her, catching Colin's attention. It approached without slowing.

If she heard the coach's entrance, she did not acknowledge such and continued her stumbling speech of justification.

"Your skill, I confess, is most impressive," she said. "I want to ensure the men are learning what needs to be done in order to replicate your tactics. It's still so early yet, you see, and I felt I must—" Her jaw clenched.

The carriage continued forward with extreme haste.

Her fingers smoothed down the front of her bodice. "I have many tasks that require me elsewhere. Continue your training."

She didn't wait for his response before turning abruptly on her heel and stepping away from him. Directly into the path of the speeding coach.

• • •

Someone shouted Brianna's name, but the sound was too distant to register. Her focus was locked on the four great black horses charging toward her. Their musty odor assaulted her nostrils. The clatter of their hooves thundered in her ears. Their black eyes met hers with bestial indifference.

Sweat prickled her flesh and the hair on her scalp rose. Her delicate shoes slipped against the slick cobblestoned surface, and her feet were suddenly no longer beneath her. There was nothing to grab, nothing to hold onto. Her world spun around and her stomach dropped. She was falling.

Fear ripped through her heart.

This was how she would die.

Chapter Seven

Strong hands gripped Brianna's waist, halting her abrupt descent to a grisly fate.

Her backside pressed against something solid. A body hardened with muscle—warm, firm, and smelling divinely of soap and musk.

"Are ye hurt, lass?" Colin's deep voice sounded against her ear.

Her nipples tightened against her bodice, and heat flared in her cheeks.

He turned her to face him and drew her protectively into his massive arms.

Brianna licked her suddenly dry lips. The pressure of his touch burned through the fabric of her gown and left her breathless with an excitement she didn't recognize.

Her hand braced in front of her, against the heat of his naked chest. His skin was slick, and his heartbeat thudded beneath her fingertips.

She snatched her hand back, but not without an embarrassing squeak.

Brianna cleared her throat in a pathetic effort to mask the unladylike sound. "No. I'm unharmed." Her hand balled into a fist in front of her chest. The burning sensation of his naked skin against her palm did not fade. "Thank you."

He cradled her waist still, an act highly inappropriate for his station, and yet she could not find the strength to order him to release her.

His eyes glinted with a hint of mischief. "I'll make sure I train the soldiers to watch out for carriages, as well." His voice carried an intimacy that should have left her uncomfortable.

Should have, but did not.

That's the part that *did* make her uncomfortable.

"For continued safety after you leave?" she murmured, more to herself than to him. Six months would be over quickly, and he would be gone. She would be free of him.

Somehow that idea did not seem as pleasant as it had only minutes before.

"Aye, for when I leave." He smiled down at her, and a small dimple appeared in his left cheek. She hadn't noticed that before.

Her gaze lowered to the sensual line of his lips. They looked soft and supple, the way poets described them. Would they feel as soft and supple against hers? A low pulse warmed between her thighs.

"Unhand her, you savage!"

Her cousin, Lord Robert Lindsay, stepped from the glossy black carriage. He strode forward with a proud gait, his head lifted with self-importance.

Colin's fingers slid from Brianna's waist, his movements slow, caressing where his fingertips lingered on her hips.

A delicate shiver danced across her flesh. Was he so hesitant to let her go?

Her pragmatic side stepped in then, declaring her a romantic fool. And rightly so. Colin was the kind of man who flattered all women.

She was no different.

"I said unhand her," Robert repeated, stopping before them.

Dread slithered into Brianna's stomach at his presence. He would ask to see the earl. He always did. This visit from her errant suitor was wholly unwelcome.

Robert placed his hand on the decorative sword he wore at his side.

Brianna bit back a retort and offered a friendly smile. She hoped it looked more convincing than it felt. "Robert, this man is Edzell's new Captain of the Guard." Her words were spoken with measured patience. God knew she would need much of that this evening if Robert intended to stay for supper.

"I was saving her from being run over by yer horses," Colin said in a strong voice, coming to stand beside her. "I'd suggest ye no ride through here with such haste next time."

A sense of comfort slid over Brianna like a cloak. Perhaps she was not so alone in her stand against Robert after all.

"A new Captain of the Guard?" he asked incredulously. "One who is threatening his betters, no less." He snorted. "If I knew Edzell was so short on funds, I would have given you coin rather than have you select your servants from rapacious mercenaries." His eyes narrowed. "You *aren't* short on funds, are you?"

Brianna bit a sharp comment from her tongue. The last thing she needed was to offend her cousin and arouse suspicion.

Alec appeared silently beside Colin and settled into a wide stance that begged for challenge. He stared down at Robert, unblinking, his gaze hard as ice.

"At least these barbarians are a far cry better than the old goat you had here before." Laughter wheezed out of Robert's thin chest.

Brianna's throat constricted at the slight against Bernard. Poor, wonderful Bernard who had died for her.

Colin folded his arms over his chest, all the playful merriment gone from his gaze. "As Captain of the Guard, it is within my rights to know who ye are and why ye are here."

"I am Lord Robert Lindsay, cousin to the beautiful Lady Lindsay." His arms shot out, gripping her around her waist and pulling her against him. "Her betrothed."

Brianna tried to carefully extricate herself from his grasp, but his grip on her was too strong.

Before she could speak to defend herself, Colin did so, his eyebrows lifting in bored disbelief. "I am certain the lady would no agree with what ye claim, and if ye dinna release her, I'll be forced to draw my weapon."

Alec pulled his sword from its sheath behind his back, revealing black-tinged steel that reflected purple opalescence in the sun's rays. The upturn to his usually grim-set lips evidenced his hope that Robert would ignore Colin's request.

Robert's arm eased from Brianna's waist, freeing her. She sidestepped him and gasped discreetly for clean air.

"Uncivilized barbarians." The words snarled from his throat like a dog's low growl. "That's what you get when you take cheap labor, cousin. I suggest your father consult me next time before hiring anyone."

"Is there a purpose for your visit, Robert?"

"I've come to dine with you and to ask after your father."

Of course by asking after him, Robert meant speak to him. A most impossible task. Her heart and stomach churned together in a dizzying rush of anxiety.

"Very well," she said. "I'll have the cook informed of our unexpected visitors."

"I knew you would be welcome to the idea, Brianna." His dark gaze slithered down her gown and made it feel invisible.

She fought the urge to fold her arms across her breasts. Instead, she tightened her hands into fists until her fingernails bit into the softness of her palms.

With a guest like him, the evening promised to be long and arduous.

* * *

Brianna admired the small white marzipan flower set atop a precious orange, a note of beauty in an otherwise horrendous day. Having Robert at her side was unnerving, but his visit had been blessedly uneventful thus far and was drawing to a close.

Hopefully.

Magda lifted the delicate confection from her orange, her eyes bright with excitement. "What a delicious end to a remarkable meal."

Robert smirked. "I'm sure it's so good you'll want to say it twice."

Magda laughed with naïve joy at his joke.

His spiteful comments were becoming more and more unbearable.

"Perhaps she says it twice so ye can understand." Colin sat

beside Pastor Thomas at the end of the table, but Brianna still heard the barb. The pastor snorted a laugh, but quickly covered it with a muffled cough.

"This orange is as sour as the company." Robert spat a mouthful of the fruit onto his plate and rose, his hand extended toward Brianna. "Walk with me in the garden, my sweet."

She glanced toward the windows. The sun was sinking and darkness would soon descend.

"Thank you, but I'm enjoying my dessert," she said politely and bit into her orange. The juicy nectar exploded against her tongue with a tangy sweetness, cool and refreshing on the warm summer evening. The bitterness of Robert's fruit doubtless lay with the man eating it.

"In that case, I shall seek out your father. He left me waiting in the solar the entire afternoon." Robert's statement ended in a petulant tone.

Brianna did not turn toward her pastor. Not when the young man knew so much. He'd given her father his last rights and watched him die. He knew of Brianna's decision to keep her father's death secret and let himself be sworn to secrecy.

She raised her eyebrows in mock surprise. "Father did not come down at all? Poor man has taken a turn for the worse and was most likely sleeping off his fever. Please do forgive him."

"He can beg forgiveness himself tonight when I speak to him." Robert turned away from the table. "My father wishes me to convey a message." He paused, his back still turned. "One of great import."

This time Brianna did meet Pastor Thomas's gaze, and found his gray eyes wide with fear. "Perhaps I shall join you for a walk after all." Brianna slid her chair away from the table. If her cousin possessed important information, she would need to convince him to share it with her.

She cast a regretful glance at her dessert and made her way to where Robert stood with his annoying smirk.

Together they walked outside where everything was quiet and still. The gentle pink notes of dusk settled over the lush garden and subdued the floral hues to muted grays and violets.

The oppressive heat of the day had gone with the sun, and a cool breeze stirred the leaves of manicured bushes. Brianna closed her eyes and breathed in the familiar perfume of blossoming roses. Her mother's memory would forever live on with each vibrant bloom, season after season.

"You look ridiculous when you do that." Robert's comment broke through the gentle lull of comfort and remembrance.

Despite her determination not to let his criticism bother her, his words hit their mark, and self-consciousness edged through her.

She opened her eyes and found his face an inch from hers. "Marry me, Brianna."

"No, but thank you." She backed up, and a marble bench caught her behind the knees. She sat down hard. The tight grin on Robert's face told her everything she needed to know.

He dusted off the bench and settled beside her.

She glanced around the darkening garden. Robert's men were not present, nor was Magda with her.

Apprehension tightened a hard grip around her spine.

She and Robert were completely alone.

Chapter Eight

The silence of the garden seemed to swallow Brianna in its dark obscurity. No one could see her or Robert where they sat, no one could hear them.

She shifted uncomfortably on the bench and tried to devise a way to escape her predicament without being rude. The warmth of the sunbaked marble seeped through her gown.

Robert's cheeks were flushed in the dying light, his eyes bright. "Why must I keep asking you to marry me?" he asked in a clipped tone.

Brianna considered her reply with great care to avoid enraging him further. "I have no wish to marry."

Robert sneered down at her. "That's ridiculous. Don't you want a husband?"

She folded her hands in her lap and paused to collect her patience. The less she explained to him, the better. Not that he would ever understand.

She had no wish to yield her freedom for the shackles of matrimony, for vows that would strip her life of books and fill it with mindless days of needlework, her belly swollen with children she would seldom have opportunity to visit. Her every decision would hinge on the approval of a husband who would fail to appreciate her efforts. Her mother had lived thus, and it had robbed her of her spirit before slowly killing her.

No, Robert would never understand. No man would.

"Your father doesn't want you to be a spinster. He wants you to have a husband to care for you." He leaned close to her. "He's promised you to me."

Robert's words in her ear sent an unpleasant shiver down

her spine. "I was not informed of a betrothal." She spoke with a confidence she did not possess. There had been too many times when Edzell's laird had been so taken with pain that his speech was almost incoherent. Too many times when he'd agreed to something, but did not fully understand what was asked.

If such a thing were true, there would be a signed betrothal. Something she'd not yet come across in her search through her father's documents.

Robert scooted toward her until she was forced to teeter on the edge of the bench. "There's an attraction between us, Brianna. You feel it too, don't you?"

His eyes shone in the moonlight, his breath quickening.

Before she could redirect the conversation toward the information he'd said he had for her father, Robert grasped her shoulders and pressed his mouth to hers. His tongue probed her closed lips, slicking her face with saliva.

Brianna jerked her head back. "Robert!"

His small eyes narrowed and almost disappeared in his face. "It's him, isn't it? I saw how you let him hold you."

"What are you talking about?" Her mind reeled. Was that what married women endured from their husbands?

"The barbarian." Robert sneered down at her. "He's put his hands on you, hasn't he?" His hands locked tighter on her shoulders. "Has he taken what belongs to me?" He looked pointedly to her lap.

Realization dawned on Brianna, and she drew back in horror. "How dare you—"

"No, cousin, how dare you?" His fingers bit into her flesh, and his free hand slid down her waist. "You will not refuse me again, beautiful Brianna."

She sucked in a breath and tried to push his groping hands away. "Stop, Robert."

"You will not deny me," he growled. "You will marry me."

His fist tangled roughly in her hair and yanked her head back. His lips ground against hers once more. This time she tasted blood.

She shoved at him and twisted against the grip on her head.

Robert's hand tightened, securing his hold, and his arms came around her. She pushed at him once more, but the velvet of her dress was unyielding where it stretched tight over her shoulders.

Then she remembered the dagger that lay in her pocket, the one she'd started keeping on her after her father had died.

She jerked her elbow toward Robert, as far as the dress would allow, and patted the voluminous skirts with a frenzied panic.

Where was the entrance to her pocket?

Robert twisted an arm behind her back, but she didn't stop her frantic search for the slit with the hand still free.

Where was the entrance to her damn pocket?

Her bodice jerked forward, and cool night air assaulted the tops of her breasts. Surprise stilled her search for the dagger sagging heavy and useless against her thigh.

Humiliation lodged in her throat and scalded her cheeks. She couldn't cry out, couldn't stop the attack. Her fingers now clawed at the sagging fabric of her dress in a vain effort to preserve her modesty.

The hand on her shoulder was an unyielding vise, and she was held captive. Stars of pain danced before her vision, brilliant white against the darkness shrouding the garden.

When had he become so strong?

A movement caught the corner of her eye, and the hollow, muted thud of a hard fist to soft flesh sounded in her ears. The relentless grip loosened and Robert slid from the bench.

• • •

The impact of his fist connecting barely registered with Colin. However, confirmation of his aim lay in a pathetic pool at his feet. Had Brianna not been present, he would have beaten the man within an inch of his life.

Alec would not have stopped him.

As it was, Brianna's frightened tears shimmered in the fading light.

An ache tugged at his chest. Colin offered his hand to help her to her feet and averted his gaze as she tugged her gown into place over the exposed part of her corset.

She placed her hand in his. Her palm was hot, moist with her tears. She rose to her feet in a rustle of fine skirts and faced him, her back straight and her shoulders squared with authority.

"With your permission, we will remove him from Edzell, my lady," Colin said. Alec drew closer, obviously anticipating the task he would deem a pleasant one.

Brianna stared down at the pile of wasted nobility. It shifted to life with a low groan.

She nodded with closed lips. "Please," she said. The word was breathless, desperate, as if speaking any more would break the composure she struggled to maintain.

"Alec," Colin said compliantly. "Escort the man to his carriage and ensure his immediate departure."

The bastard was beginning to rise, and Colin did not want Brianna to face him after her ordeal.

"As ye say, Captain." Alec scooped up the fallen lord and draped him over his shoulder like an errant flap of plaid.

"And double the guards on watch for the night," Colin added in Gaelic. Offending vain men was a dangerous game.

Alec pushed his dark hair from his forehead and turned away.

Lord Lindsay's voice rose in the night air, high pitched with his offense. "Unhand me, you vile beast!"

Colin placed himself between Brianna and the sight of her cousin being carried away. "Come now, let's get ye to yer room."

He turned her toward the castle and she moved without protest. Her shoulders were stiff beneath his fingertips, but she did not flinch from his touch.

They walked to the castle together in a press of heavy silence. He followed closely behind her, through the halls of the lower floor, up a winding staircase, and down a narrow passage. Rush nips mounted on wall sconces lit their path, and the painted stone around them echoed with their footsteps.

Brianna stopped in front of the door at the top of another flight of stairs and turned to face him.

She stared up at him with her large brown eyes. "You saved me twice today." She glanced away for a split second, long enough for her lashes to sweep across her cheeks before her gaze returned to his. "I underestimated your worth and I underestimated you. When I'm wrong, I admit to it and—" The tip of her tongue touched a small cut on her upper lip. He regretted not killing the damned noble.

"I was wrong about you," Brianna said softly.

"I intend to save ye any time ye need it, lass. I'm yer Captain of the Guard." He leaned over her to open the door. "It's my job, aye?"

And then he saw it, that frantic glint unmasked in her eyes, the way she swayed toward him, the subtle parting of her lips. He'd been around enough women to know when one was in need of comfort.

With deliberate slowness, he opened his arms in silent offering and waited. Her hands tightened around the torn fabric she gripped to her chest, and she took a timid step forward. Her white-knuckled fingers almost touched him with her closeness.

Almost.

Carefully he brought his arms around her, wrapping her in a gentle embrace. She stiffened, and he thought she would pull away, but then she melted against him. The sigh she elicited was sweet, feminine, and warmed the fabric across his chest. He brushed a chaste kiss to the top of her head. Her hair was like fine silk beneath his lips. Exactly as he had imagined.

Her scent curled around him, intoxicating, thrilling.

Arousing.

Lust slammed into him, hard, fast, and completely unexpected. Suddenly, she was no longer a woman he wanted to woo for his wife. She was a woman he wanted to possess.

But not here. Not like this.

He relaxed his hold on her in preparation to step away.

That's when she rose on her toes and pressed her warm lips to his.

Chapter Nine

The empty hall was cast in a low golden light that concealed Brianna's bold kiss from any unexpected visitors—not that she would have noticed with the way Colin consumed her vision. Nor would she have heard them climbing the stairs with the way her heart raced in her ears.

Their mouths but touched, and yet she could feel how soft his lips were against hers. The light, spicy scent of him whirled through her body and set her pulse racing. She leaned into him without intending to, using his solid body for balance and sating the intensity of her need for the closeness of his strength.

His lips did not move beneath hers. Had she expected them to?

She broke off the delicate kiss, but did not turn her face from Colin's.

The soft breath from Colin's lips washed over her chin, and her mouth went dry with the desire to feel his mouth against hers. She tilted toward him in an attempt to kiss him once more. If only she were less awkward in her approach, if only he would take the invitation for what it was.

Though truly she didn't even know what it was, only that she wanted him close. His power, his strength, the way he somehow made everything on her shoulders feel that much less cumbersome.

Colin's dark green gaze trailed down her face to her lips, and her breath caught. He was going to kiss her.

Heat flared in her cheeks, and every part of her felt shaken, overly aware of every part of him—from the warm masculine scent of him to the way his heart thudded beneath her fingertips.

She couldn't breathe, her mouth dry with an incredible anticipation unlike anything she'd ever known.

Why was he taking so long?

She rose higher on her toes, giving him better access to the hungry anticipation of her lips. Her hand shifted on his chest, desperate to press the outline of his muscled torso. The plaid over his shoulder rasped against her fingertips. Though he wore a leine, she knew what lay beneath. She had seen it. God save her, she wanted to touch the power she'd but glimpsed that very morning.

His hand rose to her cheek, cool and calloused against the flaring fire of her skin. He caressed the line of her jaw with a tenderness she thought only existed in stories.

"Ye've had a trying day, lass," he said in a voice so soft she almost did not hear him. "Ye need rest, aye?"

The realization of being deprived of the kiss was crushing. She wanted to argue, to curl her arms around his massive body and hold him captive until he gave her what she wanted.

His gaze settled on her mouth once more, and for a heart-stuttering moment she almost thought he would fulfill her wish.

He turned his head to the side, as if staring at her was painful. When he returned his eyes to her, they met her own steady gaze. He stroked her cheek again, and it was all she could do to keep from turning her face toward the caress. "Get sleep, aye? I'll protect ye."

She nodded, unable to speak and too hesitant to go. Though his words were spoken gently, the rejection cut her deeply.

He leaned forward and pressed the warmth of his mouth to her forehead, the way one might to a cherished child. Perhaps that was how he saw her, a child to look after.

"Sleep well, Brianna." Her name was velvet in his hypnotic burr.

She nodded, unable to speak for the knot in her throat and foolishly unable to pull her gaze from the way the collar of his leine fell open. The small bit of naked chest visible was powerful, lined with a sinewy muscle.

She walked backward into her room, keeping her gaze fixed

on him. His hair was copper-colored in the firelight, unbound and hanging around his shoulders in soft waves. The muted light turned his eyes a deep green, like a fine emerald.

Was he always so handsome?

How had she never noticed it before now?

"Sleep well, lass." He pulled her door closed with a quiet click, and his footsteps echoed down the hall.

She stood rooted to the ground, unable to move beneath the complicated tangle of new emotions. The deep ache for his touch, the softness of his lips upon hers, the solid wall of his chest pressed against her breasts.

Desire pulsed sweet torment between her legs and filled her mind with sinful images of Colin shirtless, as he had been earlier that day. She closed her eyes and leaned her forehead against the door. Her lips burned where she'd touched her mouth to his. She drew a slow, deep breath through her nose. His scent still lingered on her skin, clean and undeniably male.

But she could not give in to such emotions. She was, after all, mistress of the castle. Lives depended upon her in a time of much turmoil. Much as she hated to admit it, he had been right in not returning her kiss. He was her Captain of the Guard, not some wealthy suitor who could bring the protection of a powerful name.

Naught could ever blossom between them, an important fact she'd do well to remember.

* * *

Several drops of rain spit from the sky and flecked Colin's bare arms. He glanced overhead to where the sky was still a brilliant blue and the clouds fluffy white. There would be no downpour.

Alec's heavy breath panted several feet away from Colin and mingled with the grunts and calls of the guards training to their left. The fierce burn of the sun could not touch them in the shade of the large castle wall. Despite Colin's observations, it was not anything outside the castle which occupied his mind. Rather it was inside. *She* was inside.

Brianna.

A blunted weapon smacked into the back of his knees and sent him crashing to the grass.

Alec's shadow loomed over him. "Ye're distracted today."

Colin got to his feet and scanned the lawn to where the men practiced around them. Their battle skills continued to improve. A swell of arrogant pride lodged in his chest at their fluid formations. He had relocated their training to the latter side of the castle for the remainder of the day to avoid the glare of the sun.

"Aye, I'm distracted," Colin confirmed.

"Is she too intelligent for ye?" Alec gave his shoulder a shove.

Colin smirked. "That's no what distracts me."

Alec's eyebrow arched in disbelief. "Dinna tell me she actually likes ye."

Colin lifted his shoulder in a noncommittal response. "Are ye saying I'm no charming?" He jabbed his sword at Alec.

His friend batted the blunted edge away with a flick of his wrist. "I'm saying ye're no as smart." Alec gave a menacing grin and lunged forward.

Brianna was a woman well known for her learning as much as for her dowry. Colin had expected a sour woman sagging with age and prudent in action. He had not expected Brianna. Coupled with her sharp mind, she was an intimidating catch for any man.

Any man but him.

Her innocent kiss rushed forefront to his mind. The soft brush of her lips against his, the way she'd looked at him so imploringly.

She'd wanted him to kiss her back.

And God how he'd wanted to. Her lips were so damn soft, so warm and tempting. He tightened his hand on the hilt of his blade with the fierceness of his wanting. Her body had been close enough for him to feel the curves beneath her dress, to see the swell of her full breasts.

She'd wanted him, he saw it in her eyes. While he did want

to woo her into marriage, he refused to do it by taking advantage of her desperate state. He'd given her what she needed—comfort. The rest could come later.

Then he could prove to his father he was worthy of a woman like her, that he was worthy of being laird to an estate, and that he was worthy of the MacKinnon land back on Skye.

Alec poked Colin in the shoulder with his practice sword. "Distracted," Alec muttered and dropped his weapon. The tight pull of his lips said the mock battle wasn't worth the effort.

Jonathan ran toward them from the corner of the castle wall. "Captain," he shouted with urgency. "Lord Robert Lindsay arrived demanding to see the laird. My lady meets with him now. I tried to stop her—"

"Are they alone?" Colin demanded.

Jonathan nodded.

Colin swore and sprinted toward the castle entrance. As much as the soldiers had improved, their lack of forewarning about Lindsay's arrival was an oversight he'd see reprimanded. His thighs burned with the effort of his sprint, but he only cared about one thing—that he was not too late.

Chapter Ten

Only an open door and several windows allowed light to cut into the entryway of the castle. Brianna had never realized the front part of her home was so dark.

The impatient tap of Robert's toe against the stone floor clicked off the walls around them and mingled with the frantic beat of her heart.

"I'm afraid seeing Father is impossible," she repeated. She kept her voice soft in an effort to lend a privacy to their conversation the open area did not provide. Her words, nevertheless, echoed around her.

Robert's face flushed, and he paced the floor in front of her with the restlessness of a caged beast. "Why do you deny me an audience? Is he not here and you are covering his absence?"

Unease snaked down Brianna's back. Robert was getting too curious, coming too close to the harrowing truth.

"He is very ill." She looked away, unable to meet his eyes while the lie fell from her lips. Dishonesty was unpalatable, even with someone like her cousin.

His pacing stopped, leaving the upper half of his body bathed in a stream of sunlight sluicing in from the doorway. His eyes were almost unnatural in the brilliant light, the black center little more than a pinprick in a bright sphere of yellow brown.

"I demand recompense for the offense brought to me last night." Spittle dotted the sunbeam with flecks of glowing white, and his fury echoed throughout the stonework surrounding them.

The last thread of Brianna's patience pulled taut and snapped. "You demand recompense for the offense brought on you? What of the offense to me?"

Perhaps the conversation would have been more appropriate behind the heavy doors of her solar, but she refused to be alone with him.

His eyes widened. "Offense to you, my lady?"

"My bodice still bears the tear of your actions," she hissed. A cursory glance around the open area confirmed no servants lingered, but that did not mean the conversation could not be overheard.

His gaze narrowed. "I took nothing that wasn't promised to me."

"You tried to steal what would never be given." Her voice rang sharp against the stone with a volume of rage that surprised even her.

He took a purposeful step closer and stared down at her breasts. "Then perhaps I should have taken more and forced you to wed me."

Brianna's hands trembled, but not with fear. Never again with fear.

He stalked closer, until his familiar, overly rich perfume enveloped her.

She stood tall with her head lifted at an austere angle. "You are not my betrothed." The lie did not feel convincing, even when she knew there was no document declaring such. If there had been, she would have found it.

Robert's eyes widened with injustice. "You were promised to me. He said when he got better, but he's not getting any damn better, is he?" His hand caught her upper arm in the same viselike squeeze as before. "If he won't see me, if he won't give me what he's promised me, I'm going to take it."

Her heart raced with the power of her courage, of what she was about to do. Robert would not have the control this time. She had come prepared for battle.

Her fingers dipped into the wide sash at her waist. Before he could suspect her actions, she wrenched her dagger free and pressed it to his soft belly. Sunlight glinted off the edge of the sharpened blade and reflected on the far wall.

"If you even attempt to do as you have threatened, I will

ensure I am the last woman you touch." Her fingers squeezed the dainty handle of the weapon, crushing the velvet beneath her sweating palm. "I want you to go home. Return only when you've recovered your senses, cousin."

A shadow fell across them both. Something massive flew through the doorway and crashed against Robert with a force that sent him sprawling to the floor.

Brianna jerked toward her cousin's attacker and settled on familiar green eyes that made her heart leap.

Colin stepped between her and Robert—between her and the threat of danger.

Relief washed over her. Or perhaps it was something else that fluttered in the pit of her stomach. She wanted to fall against him, to breathe in that familiar, addictive scent and feel the wall of his protective strength surround her.

"Did he hurt ye?" His gaze skimmed down her gown, not with the leering lust Robert had, but with concern.

"I'm not hurt."

Colin stared at the dagger clutched in her hand, and a warm chuckle sounded from deep in his chest. "Looks like the lass could have handled ye on her own." He turned toward Robert and jerked him to his feet.

Robert yanked his hand back after he was standing and let it drop to his side. Malice poisoned the stab of his glare. "My father was right. There is something amiss at Edzell. And you aren't telling anyone, are you, cousin? Is your father truly here?" His eyes narrowed. "Truly alive?"

Brianna kept her face emotionless despite the frantic squeezing of her heart. Why would he say that? Why would such a thought even cross his mind? Did he know?

And her uncle. Air no longer found its way into her lungs. Would her uncle come to Edzell? He wouldn't be as easily put off as Robert. What would she tell him?

Several of Edzell's guards appeared in the doorway, saving her from having to respond. Colin nodded toward Robert. "Escort him out. Again."

Robert stumbled forward, his palms up in a sign of

surrender. The guards stayed back and let him walk from the room, his head held high with pride he didn't deserve.

The soldiers followed behind him, and a heavy quiet descended upon the large open area.

Brianna focused on calmly tucking the dagger back into the sash of her dress and intentionally kept her gaze averted from Colin's. He was too observant. He would see the fear simmering inside of her, the turbulent seas of anguish tipped by injustice. Her palms were slick with it and her fingers shook. Doubtless, he would see that too.

She was tired of the lying, the deceiving. If the earl had but made her legitimate, she would never have been forced to cover his death to preserve the safety of her home.

"Can I talk to ye, lass?" He leveled an intense gaze at her. "Alone."

Her heartbeat thundered through every part of her—it pounded in her ears and spread heat through her body. Her cheeks, she knew, must bear its stain. "We can speak in my solar," she said, her voice throaty with anticipation. "Alone."

* * *

Colin found himself walking the same rich hall toward Brianna's solar as he had before. Thick tapestries lined every wide expanse of stone, and sunlight poured in through countless windows. There was not a part of Edzell that was not lavishly decorated. He had noticed all of this. What man would not?

But this time, it was not Edzell's wealth that held his attention, but her mistress. She wore silk again today. The red gown hugged her slender waist and cradled her breasts in a sheen that made him want to glide his palms over the slick fabric. Her hips swayed with each step ahead of him, restrained enough to mark her as the noblewoman she was, but loose enough to announce her desires.

He tightened his hands into fists to fight the overwhelming desire to grab hold of those sweet hips.

Her head turned to the side, away from the windows, so

her face was hidden from the light. But the cover of darkness did not prevent him from seeing her gaze slide toward him, nor did it conceal the way she tucked her lower lip into her mouth before she turned forward once more.

She stopped before the solar door and unlocked it with a heavy iron key pulled from her sash. Her eyes caught his, and a shy smile spread over her lips before she entered the room. He stepped in behind her and let the door close softly, leaving them blessedly alone.

Brianna turned toward him, a pink flush creeping across her bosom and blossoming in her cheeks and lips. God, she was beautiful.

Her firm breasts rose and fell with her quickened breath. He was not the only one who wanted to resume what had been left off the previous night.

She stood several steps away. Too far. He would see that issue remedied.

"I wanted to apologize to ye," he said.

The small smile on her lips wavered. "Apologize?"

He took a step closer, making the conversation more intimate. "Aye, for last night."

A slight crease appeared between her eyebrows. "You are apologizing for last night," she repeated slowly. "Do you regret it?"

"Only if it caused ye unease, my lady. I dinna want ye to feel I took advantage of ye as yer cousin had attempted." He took another step closer. "It wasna my intention."

"You are nothing like Robert." Brianna's eyes flashed with conviction. "And you did not take advantage of me. If I remember correctly." Her cheeks flushed further still to a deep red that matched her dress. "I kissed you."

Another step. One more and she would be staring up at him, her warmth close enough to feel. Her perfume close enough to tease.

Colin's pulse hammered. "Are ye apologizing for taking advantage of me?" he asked with a grin.

"Should I?"

"Ye could," he said, closing the space between them with one final step. He traced the line of her jaw with his fingertip until he reached the delicate edge of her chin. Her head tipped back, her face turned up toward his, her eyes hooded.

He stared down at her generous mouth and his blood roared through his veins. He had no doubt she'd taste as sweet now as she had last night. "Or I could kiss ye and relieve ye of yer guilt."

Her lips parted, and he knew she would not dissuade his affections.

In fact, he was counting on it.

Chapter Eleven

Her solar hummed with an intimacy that tingled awareness through every part of Brianna's body. Her senses danced with desire, and she greedily took it all in, savoring every sensation. The aroma of sun and grass from the open window, the way it mingled with Colin's clean, masculine scent. The warmth of his body, so close to hers, the intensity of his gaze as he stared down at her, as though he truly did intend to kiss her.

He lowered his head and paused. For one agonizing second, Brianna thought she might die of impatience or perhaps disappointment if he walked away.

His mouth hovered over hers, as if he were relishing the moment as much as she. He kissed her top lip and then the bottom in sweet succession.

His tongue swept across the seam of her mouth, unhurried and deliberate. One strong hand curled around her waist while the other slipped down her dress to cup her bottom. This time, she knew what to expect. This time, she readily leaned into him and arched toward the demanding press of his hardness.

A groan tore from him, and his grip on her tightened. His tongue swept into her open mouth, mating against her own with stroke after heady stroke.

Her fingers splayed across his powerful chest, greedy to sample what she had seen glistening in the sunlight. The chiseled lines of his muscular physique were evident beneath his leine, hard and solid beneath soft, yielding fabric.

She wanted more. To touch more. To taste more. Her trembling hands continued her brazen exploration, taking her lower, tracing the rigid contours of his abdomen.

He groaned, a strangled, hungry sound that sent excitement tingling through her, arousing, powerful, and encouraging. She wanted to caress him, all of him. Elicit the same reaction again and again.

He caught both her hands in one of his. "That isna a good idea."

His gaze dipped to her bosom, and her lungs stopped bringing in air. She was his willing captive, subject to the mercy of his desires.

The muscle in his jaw leapt and he released her hands. His fingers slid up the tight bodice of her gown, inch by slow, burning inch until he reached the squared neckline. He paused. A lifetime without breath or thought passed before his fingertips skimmed over the tops of her breasts.

Her flesh prickled beneath his touch, blossoming from her bosom and spreading through her body in a wave of such pleasure, her eyes fell closed. His touch was not so light the second time. He closed his hand around her breast and his palm pressed hot against her hardened nipple beneath the layers of bodice and chemise and corset. Her breathless gasp muffled beneath the heat of his mouth.

Colin buried his face against her neck, inhaled deeply against her sensitive skin, and exhaled on a groan. She rolled her hips against his muscled body without thought, seeking reprieve from the need that burned with an urgency she could not ignore.

* * *

The fine silk of Brianna's gown was cool against Colin's palms where he held her perfectly rounded bottom, encouraging the undulation of her hips. And those arousing little breathless whimpers she gave.

His cock throbbed painfully beneath his kilt, desperate to lay claim to the woman he'd resolved to possess.

He gave a low growl and captured her lips once more, his kiss fiercer than he'd intended. By Brianna's breathless moan, she did not mind. Quite the opposite actually.

"Please." Brianna murmured against his lips.

Her hands trailed that maddening path down his stomach again.

"Please?" He drew a steadying breath. "What do ye want, lass?" He'd give her damn near anything right now. Hell, he would give her the moon if she asked for it.

But it was not the moon she wanted.

She pulled back and looked up at him, her eyes bright with desire, her lips pink and swollen from their kisses.

"I know not what I want." Her hurried words came between pants and kisses. "My body aches in a way that is unfamiliar. There is more to what we do." Her body arched against him in innocent frustration.

Sweat beaded his brow. He taught his men self control and now felt his own slipping. "There is much more to what we do," he ground out. "But ye are a maiden."

"And I've never been sorrier for it." Her fingers trailed across the top of his chest where his leine lay open, teasing the bare flesh with her feather-light touch.

God, she was so innocent, so pure. And it was his affection she welcomed. The temptation to take what she suggested was almost more then he could bear. Her kisses trailed over his chin and down his neck until his skin sizzled beneath her plump, enticing lips.

His cock was impossibly hard with the force of unslaked longing.

Not yet though.

He would not pluck her flower until their wedding night, when Edzell became his land and Brianna became his wife. He ground his teeth against the pain of his desire.

His lips nudged the delicate curve of her ear. "I can still give ye a sample of the pleasure ye crave."

Her low moan in response to his suggestion shot an arrow of lust straight to his tortured loins.

"Ye'll need to trust me, aye? I willna take yer maidenhead."

He felt her nod against his cheek and his mouth went dry. Soon, his fingers would be sliding up her thighs, seeking the source of her need, teasing the cries from her lips. His cock pounded in time with his erratic heartbeat. He needed this as much as she did.

He gripped the light silk of her skirt and eased it upward. The fabric whispered to him in the silent room, begging to be swept from her body. Her hooded gaze followed his progress.

The hem of her gown rose higher, exposing the sensual arc of her calf. He moved slowly. Not so much to keep from frightening her as to savor the alluring unveiling of her legs. He'd felt the curves of her waist, her hips, her breasts and suspected she would be beautiful beneath her skirts.

He was right.

She knew he openly admired her, he could see that in the flush of her cheeks, in the way her head ducked shyly to the side. But she did not stop him. Not when he revealed her delicate knees, nor did she look away when he stopped the ascent of the fabric at the top of her slender thighs.

He lowered his head to hers and tugged her full lower lip into his mouth. He caressed the silky smooth skin on the inside of her thigh. Her sharp intake of breath passed between their mouths, fueling his desire.

He slid his hand higher, toward the source of her need, and his cock strained against the rasp of his plaid. He pressed his lips to hers once more, a final branding kiss before pulling his face from hers. If he could not possess her, he would at least watch her expression as he brought her pleasure.

His hand trailed up to the juncture between her legs until his fingertips brushed the downy hair of her sex.

"Yes," she moaned. Her thighs tightened. "Please."

He cupped her mound in his hand and slid his middle finger against her slick opening. She bit her lower lip, cutting off her husky cry.

Colin felt the groan tear from his throat and focused on each subtle movement of his fingers. She was so wet. So ready. And if everything went as he intended, so willing.

His fingertip eased inside of her, careful not to go too deep. Her eyes shone bright with yearning beneath hooded lids, and the swell of her breasts rose and fell with each hastened breath. His thumb stroked between her swollen folds and found her sensitive bud.

Her eyes went wide, and her hips jerked against the heel of his hand.

"There?" he teased.

"Yes." Her reply was little more than a gasp.

He rolled the pad of his thumb against the tiny nub.

"What are you doing?" she panted.

"Pleasing ye."

Her cheeks were scarlet red now. "With your hand?" Her eyes glinted with fevered heat.

Despite the torrent of desire throwing him into a world of barely hinged control, an amused smile tugged at his lips. "Stop thinking so much. Just *feel*, aye?"

She nodded and her thighs relaxed around his hand. Her hips rocked in a fluid motion, matching the rhythm of his strokes. Gone was her tight-eyed expression borne of concentrated confusion. Her face was smooth, relaxed, her lips soft in sensual surrender.

The gentle huff of her breath grew more rapid and her body stiffened. She was so damn close.

Her hips ground hard against his hand, and her wet heat spasmed around his fingers again and again as the soft cries of her climax filled the room.

Her gaze remained locked on his, letting him witness the beauty of her release and glimpse deep into the soul of everything she had ever longed for. Without ever having to possess her, he knew without a doubt, she belonged to him.

He slid her skirts down and drew her toward him. His erection pulsed between them, painfully hard with need for release.

She arched her body against him, and it was all he could to do keep from lifting her skirts once more and thrusting deep within her.

"It was divine." Her eyebrow raised with emphasis.

God help him, he would have her where they stood if she

goaded him any further—inadvertently or not.

"If I dinna leave now, I dinna think I will be able to hold myself from ye, Brianna," he whispered. His lips brushed the top of her silky head before he released her and stepped safely back.

She leaned toward him. "I understand." The glaze of desire in her eyes told him she understood and did not care.

Unfortunately, he did.

He mumbled an apology, something lacking in wit and completely unmemorable. Before she could reply, he turned and quit the room.

* * *

Brianna watched Colin's broad back disappear out the door. Perhaps if her knees were not so unstable, she might have chased after him. She might have begged him to stay.

As it was, remaining upright consumed her full energy. Her feet staggered beneath her weight, carrying her backward to the hard edge of her desk. She waited for her solar door to close before she sagged against the solid surface. Her core tightened in sensual reminder of what Colin's fingers had wrought. Never had she known sensations could be so decadent. She closed her eyes and squeezed her thighs together. Another wave of pleasure rippled through her.

She dropped her head back and drew a deep breath to clear her head.

They could not keep doing this. Not when she already skirted danger with her terrible secret. Not when her uncle might show up any day.

Her borrowed time was running out, and she had no plan.

Chapter Twelve

The garden sprawled on either side of Brianna, every plant growing exactly as it should, exactly where it should. Vibrant red, pink, and yellow blooms glowed in the sunlight, as if mocking the colors of its rise and fall, and marble statues and benches scattered the grounds in symmetry. Even the bushes outlining the garden in a wall of waxy green leaves were shaped to perfection.

Brianna's own life had once held such order.

She shifted on the hot bench and ran her hand over the worn leather spine of *The Gardner's Labyrinth* where it lay heavy in her lap. The book had been an incredible help once again. Every year she referred to the knowledge printed on the pages, and every year her efforts were rewarded with nature's bounty.

Her fingertip traced the smooth lettering on the cover, and she drifted back to a time when her own mother had cradled this same book while toiling in Edzell's rich, black dirt.

Had it been in a garden such as this where her mother met the French noble?

A familiar ache clenched Brianna's heart. She did not know the full story, but from the rumors she'd overheard, her mother and father had arrived in France not long after they were wed. It was there her mother met a French noble who shared her love of learning.

An image of the earl rose forefront in her mind, his face purple with rage. "You have her mind, her curiosities. I refuse to allow you to end like her. I refuse to allow you to become a selfless whore."

A shadow fell over Brianna and pulled her from memories

best left forgotten. Relief was quickly replaced with slithering disappointment.

"Good day, Brianna." Robert's jagged smile leered down at her.

He sat beside her without invitation, and his beady gaze darted to her waist. Did he fear she carried her dagger?

A surge of power rushed through her. For all the fear he instilled in others, he was afraid. Of her.

She bit her lips in an effort to temper her impending grin.

His yellow gaze returned to her face. "I have been rude, cousin. My actions have been," he held his hands out in a show of helplessness. "Deplorable."

Brianna remained perfectly still, unsure of what to make of his apology.

His eyebrows knit together. He appeared to be serious.

"I have hurt you."

There was a warmth to his eyes that had previously been absent. Was he truly serious?

He smirked. "You don't know what to make of this apology, do you? I suppose I wouldn't either if our roles were reversed. I know I offended you, and I want to make amends."

His hand waved the air beside him, and a young servant emerged from the open doorway of the summer house, a silver goblet in each hand.

"Allow me to present you with a gift." Robert lifted the decadent cups from the servant and held one toward Brianna in offering.

Her fingers curled around the cool stem. Deep red stones adorned the goblet and glinted like glowing fire in the sunlight. The sweet spice of wine rose to greet her from the silvered rim.

"A beautiful goblet for my beautiful cousin, and the finest drink coin can buy." He glanced down at his own chalice, and his lips drew in with an expression bordering on sheepish. "This is the only way I know to express my sincere apology." His eyes turned toward her, eager, hopeful. "Please accept."

It was on the tip of Brianna's tongue to refuse, to give in to the temptation to throw the proffered gift on the soft ground.

Guilt twisted inside her, her wish to refuse warring with the instilled need to be polite.

She and Robert had been playmates when they were young. They had laughed together and made up the same silly, childish games. That is, until he grew older and his tricks turned cruel.

She stared into her own goblet of blood-red wine. Unfortunate though the truth may be, Robert and her uncle were her only remaining family. If Robert's apology was indeed genuine, she should allow him the opportunity to make amends.

Her fingertip grazed the smooth face of a precious gem. His attempt to woo her with gifts and kindness was markedly obvious, but she appreciated the effort.

His expectant gaze weighed on her.

"Of course I forgive you, Robert." Her lips stretched in a smile she couldn't force herself to feel. Perhaps in time, forgiveness would come. "Thank you for your apology."

He raised his goblet in the air. "I'd like to propose a toast to us."

"To us," she repeated and let her cup gently tap his before she brought the metal edge to her lips.

The wine was sweet on her tongue, its spice rich and bold, before fading to bitterness. Most unusual.

Robert grinned at her. "Interesting flavor, is it not?" He swirled his own jeweled goblet, sending shards of red light dancing around them. "Comes from India or some barbaric place."

"Interesting is exactly the word I would use to describe it," Brianna said slowly.

His face fell. "You don't like it."

"No, but I do." She tipped more of the terrible wine into her mouth and swallowed.

A wide grin split his face and turned fuzzy.

Fuzzy?

Brianna blinked hard, but her vision did not clear. The wine grew hot in her stomach, and sweat prickled her brow.

"Are you ill?" Robert's voice sounded distant.

The sun beat down on her, pressing her with its unbearable

heat, robbing her of air. God save her, she was so hot. The cup fell from her hands and flecks of red glared up at her, clawing into her heavy eyes. "Hot," she murmured.

The deep notes of Robert's voice swam in her ears, indiscernible sounds against the thickness of her thoughts. Her stomach clenched, and her mouth watered as if she were about to be sick. Hands grasped her arms and she felt herself lifted. Her legs dragged uselessly beneath her.

Light glanced off the goblet on the ground and sent red whirling in her vision, swirling and spinning until she had to shut her eyes to block it out. And then sweet darkness drew her into its embrace.

* * *

The courtyard was empty, as was the garden and the solar. Colin strode across the expanse of cobblestone, toward the stables. Perhaps Brianna had decided to take a ride. He had been tempted on such a fine day.

The sweet musk of hay filled his nostrils even before he entered the shaded building. Her brown steed occupied its usual stall and regarded Colin with a mournful gaze that made him regret not arriving with a treat for the spoiled beast.

Something didn't sit well in Colin's gut, an unease that grew stronger by the second.

"Help, someone please." A plaintive voice carried through the stable entrance.

Colin shot forward with a burst of energy and ran back out into the courtyard. Magda swayed at its center, her hands clasped to her chest. She turned toward him and sprinted with a speed he had not thought the old woman capable.

"Help, please, sir." Her feet skittered across the stones and she staggered.

He caught her thin shoulders, steadying her before she fell. "What's the matter, Magda? Where's Brianna?"

Her eyes were wide and her fingers plucked at one another. "Please help. Men took my mistress."

His body tightened, the way it did before battle. The way that steeled his heart against the call of fear and engaged his mind with strategy. "Who were these men? Where did they take her?"

Tears rolled soundless down her cheeks. "Toward the summer house." She shook her head miserably. "But I don't know who they are."

The old woman might not know the men, but Colin had a strong idea whom to suspect. And the bastard would pay for his offense.

"She'll be fine, Magda." He gently squeezed her bony shoulders one last time before releasing her and racing toward the garden.

His thundering boots on the hard ground fell to a hushed whisper over the lush grass. The garden was still. Too still. No screaming, no cries for help, no crashes of struggle.

He shoved through the door of the summer house and found only silence in the dimly lit room. Empty, save the massive stone table at the center.

His stomach twisted. If she was here, she was on the second level, in the isolated bed chamber above.

He leapt up the stairs, taking them two at a time, and slammed his weight into the second door. It gave without resistance, and his body burst into the room. Brianna's cousin stood at the opposite end, before a bed.

Colin's heart compressed. Milky white legs hung limp from either side of the bastard's hips.

Robert looked over his shoulder with a smirk that dropped open into a look of surprise. "You're not—"

Colin didn't remember crossing the room, nor did he remember cocking his arm back, but he would always remember how satisfying it felt to have the whoreson's head snap back beneath his fist. Once again, Brianna's pathetic cousin lay motionless at Colin's feet.

Brianna.

She lay on the bed, her heavy skirts pushed to her hips and her long legs spread. Her face was turned to the side, deathly pale. Her chest did not rise.

Fear gripped Colin in its unfamiliar grasp.

He leaned over her and caught her face in his hands. Her flesh was cool and slick with sweat beneath his fingers. A soft exhale tickled the hair on the back of his hand.

Relief crashed through him. She lived.

"Brianna." His voice was loud in the stillness of the room.

Her lashes fluttered.

"Captain!" A voice shouted behind him, shocked, full of rage.

Brianna's eyes flew open and found Colin's. "What—?"

"What is the meaning of this?" The voice was familiar, and yet Colin could not bring himself to tear his gaze from Brianna. He wanted to feel her pulse beneath his fingers and see her breath pull in and out of her chest.

"Captain, what have you done?" The young pastor's hissed voice cut through the haze of Colin's shock.

He froze between Brianna's naked legs where he leaned over her with Robert laying at his feet. No matter how he could try to explain this, one thing was certain.

Brianna's reputation was ruined.

Chapter Thirteen

The air hung thick with accusation and pressed into Colin. He did not have to turn to see the pastor's gaze on him. He could feel it slicing into his back.

Colin grabbed the hem of Brianna's skirts and jerked them over her legs in a belated effort to preserve her modesty. Had he not been so panicked when he entered, he might have thought to have done that first.

Her glassy eyed stare drifted down. "Why was I—" She clenched her jaw, cutting off the slowly slurred words.

The shutters banged open behind him, and Thomas's shouts rang through the room. "Send for the healer. Our lady is ill."

Robert rolled to his feet beside Colin. "You barbarian! How dare you touch her?"

His meager fist pulled back, but before he could land a blow, Colin caught his wrist and shoved him back two steps, against the wall. "Dinna try it, Lowlander—ye willna like the end result."

Thomas appeared between them, his arms spread wide. "Cease this immediately. I will have answers and I will have them now." His usually jovial face was red, his mouth drawn tight.

A pitiful whimper came from the bed where Brianna lay. Regret splintered through Colin's anger. He would properly deal with Robert later.

The sooner the conversation at hand passed, the sooner he could do as he desired.

Robert spoke first. "I came in and found the Highlander hovering over Lady Lindsay. I tried to stop him and managed a few blows before the beast turned uncontrollable and slammed into me with such force, I was knocked from my wits."

Colin stared down at the lesser man. Were the situation not so serious, he would have laughed—especially when Thomas's eyebrows furrowed in a show of mild disbelief. Colin glanced at Brianna. Her eyes misted with tears and confusion.

Certainly this was no laughing matter.

"And you, Captain?"

The pastor's voice pulled Colin's attention. "What is your account of the story?"

The muscles along Colin's back drew tight at the recent memory. "I was informed Lady Lindsay had been taken. When I came to the summer home, I found him," he nodded toward Robert's smug face. "He had her dress pulled up." His hands clenched into fists. "And he was between her legs." Each word came out short and hard between clenched teeth. "I knocked the bastard to the ground and tried to ensure Lady Lindsay was safe."

Thomas tucked his lips in his mouth and furrowed his heavy brows. He leaned around Colin and looked to where Brianna lay. "I believe we shall have to ask Lady Lindsay what transpired and we'll have a full account of the truth."

Robert rolled his eyes. "She'll have no idea what happened, she was unconscious when I came in here." His chin tilted up at a cocky angle that would be perfect to catch with the sharp edge of an elbow. "Clearly her innocence is in question. No man of noble bearing would want her now." His lip curled. "She's ruined."

"Dinna speak of her like that," Colin growled. Were this a different time and place, the Lowlander would be crushed beneath his boot for the offenses spoken and committed against Brianna.

Lindsay narrowed his eyes. "I'll marry her even though her reputation is in shreds." He wrinkled his nose. "From the acts of a *commoner*."

A sharp cry sounded from the bed. Brianna lurched upright and immediately doubled over. Her hands cupped her face and a low moan sounded from behind her fingers. "Where am I?"

She lifted her head, her eyes wild and distressed. "What's happened?" She shook her head. "I don't understand any of this."

Her shield was stripped away, and every fear lay evident in her anxious stare.

Colin's explanation caught on his tongue. She looked so innocent, so exposed.

Before he could go to her, Thomas stepped forward and placed a protective arm around her shoulders. "My lady, I'm afraid your virtue has been compromised."

Her mouth worked soundlessly and her gaze darted to each man. "That's not possible, I haven't-I would have…have felt—"

Robert edged toward the bed, his sunken chest puffed out. "I have agreed to save your reputation. You are to become my wife."

Colin cursed inwardly. This was not how he wanted Brianna to know who he was. This was not how he wished to propose marriage.

"No," Brianna whispered. "I can't."

A victorious smile erupted on Robert's pocked face. "You have no choice but to marry me."

"That isna true," Colin said. "I was the one found with her. I am responsible." He steeled himself and met Brianna's wounded gaze, wishing he were alone with her. Perhaps then he could explain.

Robert's sharp bark of laughter reverberated off the plastered walls. "You? Marry her?" His mirth contorted into a dark glower. "A commoner like you will never know the touch of a lady like her." He stepped closer to Colin. "A commoner like you will die for your offenses."

Colin widened his stance and crossed his arms over his chest. "Good thing I'm no a commoner then, aye?"

The nobleman's confident posture faltered.

"Laird MacKinnon is my father. I'm a noble in my own right, and I'll be claiming Lady Lindsay as my wife." He stared hard at Robert without blinking. "And she will be under my personal protection from this moment forward."

POSSESSION OF A HIGHLANDER

* * *

Brianna gripped the sumptuous velvet coverlet beneath her. It felt real. Certainly the heat of her cheeks was real, as was the painful churning in her stomach.

But this could not be real.

Her innocence was compromised.

Her Captain of the Guard was a noble.

She would be married.

No, this could not be real.

She squeezed her eyes shut. When she opened them, she would find the events had been nothing more than a horrible, horrible night terror.

Her eyes flew open and her heart plummeted. All three men stood over her, glaring challenges at one another.

Rage tore through her cloud of hopelessness. Her hands fisted the coverlet beneath her fingertips. How dare they plan her life?

"No." Her protest was feeble, a gasp in a room with little air for breathing. "No," she said again with more strength.

Thomas's hold on her tightened. The comforting gesture felt like a yoke falling over her shoulders.

"Be still, my lady." His concern was evident in the softness of his tone. He looked toward Colin and Robert. "The two of you should leave and ensure the healer comes to see her posthaste."

Robert skulked out of the room, but Colin remained. His cool hand clasped her fingers and eased the overwhelming heat of her palms. "Ye'll be safe with Thomas, aye?"

She bent her head, unable to look into the green eyes that had once made her heart race with excitement.

"I would speak to ye later if I may," he said softly.

A tear slipped from her eye and splattered against the back of his hand. He drew a deep breath and squeezed her fingers once more before releasing her.

"I'll have yer life if ye let anything happen to her, pastor." The threat in Colin's voice was blatant.

"She will be safe and well cared for."

Colin's boots echoed off the wooden floorboards, and the door clicked closed behind him.

She waited until the sounds of his departure could no longer be heard before she spoke. "Thomas, I have no wish to wed."

"We do not have to discuss this now."

Brianna looked up at him and focused on his friendly gray stare in an effort to keep her world from spinning. "We must discuss this now. I do not wish to wed."

Thomas gave a heavy sigh. "My lady, you do not have a choice. Lord Robert will ensure your reputation is destroyed until you are forced to wed him. Marriage to the Captain is your only option."

Desperation rattled inside her. Her palms prickled with sweat, and a swell of nausea rolled through her once more.

Marriage. The loss of her freedom, the sacrifice of her books, the surrendering of her will to that of her husband. It was a fate worse than death.

She offered a faint smile of hope. "Perhaps Robert will tell no one."

Thomas studied her for a moment, and his lips thinned into a hard line.

She tensed, suddenly wary. "You aren't telling me something."

"My lady, it was Lord Robert's servant who bade me enter this room under the assumption I was to find a soul in need of help." The vein in the center of his forehead stood out prominently, his only indication of anger. "He wanted me to find you thus, only I think the Captain interrupted the deed."

The reds and yellows of the painted walls around her spun. "You mean—"

"He saved you from being forced," Thomas finished for her.

Her fingers ached from gripping the blanket beneath her, but she feared she would slide to the hard floor if she let go. "I cannot wed, Thomas." Her voice trembled. "Please do not force this on me."

He crouched on the floor in front of her so his face was level with hers. "Lord Robert will publicly accuse the Captain of rape." His gaze turned hard with sincerity. "If you do not wed him, Colin MacKinnon will hang."

Chapter Fourteen

Brianna stared into Thomas's eyes, hoping to find something other than truth in the gray depths. Hoping, but not succeeding. Chills left a prickle of bumps across her skin.

"He can't hang for a crime he did not commit." Her voice was almost lost beneath the crush in her chest.

Thomas's brow creased with sympathy. "Your uncle's influence with Parliament is too strong, and all will assume you lie to preserve your honor." His hand rested on her arm. "He will die if you do not marry him."

She turned away from him. "Then I'm presented with no choice." Sorrow rose thick in her throat and threatened to choke her.

Colin would be spared and she would be sacrificed.

"The Lord has provided you with the opportunity to legally save Edzell and be free of the constant proposals from your cousin."

The walls of the room pressed in on her and she could no longer breathe. Her heart launched into panic and slammed fast in her chest. Sweat dampened her skin.

Thomas's voice continued. "Your people have already accepted the Highlander. In the short time he's been here, he has earned their respect. He will be a fair laird and, I believe, a good husband to you."

The weight of his hand on her shoulder jarred her raw nerves, and her body snapped away at the slight touch.

"Please be calm, my lady." He leaned close and lowered his voice. "My lady, your father has been dead not two weeks. With each passing day, the threat of discovery grows. Once you are wed, we can perform the funeral and your father can finally be buried with the honor his title warrants. We can be free of the guilt."

She turned her gaze back toward him and noticed for the first time the strained lines around his eyes.

We can be free of the guilt. Thomas bore the burden of her father's death on his shoulders the same as she. Her request of him had been unfair, and his acceptance was beyond what any pastor should be expected to do.

His words rang true. Marriage to a noble would render her illegitimacy a nonissue, and the earl could finally be put to rest. She and Thomas could both be free of their secret.

The scuff of footsteps scraped the stone stairs outside the door. Thomas stepped back and regarded her with the kind expression she usually received when she sought his advice.

"Perhaps the Captain will be an understanding husband," he said. "He appears to be a reasonable man. And if I may be so bold to say so, my lady, I think he will see you as more than a title and wealth, unlike the way others have viewed you."

His words struck sharp in her chest. "How did you—"

"Do you think I didn't realize your fear?" he asked with a tender expression.

A gentle knock sounded at the door before she could answer.

"That will be the healer. After you've seen her, if you feel up for it, I believe your future husband would like to speak with you."

Brianna remembered the cool caress across her fingers before Colin left her. She knew he wanted to see her. But what did one say to the other when a misunderstanding of shame led to a forced union?

· · ·

Colin's feet pounded down the stairs of the castle. Light slanted in through the windows overhead and streaked the hall. He needed to get outside. He needed to find his men and rip into his fury in mock battle lest it consume him.

The castle's shaded interior offered no comfort, and he felt only relief when he was free of its closing walls. Energy fired through his body with each step, burning like hot metal in his tense muscles.

He hated being sent away, being forced to leave Brianna's side when she needed him most.

In the distance, the band of guards was slowly dispersing.

Though their training for the day had finished, several men milled about. Alec stood off to the side, overseeing the proper storage of the practice weapons. He raised an eyebrow as Colin approached.

"What's got ye so riled?" he asked.

The image of Lindsay standing between Brianna's naked legs slammed into Colin. "Is my anger so obvious?"

Alec smirked. "It is when I know ye well enough." He stepped closer and spoke in Gaelic. "What happened?"

Colin glanced toward the lingering men. "If ye knew me well enough, ye'd know I'm no in the mood to talk."

"Ach, that doesna happen often."

Colin wasn't in the mood for jests. He braced his hand against Alec's shoulder and shoved hard, sending him staggering backward.

Alec's face went dark. "Ye missed practice earlier." His black blade slipped from its scabbard with a menacing hiss. "And now ye pick a fight with yer better?"

Colin's blood sizzled in his veins, blending frustration and anger into one raw emotion. He gripped the handle of his sword and slid it free. "My better?"

He lunged, and the sharp edge of his blade slashed the air. Alec blocked the blow and darted left.

Colin's attacks were automatic, motions borne of impulse rather than thought. Alec's weapon crossed in front of him and blocked the attack. Still, Colin did not relent. He pushed forward with his sword, bending his friend backward.

"What the hell is wrong with ye?" Alec asked raggedly.

Colin grunted and shoved with all his might until Alec bent backward once more. "That cousin whoreson of hers tried to force himself on her, and I walked in on him," he growled in Gaelic.

Alec's sword dipped. "What?" He managed to pull his weapon up before Colin struck again.

Their blades crossed once, twice. Colin took a step back and drew a lungful of air. The swords they fought with were not blunted for practice; they were sharpened for killing. "I tried to save her and now I appear guilty."

"They think ye raped her?" Alec asked.

Colin shook his head. "But she's compromised now, aye?"

The concern on Alec's face gave way to nonchalance. "Well, ye wanted to wed the lass anyway." He flicked the tip of his blade against Colin's sword. "Dinna let the fight go out of ye yet. I'm finally getting some good practice." He grinned and caught Colin around the back of the neck with his hand.

Colin ducked from Alec's grasp and brought his sword up once more. Damn it, Brianna was supposed to fall in love with him, or at least desire him enough to agree to marry him. He was not supposed to have to force her to be his wife. He sidestepped Alec's jab.

He needed the land, but he wanted her trust.

His blade lashed out and skittered against Alec's block.

Now she thought he'd taken advantage of her. Now she knew he'd kept his identity from her. His only hope was that she would assume he was next in line for the MacKinnon lairdship.

Alec's sword rang against his.

Years of his serving beneath Kieran MacDonald had not been enough to impress his father, nor apparently had the fortune he'd accumulated in his travels. Colin tightened his fist on the pommel of his sword and swung at Alec.

Colin's father had remained unimpressed and deemed him a poor choice for laird.

Selfish.

He thrust his weapon, and Alec narrowly evaded the blow.
Reckless.

Colin's blade whistled through the air as he struck again.
Impulsive.

The impact of Alec's block vibrated against Colin's palm.

Alec stepped back out of his path and held up his hand.

"I thought ye wanted a fight," Colin ground out between his teeth. His father's words raced through his head, each one pounding with the rage already pulsing there, mingling with the offense of his father's choice for future laird. A rare spark of humiliation burned through Colin. His younger twin brother would be laird.

Alec lunged forward once more, his dark blade nicked with silver glinting in the late afternoon sun.

Colin evaded Alec's blow, his muscles singeing with heat. His friend had not yet had time to recover before Colin swung his weapon once more.

No father left his land to the second son. No father, but Colin's.

A brilliant spot of red appeared on Alec's forearm and broke through the fog of Colin's anger.

He dropped his blade and caught Alec's arm in his hand. "Why dinna ye say something?"

Alec grunted. "And admit I let ye beat me?" He slid his sword into the scabbard behind his shoulders.

Colin pulled back the sleeve of his friend's leine. A narrow ribbon of blood appeared where he'd been caught with the sharp edge of the blade.

"How 'bout ye find a fair lass to croon over my battle wound and then tell me the rest over an ale, aye?" Alec lifted his eyebrows in an uncommon show of playfulness. "Yer coin."

Colin stared down at the cut. He was fortunate it had not been deeper, more debilitating. He glanced back to the garden entrance, and his heart shuddered with an angst he could not give name to. Brianna had still not emerged. The healer's hunched figure slowly ambled across the cobblestone.

"Aye, I'll do all those things with ye, Alec. After I see to Brianna."

"All the better. That way we can celebrate yer marriage too." Alec slapped Colin on the back.

If only it were so easy. Something told Colin his future wife would not be as comfortable with the idea of their union.

Chapter Fifteen

Did there have to be so many halls in Edzell? Colin quickened his pace and turned yet another corner toward Brianna's solar. The aging healer had assured him she was well, but he needed to see for himself. To ensure color touched skin that had been too pale, and that her labored breath came now with ease.

His knuckles rapped upon the heavy wooden door.

"Enter." The feminine voice on the other side was surprisingly strong.

He pushed the door open and crossed over the threshold. She stood by an open window, her stiff back facing him. The door thunked closed behind him. Still, she did not turn.

"You came more quickly than I'd anticipated you would," she said, her tone flat.

Everything about her stance indicated she did not wish him to be near her, yet he could not force himself to stay away. He strode toward her, the consequences be damned. "I have been worried about ye."

"I'm well. The healer said I had been poisoned." Her head lifted sharply. "I no longer feel its effects."

Colin stopped just behind her and followed the graceful curve of her neck with his eyes. He wanted to stroke his fingertips against the exposed flesh, to confirm her skin was of a normal temperature. To feel her sweet softness once more.

Brianna turned toward him, her face a practiced mask of indifference. "Why did you not tell me who you were?"

But her eyes were not indifferent. Hurt showed there. She had trusted him, and what he saw showed she felt she'd been betrayed.

"Ye dinna ask." Colin inwardly cringed at his own words.

She stared up at him without saying a word. He tensed in preparation for her anger, her frustration at what he knew she'd see as him lying. But he got none of those. Instead, her shoulders sagged beneath the sigh of an exhale, and her head dropped forward in defeat.

"It matters little why you chose not to tell me. If you came here to propose marriage, you are getting what you wish, regardless of what I desire." Sorrow laced her words, and the weight of her regret settled on his shoulders.

Damn that Robert Lindsay shite. Colin had been doing well with Brianna before this. Now she was being forced, and the shield he'd worked so hard to disarm was back with a vengeance.

God, she'd been bonny with her guard stripped away, her face soft with passion, her eyes bright and carefree. He would see her thus again, no matter what it took.

"Ye still have a choice, Brianna," he said.

She folded her arms tight over her chest and curled her shoulders forward. "I will not have you hanged for a crime you did not commit."

So she knew he was innocent in this. That knowledge meant more to him than he thought it would.

He lowered his voice. "Ye know what happened?"

She gave a terse nod. "Thomas told me."

He captured her hand in his, and, while she remained aloof, she did not pull away. "Let us work through this together. Marry me, and we can put everything behind us."

Her face was impassive, but her breasts rose and fell rapidly with her quickened breath. "You ask me to marry you as if we have a choice."

"Aye." Colin watched her with careful consideration, noting the white lines around her lips.

"I care for ye, Brianna." He longed to cup the warm silk of her face in his hand, to show her just how much he cared. "I want ye," he said softly.

She gave him a sharp glare and pulled her hand from his grasp. "And you want Edzell." Her shoulders straightened. "To think, all the men who sought the power of my wealth, and it's the man posing as my Captain of the Guard who secures it."

"And a Highlander, no less," he teased.

Her cheeks flushed to a bonny pink. "How can you joke about this? We are being forced to marry."

"No one is forcing me to ask ye."

Her gaze settled on her fingers clasped within his. "I'm educated. I can speak and write in seven languages, and I prefer doing numbers to needlework. I have no desire for children." She thrust her jaw out in that stubborn way she did. "I'm not an ideal choice for a wife."

Her palm was hot and moist in his hand. It was obvious she did not want this and was trying to talk her way out of it. Insulting him, however, was hardly the way to accomplish that.

His thumb brushed the underside of her exposed wrist, where her skin was softer than the finest silk. She drew in a soft breath, and he knew she was not as unaffected as she perhaps wanted to be.

"Companionship will come with time," he said. "We share something deep, something compulsive." He leaned over her so the delicate scent of lavender tickled his nose, and his skin sizzled near the warm heat of her body.

He felt her proud stance soften. "You are not a good fit for me," she whispered.

It was a paltry defense. One he would see stripped away.

He traced the gentle sweep of her neck with the back of his fingers. "I disagree." He brushed a stray lock of hair from her brow. "We are a perfect fit for one another."

Her face tilted toward his, and the glint of desperation melted away.

His fingers trailed along the sides of her narrow waist. "There is a pull between us that I've no ever felt before." He gently tugged her toward him. "I dream of yer lips against mine, of your scent surrounding me as I caress every soft curve of yer body."

Her lashes swept across her rosy cheeks. He bent over her, nuzzling her ear, and whispered in Gaelic. "*Nuair a bhios sinn ceanailte, chuiridh mi mo theanga far an robh mo mheoir."*

She stiffened beneath his fingertips.

When we are wed, I cannot wait to slide my tongue where my fingers have been.

Her eyes went wide and her head jerked back in disbelief. Apparently, one of her seven languages was Gaelic. Quite the pleasant surprise.

He caught her hand again before she could push away from him. "Just because I can say it in a different language doesna make it any less crude, aye?"

She yanked her hand back and crossed her arms once more. "You've made your point."

"Brianna, I canna promise I will be the best fit for ye or that every day of our lives together will be perfect. I can promise ye that I will try to be the best husband to ye that I can. I will protect ye with the last breath in my body." He grinned down at her, "I may even let ye win at a debate with me—in Italian. If ye ask nicely."

A small smile crept over her lips. "Impossible. You don't speak Italian, do you?"

"No," he confessed. "But perhaps ye can teach me something new." He stroked her velvety cheek and leaned close to her once more. His finger skimmed across the petal softness of her lower lip and trailed down her slender throat. "Until our wedding day, my lady."

With a delicate, nibbling kiss to her neck, he stepped back and bowed low before quitting the room, leaving a red-cheeked Brianna staring after him.

Chapter Sixteen

Stained light poured in through the chapel's windows and cast an assortment of colors over the sea of faces staring at Brianna. Flowers dotted every available space, and the scent of fresh herbs stirred from underfoot.

Nervous flames flicked from the many candles spread around the room. They gave off as much heat as they did light. Her brow tingled, and she hoped she had not begun to sweat.

"Do you take this man as your husband?" Thomas repeated once more. His voice resonated over the subtle shifts and awkward squirms of the congregation.

Colin stood at her side, his confident smile never wavering, despite her obvious hesitation. He looked remarkably handsome with his rich auburn hair tied back. His sharp jaw was clean-shaven and made his skin appear surprisingly smooth and soft. Even his barbaric attire held a level of elegance she had not seen before. His leine was crisp, his kilt perfectly pleated around his waist, and a finely crafted gold pin accented the length of plaid slung over his shoulder.

Handsome did not change the fact that he would be the man to strip her of her freedom. Postponing her acquiescence to their union would not keep the event from happening. Nothing would.

She had no choice. "I do."

A collective sigh rose from the masses behind her, and Colin's dimple showed with his broad grin.

And so it was done. Her life in forfeit for his. She glanced back at the faces of the very people she had saved from her uncle, and her heavy heart lifted. Their joy was genuine, and their affection obvious in their smiles. No matter how difficult marriage would be to endure, her people seemed happy with Colin.

He clasped her hand in his, and something cold and heavy slipped onto the fourth finger of her left hand.

She glanced down and found a thin gold band with a brilliant set round emerald shining up at her. Her stomach flipped, and she covertly scanned the attendees of their wedding. Not the nobles who covered their emotions easily, but the familiar faces of her people. The congregation did not appear as shocked as she at such a blatant display of the popish old ways.

The caress of Colin's thumb against her finger pulled her attention back to him. "I hope ye like it," he said in a quiet voice. "It belonged to my mother."

Brianna bit the inside of her cheek and nodded. "It's lovely," she managed. Indeed, the ring was beautiful, but the act of presenting her with it could be construed as Catholic sympathy. Edzell would not do well with unfavorable attention from the church.

Colin's hands wrapped around her waist, and he pulled her closer toward him. "I believe I get to kiss my bride, aye?"

Cheers erupted behind them, along with several inappropriate jests.

Thomas lowered his head, but not before Brianna caught his quick smile. "That you do, laird."

Discomfort sizzled in Brianna's cheeks. She tensed at Colin's touch, unsure what to expect.

He leaned closer, and her pulse fluttered with an anticipation she could not disregard. She closed her eyes, and the heat of his mouth stopped just over hers. His hand slid behind the back of her head, his thumb caressing her cheek. Her breath came fast. He had held her thus before.

His mouth closed over hers in a kiss passionate enough to declare her as his, but tame enough to be socially appropriate. The smooth skin of his chin glided against hers, and the spicy scent of his breath sent a chill of excitement raking across her flesh. He was delicious to kiss with his face clean-shaven.

Much as Brianna hated to admit it, she wanted to stand on her toes and crush her mouth to his, to let his smooth face rub hers again and again as their tongues entangled in a fire of wild heat.

Instead, she remained straight-backed and stiff in his arms. She refused to allow herself to demonstrate the wanton behavior that was doubtless expected by the neighboring lords. The urgency of their wedding was already enough to send tongues wagging.

The tip of Colin's tongue flicked slowly between her lips, and a little whimper sounded in her throat before she could stop it.

He gave a low chuckle and broke off the kiss. "I canna listen to those sounds ye make or it will be a short celebration." His words were lost to others beneath the cheers of the congregation. "But tonight—" His lips grazed her neck, just below her earlobe. "I promise to make ye verra, verra happy."

Brianna's nipples drew tight and her cheeks stung with the force of her blush. He released her with a wink and wrapped her icy hand in the warmth of his.

She shoved aside her desire and accepted his attention for what it was. He was trying to sway her with intimacy and the promise of pleasure.

Soon he would realize she would not be so easily won. Passion would not respect her opinions or allow her freedom. She looked at him from beneath her lowered lashes. How long before his relaxed demeanor would tense? How long before his charming smiles drifted toward other women? How long before his tender touches would become cruel?

No, she would not allow herself to be placated with longing, not when her spirit was locked beneath the weight of the vows she had just spoken.

* * *

Revelers danced in their finest clothes, and the table before Colin practically bowed beneath the bounty of choice meats and decadent pies. Lively music echoed up to the high ceiling of the great hall and rivaled the spirited conversation of the wedding guests. All of this, and not a single thing brought even the slightest smile to his somber bride.

Petulant though she might be, she was certainly the bonniest thing he'd ever laid eyes on. The wedding took only two short days to organize, and yet she looked every part the well-prepared bride. Save for the way she sat uncomfortably upright with her hands clawed tightly around the arms of her chair.

Her rich brown hair tumbled unbound down her stiff shoulders and shone in the rich afternoon light. She wore a simple gown of pink satin that accented the natural flush of her cheeks and lips.

Colin had left her alone until this day in the hopes the lass would come to terms with the idea of their union. Considering her apparent displeasure, perhaps that had not been a wise decision.

"Ye look beautiful." He placed a hand over her hard-knuckled grip on her chair.

"Thank you." Her response was automatic and distracted.

Never one to be dissuaded, Colin carefully pulled her hand from the chair, one finger at a time, and turned it palm up. "I shouldna have left ye alone these last few days. I thought ye would need some time."

Her wary gaze slid toward him. "I had much to prepare. I didn't need the distraction." She pulled at her hand, but he held tight.

The pad of his middle finger circled her moist palm and trailed down the heel of her hand. He dragged three fingers across her inner wrist, slowly, sensually.

"Would I have been a distraction for ye?" He glanced up to watch her reaction.

Brianna swallowed hard, and her gaze followed his finger's path up the inside of her arm to the crook of her elbow. The woman may not have wished to wed him, but her body responded to his in a way that pleased him immensely.

She pulled her arm away and looked up at him. "I don't like

how you do that."

"Do what?" He did not give chase to the hand she tucked firmly in her lap, though he wanted to.

"Touch me but once and I feel my thoughts slide away from me." Her stare dropped to his mouth and his blood heated. "It's very frustrating."

His fingers skimmed the delicate line of her jaw. "Ye act as if ye are the only one affected."

A line appeared between her brows, and her face softened.

He eased forward in his chair, intimately close. She swallowed, but she did not lean away. He closed the scant distance between them and pressed his lips to the plush softness of hers. Conscious of those watching, he halted the kiss before it could truly start. Unleashing his passion before their guests would do nothing but bring her shame.

"If only ye knew how badly I want ye." He drew a deep breath and willed his blood to cool. "Tonight," he said into her ear.

The pink tip of her tongue parted her full lips and left them moist, glistening.

Colin shifted in the hard seat.

So much for his blood cooling.

"Lady Lindsay, congratulations on your marriage." A nasal voice shattered the fragile moment between them.

"Robert?" Brianna's head jerked toward her cousin.

"I must say, I never thought to see one as delicate as you married to something so uncivilized." The whoreson glanced around with a pretentious smile, as if looking for supporters to his statement. He found naught but curious stares. "Considering the haste of the wedding, I assume we will see your belly swell with child soon?"

Colin stood abruptly and stepped around the table. "I dinna care for the way ye are speaking to my wife."

Robert's beady eyes darted between Colin and Brianna. His cheeks mottled purple. "What does your father say of this union, Brianna? I see he is not present. That comes as little surprise." He sneered down at her in a way that made Colin want to put his fist through the bastard's face. Again.

"I suggest ye leave her alone. And I suggest ye dinna test my sincerity."

Frustration twisted in Colin's gut. There had been no asking Brianna's father for permission, not that Colin hadn't tried. Magda had offered to help, and came downstairs frantic with worry at finding Laird Lindsay's bed empty. Colin understood what the aging woman did not.

There was much to discuss with his new wife. After the wedding night.

Before Robert could reply with another offensive comment, Magda approached. She wore a wreath of flowers in her hair and pride gleamed in her bright blue eyes.

"It is time, my lady." She gently touched Brianna's hand and looked at Colin. "I must spirit your bride away, but promise you will be reunited soon."

He inclined his head in understanding and met Brianna's worried gaze before she was led away. Long shadows stretched along the walls of the castle. The sun was setting. Darkness would come soon and she would be in his arms. A stirring of desire coiled deep within him.

He turned his attention back to Robert. Alec shouldered past the pretentious nobleman and stood directly beside Colin.

"Watch where you walk, barbarian." Robert brushed at the sleeve of his jacket.

Alec's face remained cold and impassive. "Give me a reason to kill ye."

Robert's eyes went round in his long face. "You savages are as bloodthirsty as they say."

Alec bared his teeth and snarled. "Care for a demonstration, Lowlander?"

Robert turned on his heel and pressed through the throngs of revelers in his haste to escape.

"Ah, ye have a way about ye, Alec." Colin grinned at his old friend and accepted the congratulatory smack on his back.

"Colin MacKinnon wed." Alec shook his head in mock disbelief. "I dinna ever think to see the day."

Colin chuckled. He turned his gaze toward the open doorway to his left. Several halls and a short climb up the spiral staircase, and he would arrive at the room he would share with Brianna.

"Watch out lest ye be the next to wed, old friend," he said to Alec.

Alec smirked. "That isna likely. I dinna think I'd find a wife to put up with me."

Before Colin could reply, Magda's withered hand settled on his forearm. A smile creased her eyes. "She waits for you, laird."

His blood heated with anticipation. He nodded his gratitude to Magda and turned toward the doorway.

Finally, the time had come to make Brianna his wife.

Chapter Seventeen

Brianna sat on the coverlet of her large bed, her legs crossed tightly at the ankle in front of her. No longer did she occupy the center of the mattress as she had done her whole life. She'd been nudged to one side by obligation. The bed was to be shared. With her husband.

Her throat worked in a swallow that failed to wet her dry mouth and failed to alleviate her fear.

Precious wax candles dripped into metal trays throughout the room. Their flames were too bright for Brianna's liking. They exposed too much.

The nightrail she wore was a whisper of fabric over her naked body, a fine gown meant to entice love and make the wearer feel beautiful.

She did not feel beautiful.

The white silk had been woven so thin, it showed every intimate line of her body. She was bared. Vulnerable.

Heavy footsteps fell upon the private staircase leading to the room, and she knew he approached. Colin. Her husband. The breath squeezed from her chest and her pulse tripped an erratic rhythm. Once this one act was done, there could be no annulment. She would be irrevocably married. Forever.

The shuffle of feet sounded outside her door, followed by the familiar squeak of the latch. Her chest rose and fell in quick succession as panic took control.

She squeezed her eyes shut as if not seeing could make the situation disappear. The door creaked open and then shut. For all she wished it to stop, she was being plunged into a life she did not want. Footsteps approached the bed. Her heart pounded against her ribcage.

Colin was a good man, and they did share passion. But he was still a man, and men took what they wanted without thought or consideration.

"Brianna." Colin's voice was mere inches from her face, his voice gentle.

She opened her eyes and found him gazing down at her, his features soft and his concern genuine.

"I brought ye some wine if ye like." His thumb brushed her cheeks. "Ye dinna need to cry, lass. I willna hurt ye."

Was she crying? Humiliation burned through her veins. The cool silver of a goblet pressed to the heat of her palm, and she took the proffered wine with unspoken gratitude.

She craned her head over the rim and sniffed the contents with as much discretion as was possible. The heady aroma of wine met her examination.

Colin's chuckle was warm and free of mockery. "I wouldna poison ye, lass. I thought ye might like it to calm yer nerves."

Suddenly sheepish for her hesitation, Brianna lifted the goblet and took a delicate sip. The rich wine burned pleasantly against her throat and settled in her stomach with a comforting warmth. No bitter aftertaste.

He watched her carefully. "Magda dinna frighten ye, did she?"

"Magda?"

His eyes searched hers. "Did she speak, ye know, about what to expect?"

Brianna gazed down at a loose thread of her nightrail. "No, I read a pamphlet on it."

"A pamphlet?" The smile was evident in his voice.

She nodded, unable to meet his eyes. She stared down at her gown. The fabric was so thin, the pink of her naked skin showed beneath. She pressed her body into the bed, as if shrinking back from the transparent garment could make it less revealing. As if the act could quell her desire to crawl out of her own flesh and slink into the shadows.

Colin eased onto the edge of the mattress beside Brianna.

His stare was serious, focused. Something deep within her knew what that look meant. It was time.

Her heart stuttered.

She did not want this. Not the consummation, not the marriage, not the end of her freedom.

"Colin, I want to talk first." Her voice was loud in the silence of the room.

"Are we no talking now?" His eyes were almost black in the dimly lit room. She didn't need light to know exactly how green they were.

"We are. But I—I don't know that I can do this." She drew a deep breath and inadvertently filled her nostrils with the rich aroma of soap and masculinity. Her body hummed in response to his closeness.

"Ye can, I assure ye." An amused smile touched his sensual mouth.

He traced a taunting line from her elbow up to her shoulder. She watched the ascent of his finger before turning her eyes to him once more.

"I want to bring ye a pleasure I let ye but sample the other day." He leaned closer, and the ropes beneath the mattress creaked. "Ye are my wife now. I want to taste the sweetness of yer lips and run my fingers through the silk of yer hair like I've imagined since the day I met ye."

His voice was low, hypnotic. "I want to touch all of ye and see if it's possible that the rest of ye is as velvety soft as yer cheek. I want to hear ye make those sounds when I kiss ye that bring me to my knees with longing." He nudged her mouth with his, and the spicy lure of his breath set her heart pounding for a whole different reason. "I want to love ye, Brianna."

And then he kissed her, his lips insistent, his tongue coaxing as he swept the protest from her lips. The fine goblet slipped from her fingers and clattered to the floor below.

Colin sat back on his heels and pulled the shirt over his head, baring his powerful torso.

A blaring warning sounded in her brain even as her traitorous eyes feasted on the masculine flesh laid before her. "What are you doing?" The question squeaked from her tight throat.

"Taking my wife to bed," he said simply. He braced his arms on either side of her and leaned forward.

"Please." she whimpered and scooted against the cushioned wall of pillows behind her. "I do not want this. We should wait."

He pressed his lips to her neck and inhaled deeply. "Why do ye wish to wait?" Her nipples strained against her flimsy dress in response to his caress.

His tongue flicked against her hot skin between kisses, one after another down her neck, down her chest, down to where her breasts swelled against the loose neckline of her nightrail. She closed her eyes and tried to ignore the surge of pleasure. "Please do not force me."

His breath teased the responsive flesh along the tops of her breasts. She clasped her hands tightly in her lap lest she give in to the urge to stroke his chiseled flesh.

"I would never force ye." He nuzzled the fabric of her gown aside, and his mouth touched the skin above her nipple.

Her body tingled with awareness, and a steady, pulsing heat blossomed to life.

She drew a shaky breath. "You say you will not force me, yet you do not cease your actions."

He buried his face in her hair, his lips skimming her ear. "Ye want this."

She clamped her teeth together and tried to ignore the way his scent made her blood sizzle, the way his smooth chin against her skin made her wonder things a lady should not think.

"How can you say I want this when clearly I do not?" Her voice was a strained whisper.

His teeth scraped against her earlobe, his breath hot against the sensitive spot there. "Mmm...I think ye clearly do."

He pressed a kiss to the base of her throat. "Yer skin is warm beneath my lips, yer heartbeat frenzied." His fingers trailed over her low neckline, and the palm of his hand grazed her hardened nipple.

Brianna bit her lip to keep the sound of pleasure locked within her.

"Yer body betrays yer words." His fingers slid down the length of her arm to where her hands gripped one another in her lap. "I can feel yer restraint."

He caressed her thinly-clad thigh, the roughness of his calluses snagging the delicate fabric. His thumb brushed dangerously near the juncture of her legs.

She squeezed her thighs together, trying to clear her body of its wanton desire to part beneath his touch.

The heat of his mouth moved beside her ear again, his voice an intoxicating mix of velvet seduction and desire. "Ye havena stopped thinking about my threat."

Chills of delicious excitement rose on her arms, and the warm thrum between her thighs roared to a steady pound.

I want to slide my tongue where my fingers have been.

Crude words, sinful words that went against everything she had been taught as a girl.

And she had not been able to stop thinking about them. Surely he had not been serious.

"I don't know what threat you're talking about," she countered. Even she could hear the lie behind her breathy words.

Colin grasped the simple tie holding her nightrail closed. "I think ye remember."

The bow slid soundlessly from its knot, and the thin silk slipped from her shoulders. She caught the flimsy neckline before her breasts were exposed and clutched it against her. Air that had moments before been too warm now felt cool against her bared skin.

Colin's gaze dropped to where her hands were fisted against her chest, to where the only separation between his eyes and her naked breasts was a slip of ineffective clothing.

He captured her lips with his. Breathing was impossible, thinking was impossible, hearing anything other than the roar of her own heart—all impossible—all the telltale signs of an anticipation she was starting to truly understand.

• • •

Colin dug his hands into the soft mattress and nibbled Brianna's full lower lip. He needed to go slow, to fight the raging lust threatening his control.

The wisp of a gown she wore draped from her smooth shoulders like moonlight. Her hands folded over themselves in front of her breasts as if in prayer. He would see her hands removed and her body unveiled before him.

His tongue swept deeper into her mouth as he scooted closer to her. She tasted sweet. Innocent.

His.

Her mouth opened and she leaned her head back with a sigh of surrender. He covered the tightness of her furled fingers with his hand. They loosened beneath his gentle persuasion and the fabric fluttered to the bed, leaving her torso naked for his exploration. He eased back and let his gaze glide across her breasts in all their round, creamy white perfection.

His heartbeat thrummed without restraint, absent the control he typically possessed. He wanted to glide his palms over her, revel in the taste of her desire, feel every glorious inch of her body with his mouth, his hands, his everything.

He pulled her toward him with a strangled growl and pressed his lips to hers. His tongue discovered the depths of her yielding mouth, and his hands roamed over the warm, full weight of her breasts.

She was firm beneath his touch, her skin a silk so fine he worried his callused fingers might snag it as he had her nightrail.

Brianna gasped against his lips and arched her back so her breasts pressed into his palms. And then finally, finally she touched him. Fingers extended and trembling, her hands hovered over his chest.

"Touch me, wife," he said in a gravelly voice.

Her heart danced beneath her soft breast, a frantic beat that matched his own. She gave a desperate moan, and he felt the thread of her control snap. Her hands turned hungry, her palms sliding against his chest, her nails gently scraping his nipples.

Jesu, her touch was a fire that burned straight into his loins.

He trailed kisses from her lips down the graceful length of

her neck. His fingertips skimmed the underside of her breast, and everything slipped away except the woman in his arms. He wanted to taste her, to claim her as no other man had. As no other man ever would.

He curled his hand around her breast and closed his lips over the delicate bud of her nipple. Her breathing turned ragged, frenzied. The silent mark of yearning he'd been seeking.

Colin's muscles drew tight and his body screamed for her, demanding the lust raging within him be slaked. He could hardly bear the throbbing ache of his cock.

His lips moved against her soft, warm skin, nuzzling and nipping the fullness of her breasts until her fingers tangled in his hair.

She writhed beneath him. "Do what you did before. Please." Her voice was breathless, her words quick with an urgency he knew all too well.

His cock lurched beneath the stroke of her words, his body aflame with anticipation for her cries of pleasure. His hands glided over her nightrail to the cleft between her thighs.

"Yes," she whimpered. "Please."

He stroked his finger against the damp fabric. He shook with a demanding need he hadn't known before.

Brianna pressed her hips against his cupped hand, her moan insistent.

Colin grasped the nightrail where it crumpled at her waist and slid it lower, under the tantalizing curve of her bottom, down, down, down the length of her long, slender legs.

His hands slid back up her body from her shapely ankles and tantalizing thighs to the sweet temptation that now demanded his attention. Her shapely hips rolled beneath the power of her longing, her flat stomach and narrow waist gently bending and flexing with each subtle movement. She was even more beautiful than he'd imagined.

He covered her body with his, laying the hardness of his battle-scarred body upon the velvety warmth of her soft innocence. Each movement was made with a forced leisure, and his muscles ached with the force of his restraint. His lips came down on hers, rapacious in the need to catch her gasp of pleasure. His hand slipped between them and eased between her thighs. Naked, wet heat met his fingertips. Her body stiffened and she sighed into his mouth.

She was swollen. Slick.

His thumb rolled against her sensitive little nub. Her breathless cries filled the room, her hips matching every stroke, every touch.

Her lashes fluttered closed and her head fell back. Colin watched the pleasure play out on her face. This exquisite creature was his wife.

He captured her heart-shaped lips once more with a kiss that branded her as his. She tightened against his fingers and he knew she was about to come. He withdrew his hand from between her legs and grinned. It was time to savor everything his bride had to offer.

Her lips fell open, and confused injustice sparked hot in her gaze.

Colin smiled down at her. "I made ye a promise."

Before she could protest, his lips found her breasts and skimmed over each rounded globe, savoring her rosy nipples before continuing his descent downward.

Her gasp echoed off the stone wall. "What? No."

The bed creaked beneath them as he shifted his body lower to allow for better access. He kissed the tops of her legs and slid his hands across the smooth expanse of her inner thighs to keep her from closing her legs.

"No." Her hips lurched away from him, but her plea was husky with want.

He exhaled through his mouth, teasing her with the heat of his breath.

"Please." She squirmed beneath him.

Colin kept his hands fixed on her legs and kissed the inside of her right thigh before shifting to the left.

Tonight, his wife would learn he did not make empty threats.

Heat fanned over Brianna's thighs in delicious torment. She clenched her eyes closed against the image of his head between her legs.

What he intended to do was wrong. Sinful. His slight shift forward whispered against her flesh, and her breath hitched. She should push away, scream for him to stop, and yet she was locked into place by the edge of her curiosity.

The warmth of Colin's mouth passed over her, alternating kisses on either side of her innermost thighs with an excruciating slowness. He stilled between her legs. Heart hammering, she peeked her eyes open. His hot stare burned into her, watching as he ducked his head and dragged his tongue against her most sensitive flesh.

She cried out and jerked her hips away from him. Her cheeks burned and her heart squeezed the breath from her chest. His mouth was too close, too intimate. Aching hunger clawed within her, and moisture pooled where his tongue had swept.

His hands slid under her buttocks, toward her waist, and curled around her thighs, trapping her. "Let me love ye, wife."

He brushed the softness of his lips against her, and her nipples drew tight with pleasure. She shook her head against the pillow. "It's sinful. It's not-it's not…"

"In yer pamphlet?" He pulled her hips upward, lifting her slightly off the bed and the full warmth of his mouth closed over her.

The wet heat of his tongue parted her the way his fingers had done before. The way he had promised. She clutched blindly at fistfuls of blanket beneath her, and the argument on her lips slipped into an agreeable moan.

His tongue pressed the source of her delight and flicked once, twice. Fire tingled through Brianna, and her ragged breath battled the silence of the room. His tongue continued a maddening, lazy circle, and the tip of his finger gently slipped inside of her.

His muffled groan against her sent a thrilling vibration through her core.

Her body tensed and her hips arched in reflex. He pulled her tighter within his arms, his mouth following her impatient gyrations.

A gentle scrape of his teeth and she slid over the edge. Pleasure exploded within her body, beneath Colin's mouth, and mated with the flame of his merciless tongue. Quivers of bliss spiraled through her, and a breathless cry whimpered between her lips.

Colin propped up on an elbow with a lazy smile as the final waves of euphoria lapped within her.

"It wasna as bad as ye thought it'd be, aye?" His eyebrows rose suggestively.

She couldn't help her carefree grin anymore than she could keep her eyes from lingering on his gloriously naked chest. "I wouldn't complain if it were done again."

"Ah, wife, we will have a lifetime to do that again, I promise ye." He rose to his knees and rested his hand on the belt securing the plaid to his waist. "There's still more to teach ye tonight."

Her gaze fell to where his fingers pulled at the thick leaver strap, to where his hardness bulged beneath his plaid. A blend of excitement and trepidation quickened her pulse.

Colin pulled the belt from its buckle and tugged it from his waist so the kilt slipped down his narrow hips. Brianna succumbed to the tantalizing lure of her curiosity and followed the trail of auburn hair that trickled from his navel down, down, down.

She gasped and wrenched her eyes away. Not that it mattered. She could not clear her mind of what she'd seen.

Tight muscles ran rigid along the lower portion of Colin's torso, carving lines on either side of his hips. She drew a shaky breath. The thin line of hair trailed down his banded stomach to where it grew thick between his legs, where his flesh jutted proudly from his body.

Her pamphlet stated he would place his lance within the softness between her legs. It had sounded so easy. No mention had been made of a man's lance being so large, so intimidating.

She shuddered at the thought of that massive thing between Colin's legs pressing inside of her.

"Brianna." The burr of his Highland brogue was thick, and the n's in her name came out in a soothing purr. "Ye can look upon me if ye like."

She stared miserably at the rumpled coverlet and shook her head. "I would prefer not to."

There was a pause. "Ye find me displeasing?"

Her eyes flew to his face. "Of course not, I find you—"

He grinned at her, and the dimple appeared in his left cheek. "Ye find me what?"

The churl! "I find you too large."

"Ach, ye know how to warm a man's heart." He folded his hand around hers and brushed his lips against her knuckles.

The familiar heat of desire settled in her belly, and the slow, sensual pulse hummed to life once more. He guided her hand down his smooth, powerful chest to the hard muscles along his abdomen. He stared at her, his movements slow, as if gauging her reaction before continuing. Her fingertips brushed the coarse hair and she trembled. She knew where he drew her, where she would touch next.

Brianna hesitated, but Colin eased her hand lower. His jaw clenched tight and his heavy breath matched her own. He removed his hand from hers, leaving her free to touch him without aid. To make her own decision.

She looked again upon his rigid flesh. He wanted to feel her hands on him, yet she doubted she could wrap her fingers completely around him. The top of the thick column was rounded, smooth with a bead of moisture glinting at its tip.

Brianna bit into her bottom lip and tentatively trailed her finger against his length from where it rose from his body to its swollen end. Colin gave a strangled groan, a sound so tortured it drew her from her study. Pain did not glint in his eyes, but something darker, more primitive.

He enjoyed the stroke of her hand, the same as she enjoyed his. Only this time, she wielded the power.

She curled her fingers around the base and proved her initial observation correct. He was too big.

Touching his lance was not unpleasant, as she had assumed it might be. The pulse of his ardor thrummed against her palm, rigid as bone beneath satin flesh. How could something so hard possess such softness?

She continued her exploration, caress by timid, curious caress. Colin's breathing grew deeper, heavier. Moisture warmed between her legs once more.

The tip was spongy beneath her fingers compared to the steely shaft. She brushed the pearl of moisture with the pad of her middle finger and smeared it in a delicate circle around the smooth head.

Colin caught her wrist and pulled her hand away. "Enough."

He grasped her shoulders and applied light pressure, pushing her to the bed. She complied because she knew not what else to do. The coverlet was cool against her naked back, a comforting contrast to the heat of her unease. He crawled over her until his taut body hovered over hers. His skin did not touch hers, yet she could sense his warmth. Her pulse quickened with nervous anticipation. Frantic thoughts jumbled in her mind—acknowledgement of the finality of their act, fear of the unknown, primal excitement for what she sensed would come.

His mouth claimed hers and his tongue stroked hers with savage yearning. He slipped his fingers between her thighs once more, caressing, enticing, probing. She tried steeling herself against the pleasure he gave, but then he brushed that incredible place he always seemed to find, and her hips moved of their own volition. All thoughts fled her mind, save the need to quell the fire raging within her.

The weight of his body settled on top of her. Something blunt nudged her sex and replaced the teasing of his fingertips. She arched instinctively toward him, and a low groan purred in the back of her throat.

Colin nuzzled against her neck, his voice like dark velvet in her ear. "Do ye want this, wife?"

Colin silently cursed himself for even posing the question to Brianna. His cock pulsed against her slick cleft, all the desire, all the longing, poised for relief.

"Yes." The glorious word came on an exhaled moan.

He breathed a sigh against her glossy hair. If she had said no, he wasn't sure stopping would be possible.

He braced his arms on either side of her and gently pushed. Her narrow opening gripped his sensitive tip, and his hands fisted in the coverlet. Raw lust pumped in his veins, tempted him to thrust hard and fast. He tightened his hold on the bedding.

Brianna rolled her hips against him, nudging him deeper until he felt the barrier of her maidenhead.

This was going to be more difficult than he realized, especially when she was so damn tight.

Sweat pricked his brow. He needed to focus, to control himself. He leaned over her and swept his lips against hers. "Forgive me," he whispered against her mouth.

He felt her lips fall open in question, but did not wait for her to speak before he broke through her delicate wall.

She gasped sharply. Her body stiffened beneath him. He gritted his teeth against the ache of pleasure and forced his body still so she could adjust to him.

Colin looked down at her and found unshed tears glimmering in her wide eyes. He lowered his head and touched his lips against each eyelid, then caressed the sweetness of her mouth with his own.

"I dinna mean to hurt ye," he said.

"I know," she said softly. "I read this would happen."

He bit back a grin. "Are ye all right?"

She gave a tense nod. "You can do what you need to now. I'm ready."

What he needed to? What the hell kind of a pamphlet had she read?

He pressed his lips to the soft skin at the base of her throat. "It's no what I need to do, lass. It's what our bodies want." He caught the tip of her lobe between his teeth and let his breath tease her ear. "Yers as well as mine, aye?"

She nodded against his cheek, but her body remained stiff. He brushed the curve of her breast and pulled her lower lip into his mouth. The muscles along his back burned from holding his position for so long, and his cock throbbed brutally with unsated need.

The fingers of his free hand found the tender bud of her nipple and rolled it beneath his thumb. Brianna's sigh melted against his lips like a decadent sweet, and her body relaxed beneath him. With great care, Colin shifted his hips back and groaned with the jolt of pleasure firing through his body.

He pressed his fist into the mattress, his breath hissing through his clenched teeth. Slowly, he nudged himself inside her once more. Her thighs tightened around his waist, and the uncertainty on her puckered brow smoothed.

He would see her expression cleared. He did not move again. This time he teased the bud of her lust as he eased back, gently circling when he pushed back in. She arched to meet his slow plunge, and a husky moan echoed a deep desire he didn't want her to ever hide. Her eyes were glassy, her cheeks flushed. This was what he wanted.

He increased his tempo, and an incredible friction gripped her in the tightness of her sheath. She moved with him, awkward at first, her rhythm clumsy, before finding the steady pulse of their passion. Her breath came in excited pants.

She gasped and rocked against him, perfectly timed to meet his thrust. "Can I come with you inside me?" she asked between breaths.

The thought of her tight heat squeezing her release around him was almost more than he could bear. "That's the idea," he said raggedly.

He slid one hand over her hip, guiding her natural movements, and shoved deeper, burying himself in the most incredible moist warmth.

Gone were her apprehensions. Her hands roamed over his back, her body arching in fluid, graceful swells against him.

Her heavy-lidded eyes sparkled in the low light, and her kiss-reddened lips parted with pleasure. Something deep within his chest stirred. God, she was beautiful.

Her body ground against him with a sense of urgency, and she grew tense around him. His bollocks tightened in preparation for his own release. Damn it, he would not come before she did. He pulled her nipple into his mouth and swept his thumb against the swollen bud just above where they joined.

She gave a sharp cry and her core spasmed around him,

tight, tighter, tight, tighter. Colin thrust forward one final time and gritted his teeth against the pleasure exploding through him. His skin prickled, his muscles tensing with the glorious wave of release that eased out in a low growl.

His heart raced and his lungs could hold no air, not while he lay cradled between the sweet thighs of his beautiful wife.

He smoothed damp curls from her forehead and waited for her breathing to return to normal before his lips brushed hers one final time. Careful not to squash her, he rolled to the side and wrapped her small frame in his arms.

She nestled against him and lay her head on his chest with a contented sigh. His body was sated, and his woman was safe in his arms. He wound a lock of her hair around his finger. What more could a man ask for?

His chin brushed the top of her silky head.

Tonight was for loving and pleasing, but tomorrow—tomorrow would be for answers.

Chapter Eighteen

Sunlight bathed the haven of tangled sheets. A goddess had slept beside Colin. Well, perhaps not slept.

The room was silent, save the calming of their racing breaths. Pools of candle wax dotted the room, evidence of a night with little rest. Not that Colin minded.

He cradled Brianna's curvy body against him and breathed in her scent. The sun had long since been up, but thus far their only attempt to remove themselves from the private room had resulted in a kiss that quickly led to greater things.

Brianna's hand skimmed the hair of his chest, tickling the skin beneath. Her gaze was distant, her lips lifted in a soft, wistful smile.

He couldn't keep the grin from his own face. "So, was it like what ye read?"

She looked up at him and a pretty blush colored her cheeks. "It was different." Her voice was still husky, a sensual reminder of the passion recently shared.

She rolled back and peered up at him, her expression shy. Though truth be told, he found his attention drifting to the roundness of her breasts thrust out in tempting display. Desire warmed to life in his loins. He should be exhausted by now.

But she was his, and he would never allow himself to miss an opportunity to remind himself of that. His finger traced an invisible path down the silky curve of her breast to her narrow waist. Her nipples drew tight and tiny bumps rose across her skin.

"Mmmm…and how was it different from yer pamphlet?" He tore his gaze from her body and met her sleepy-lidded gaze.

"You did more than was indicated." She looked away, and a flush of color spread over her lovely chest. "The way you made me feel. I didn't expect that."

He leaned forward and brushed a kiss across her naked shoulder. "And how did I make ye feel?" Her eyes closed, her face relaxing in a look of pleasure he'd seen so many times that night. A look he intended to see so many more.

"Beautiful," she whispered. "You made me feel beautiful." Her eyes opened and locked on his. "You made me feel like I mattered."

The backs of his fingers dragged a decadent path from the swell of her hip, back up to the side of her naked breast. "Ye are beautiful, Brianna. And ye matter more than I could possibly tell ye." He traced her jaw with his fingertip. "The start of our union is no what ye deserve." He watched her carefully, gauging her reaction to his words. "And I know ye dinna welcome this."

Her stare sharpened. "It's true that I did not wish to wed, but it was not you who gave me hesitation." She pulled herself to a sitting position and tucked the sheet under her arms so her breasts were hidden from view. "My parents did not have a happy marriage."

The late morning light glinted off strands of gold in her rich brown hair.

He caught a tendril coiling beside his hand and twisted it around his finger with a movement subtle enough not to distract her. "I dinna want an unhappy marriage."

She shook her head, inadvertently pulling the curl from his touch. "I don't either."

Her gaze slid across the room and her fingers clasped in her lap. He studied the tightness of her jaw, the protective stiffness of her back.

She did not believe a happy marriage was possible.

Telling her otherwise, he knew, would not be enough. There was still much wooing to do with Lady Brianna MacKinnon. She may be his wife, but her wholehearted affection and trust were not yet his.

The more she denied him, the more he craved what she

would not give. Such feelings would be hard-won, but he was persistent and stubborn.

His fingertips brushed the smooth line of her chin and tilted her head toward his. He would show her with his actions. His mouth moved against hers in a languid caress. The tension in her body eased and the sheet fell from her breasts.

He would protect her, love her until she realized their marriage could be happy.

Until she did not regret him.

* * *

Brianna peered over the stone windowsill of her solar to where the soldiers trained below. The flushed faces were all familiar, yet none was the one she sought.

She rose on her tiptoes and nudged her hips closer to the wall in an effort to see better. If she leaned any farther, she might fall out her solar window. Or worse, be caught.

The men lined the courtyard just outside the garden, repeating the same ducking-roll motion from that morning.

Her gaze flicked from man to man, seeking her husband. Would he be without his shirt?

A bubble of giddiness swelled within her. Her fingers tingled with the memory of his smooth, muscled flesh moving above her. Of the silky heat of his hardness. Of the way it bumped against her, seeking entrance.

A sore heat pulsed between her thighs.

"Should I be jealous my wife gazes at other men with such obvious pleasure?" Colin said from behind her.

Heat shot to her cheeks. She spun around and found him standing directly in front of her. Water dripped from the tips of his darkened hair. Her wicked mind flashed to images of him in Edzell's bathhouse, his gloriously naked body slick with oiled water and caressed by tendrils of steam.

Her gaze trailed from his crisp leine down to where the muscles of his calves bulged beneath the hem of his kilt. The rest of him was as strong and powerful.

"You can be jealous only of the auburn-haired Highlander I seek below," she said.

His eyebrow rose. "A Highlander, ye say? I hear those men are barbaric." His hands slid over her waist and drew her toward him.

"Indeed. He wears no shirt at practice. Most barbaric." Her fingers splayed across his fresh leine, tracing the firm flesh beneath.

He cupped her bottom and drew her tight against his body. The hardness of his arousal dug into her lower stomach, and her knees went soft for what she had tasted again and again through the night.

He nipped her earlobe. "I think perhaps ye like a half-naked barbarian."

A decadent shiver trickled down her spine. "Perhaps I do."

He swept a kiss across her lips, a whisper of warmth that left her craving the heat of his tongue. "I shall keep that in mind for when I eventually return to my training."

Brianna stood on her toes and leaned into him, hoping his fingers might explore more, touch her in intimate places, make her cry out. "Do you have tasks that call you from the men, husband?"

She breathed in the spice of his masculine scent and suppressed a moan. Perhaps the marriage *could* be happy as he suggested. Perhaps the love she'd read of in poems existed.

Colin stared down at her. "There is much to do today."

Something hesitant lingered in his gaze. She shifted off her toes and took a step back. "You refer to something specific," she said slowly.

The expression on his face was earnest, his lips without his characteristic grin. "I need to talk to ye."

The giddy trip of her heart slammed to a halt. "About?"

"Yer father." His expression did not change, and yet her body felt as though it would burst into flame.

"What of him?" Her voice trembled, and his green eyes narrowed in that overly-perceptive way.

He took a step toward her, and she instinctively took

another step back. Away from him. A frown creased his brow. "I'm no trying to frighten ye."

She stared miserably at a sconce on the opposite wall, unable to meet his gaze. "I know what you ask." A shudder went through her. This was the first time she would speak the horrible words out loud. "Laird Lindsay, the Earl of Edzell, is dead."

If Colin was shocked, he did not appear such. His gaze was kind, sympathetic even, but certainly not surprised. "How long?"

Shame burned within her and seared her cheeks with unforgivable heat. Tears stung her eyes, and the thickening knot in her throat justified silence to her unwilling tongue. Nothing she could do would bring the earl back. Nothing she could do would erase the horror of leaving his death a secret for as long as she had. Her nails bit into her palms.

Colin's hand rested on her shoulder and pulled gently until she stepped toward him. "I know ye well enough to know ye wouldna do this without reason."

She pressed her face to the soft linen of his leine, away from his gaze. He saw too much.

He rubbed the point of tension at her neck and trailed his hand down her back, his touch supportive, lending her the strength she so desperately needed. "I need to know so we can prepare the funeral arrangements," he said. "And I need to know why ye felt ye had to do this."

Brianna nodded and drew a deep, steadying breath. The time for confession had come.

* * *

The tinny clangs of a mock battle outside trickled in through the open window. Colin had listened to Brianna's explanation with careful silence, a silence he now did not know how to fill.

He forced his features to relax lest she read his concern. Her gaze dropped miserably to the floor, but not before he caught the unshed tears clinging to her lashes.

Laird Lindsay died less than a fortnight ago. How she had managed to keep her father's death a secret for this long spoke a great deal of her servants' respect for her.

Blood pounded in his veins and roared in his ears.

Burying a man two weeks dead would not be a feat easily done. Not with a man of such political power and noble status. Especially one with a brother set on keeping the land for himself. No wonder his vile son tried to force Brianna into marriage.

Colin squeezed his arms tight to keep from running a hand through his hair. Or punching the wall.

Damn it, getting the Lindsay land was not supposed to be this difficult.

Brianna craned her head forward and gave a choked whimper, the kind a lass made when she was trying not to cry.

His chest tightened. She had done what she thought best to protect her people. The legal implications had obviously not been taken into consideration, nor did the possibility of someone attempting to charge her with murder. The only card she held in her hand was her legitimacy.

Women had no understanding of the rules of men. Nor of their ruthlessness.

He rubbed a hand against the silky back of her dress. "All will be well, wife."

And it would. He would make certain of that.

But first, there needed to be a funeral.

Chapter Nineteen

Fat raindrops pelted Brianna's cheeks and plastered her hair against her scalp. The battering downpour was fitting for the day and compensated for the tears she would not allow herself to show. She swallowed them down and let them curdle in her stomach with the bitterness of her lies.

The lush grass before her had been slashed open in preparation for a coffin containing no body. She glanced to where the newly planted roses entwined with one another in a thorny embrace over the earl's makeshift grave. The tender buds were clasped tight, as if protecting the secret laced within their roots.

Hands weighted with sympathy rested against her shoulder, and the hushed tones of random nobles murmured words of comfort. But there was no comfort for the ache within her. No words could remove the image of the earl lying with the rich dirt of Edzell forever pressed against his cold flesh rather than cradled in the luxurious, cream-colored silk of his coffin. Not buried with the lavish comforts of a nobleman, but with the crude disposal of a pauper.

Throngs of people whose names she barely remembered offered their condolences before turning away to greet friends. They cowered from the pouring rain in a huddle of rich fabric beneath the eaves of the church. To them, this was a parade to demonstrate their wealth, not a mourning of death.

The world churned in a whirl of black brocades and heavy velvets, a world of darkness threatening to swallow her up. The thud of her heart slowed in her otherwise hollow chest, and the energy needed to draw each breath no longer felt worthy of the effort. Her knees buckled.

Before the earth could draw her toward its sodden embrace, a strong arm slipped around her waist and pulled her upright. A blanket spread warm and dry over the top of her head. The clean scent of soap cut through her painful musings, and she knew without having to look up, he was there. Colin. Her husband.

"I think it best ye come in from the rain now, aye?" His tone was quiet, soothing.

The heat of his hand enveloped hers, and a strong arm caught her around the shoulders. She closed her eyes and allowed herself to revel in the sensation of his comfort.

For all she had fought against their marriage, she did not know what she would have done without him these last few days. He had taken over the funeral arrangements and ordered the servants to complete the tasks necessary. Not once had he turned blame on her or expressed frustration for the mess she had created. He had been supportive.

"Ye should go lie down, lass." The softness of his voice was a gentle interruption of her thoughts. She opened her eyes and found his gaze fastened keenly on her. "Yer guests will understand if ye dinna attend the feast."

He clearly did not know the Lowland nobles as she did. Lips would curve in sympathetic smiles while cold stares would assess her stomach to see if she swelled with Colin's babe, to confirm the rumors of their hasty marriage.

No, she would attend the feast, but not only to dispel gossip. She stared at the empty grave once more. Her attendance was the least she could do for the earl.

* * *

Conversations buzzed around Colin, and countless Lowlanders in their bizarre fashions pressed against him from all angles. Alec stood at his side with a cup of ale hanging from his fingertips. No one attempted to converse with either of them, an offense Colin found himself appreciating.

He stared across the room to where Brianna spoke to

the guests on her own. She had insisted she was well, yet the paleness of her face left unease churning in his gut. At least she had heeded his advice and changed into dry clothes.

The man she spoke to was perfectly rounded in height and girth and leaned on a cane of glossy black that bowed under his weight. His wild, dark hair stuck out in all directions, and he glared down at Brianna with a malice that set Colin on edge.

When the man's fleshy hand locked around her forearm, something dark and dangerous flashed through Colin.

No man touched his wife.

Colin strode across the room, heedless of the stares, heedless of those he shoved aside in his need to get to Brianna. He grabbed the wrist of the hand holding her captive and squeezed the spongy flesh.

"I suggest ye remove yer hands from my wife." He gave the man a look meant to convey the truth behind his warning.

"Your wife?" Dark eyes shifted to Brianna, and the meaty fist released her slender arm. The man shook Colin's grip off, his gaze never leaving hers. "This is what you married?" Five stubby fingers like sausages too stuffed for their skins splayed in front of Colin's chest. "*This* is now in charge of Edzell?"

The bastard wanted a fight, and Colin was only too happy to oblige. He flexed his chest so it pressed against the man's fat hand. "Aye, and *this* could have ye thrown out of Edzell if ye dinna show some respect."

The man's narrowed eyes appeared to sink in the folds of his face, but his hand fell away. "Now I do not regret having missed the wedding." A shallow breath wheezed from his lungs. "I don't care to see my family's land in the fists of a barbarian."

Colin leaned over the man. "Ye'll see just how barbaric I can—"

Brianna stepped between them, a slender hand held out toward each of them to hold them apart. "Colin, this is Lord Reginald Lindsay, my uncle."

"Do not introduce us as if we are equals." The words hissed in a spray of moisture from her uncle's fat lips. "I heard how he forced you to marry him."

The steady chatter of voices around them quieted. People strained to listen, and Colin didn't care. "Ye overstep yer bounds, Lindsay," he growled. His palm burned with the urge to rip his blade free.

"As you've overstepped yours, Highlander." The black cane whipped through the air and smacked against the stone floor.

Colin caught Brianna's stiff shoulders and firmly shifted her behind him. Her eyes were wide, but she did not protest.

When Colin turned his attention back to Lindsay, he found the over-proud nobleman peering around him in an attempt to address Brianna. "Your father's funeral being so close to the date of your popish wedding is a little too coincidental for comfort, niece."

Colin folded his arms over his chest. "That sounds dangerously close to an accusation."

The glittering glare slid back to him. "I think you know exactly what I'm saying, Highlander. Unless you're even more daft than you look."

The muscles along Colin's neck tightened, and a wave of hot blood rushed to his face. "I am laird here, and I will have yer respect."

Her uncle gave an exaggerated smirk and jerked his head to the side, addressing the people around them rather than Colin. "A title earned through the death of her father. The *convenient* death of her father."

Brianna's gasp sounded behind Colin, and the stiff fabric of her gown rustled.

"Indirect words spoken by a man who lacks the strength to speak plainly." Colin stared down at Lindsay in a challenge he hoped the bastard would take him up on.

Lindsay did not cower beneath Colin's intimidation. "I would not be surprised if Lord Lindsay's body bore the markings of a claymore."

Colin's control unwound to a single, solitary thread. His body surged with the force of everything necessary to kill. The slightest provocation and Lindsay would feel the MacKinnon wrath. "I suggest ye remove yerself from my lands."

A smug smile imprinted her uncle's doughy chin. "And I suggest you confess to your crimes or have them laid open for all to see."

Colin's chest filled with a steadying breath. Killing the man would only exacerbate Edzell's problems. "Get out."

Lindsay's hands mottled red and white where he gripped his cane. "You can throw me out now, but I'll be back when I have a missive from Parliament." He craned his head up toward Colin, the threat in his eyes unmistakable. "When I've received permission to dig up my brother's body."

"No," Brianna cried behind Colin.

Her hand grasped his, slick with cold sweat. The weight of her body sagged limply against him.

Chapter Twenty

Dark. Everything around Brianna was dark. Empty. The squeal of hinges broke through her world of nothing, followed by the thud of heavy footsteps on stone.

She was weightless, floating. No. Her brow furrowed. Not floating. Being carried.

Not again.

Her eyes flew open and she jerked upright, her legs kicking against her heavy skirts, arms shoving against the strength holding her aloft.

The strength tightened, and a soothing shush broke through her panic. "I have ye lass."

She stilled, her body locked, tense.

"Are ye hurt?" Colin asked. His step did not falter.

She dragged air into her lungs in an effort to slow the frantic rush of blood. "I awoke to being carried, like before, like with Robert. I thought…"

Her gaze swept across the large bed, the carved chest, the beautiful tapestries threaded with gold. Tension melted from her body. Her room. Warmth replaced the vestiges of icy fear. *Their* room.

"Ach, forgive me, lass. I dinna mean to frighten ye." He stopped beside the bed and lowered her to the soft mattress. "Ye fainted."

He stroked her cheek and Brianna turned into his palm. "Thank you," she murmured. "Thank you for taking me away from…"

Her uncle. Anxiety threaded her body once more.

"Ye dinna need to worry about him." Colin's thumb swept

across her face, a slight, tender touch.

The acidic churning in her belly could not be soothed so easily. If her uncle dug up an empty grave, he would have Edzell in his grasp. "My uncle will stop at nothing—"

The bed shifted and Colin's warmth settled beside her. "Not even the king would issue such permission, Brianna. To do something so vile would be to go against God himself."

He spoke with a conviction that made her want to believe him. She would look up the laws later when she was alone, to confirm for herself the protections in place.

"Ye're too pale. Are ye sure ye're well?"

Her fingertips caressed the smooth emerald on her finger. She had grown accustomed to the ring's weight, and felt reassurance in its tight embrace.

"My uncle accused you of murder, Colin." She blinked slowly against the squeeze of her heart. "Publicly."

He chuckled. "It takes more than a few feeble words to frighten me. Dinna worry yerself, wife. I have no ever found myself in a place I canna get out of." He lowered his voice to a gentle burr. "But I dinna think that is all that weighs on yer mind."

She stared at the muted blue bedding beneath her. Words burned in her throat, trapped, and her vision blurred.

His hand covered hers and his comforting scent embraced her, encouraging the tears she fought so hard to keep at bay. She let his fingers tilt her face so she met his warm stare once more. In the beautiful green depths of his eyes shone an unyielding strength, one she shamelessly borrowed.

"My heart aches with guilt." Her throat strained to speak around the swell of threatening tears. "I did an awful thing. I lied for weeks, and now the earl pays the price of my deception with the grievous dishonor of a pauper's burial."

"Ye did it to protect yer people. There is no shame in that." His tone was calm, as if he were afraid of frightening her.

She shook her head vigorously and did not bother to wipe the strand of hair clinging to her cheek. "I was selfish." Her stomach knotted at the confession, and the ache blossomed to a fierce blaze within her chest. "I did not want to give up my freedom."

He tugged her toward him and coaxed her head to his chest with a subtle caress of her cheek. She wilted against him and succumbed to the weight of her heavy, swollen eyelids.

"Ye had no other option unless ye wed yer cousin, and I think having him as laird would be as bad as yer uncle ruling, aye?" His hand moved in soothing circles against her back. "Ye did what was necessary to preserve the safety and comfort of yer servants. I know ye are ashamed of yerself, lass, but ye shouldna be." He pressed a kiss to the top of her head. "I'm proud of ye."

"Proud of deception? Of placing him in an unmarked grave?" she choked out.

"Of saving yer people, Brianna. Of salvaging yer home. Now dinna worry about it any longer. I'm yer husband—let the worry fall on my shoulders, aye?"

He leaned back and tilted her chin so she looked up at him. "Aye?" he repeated.

She nodded slowly, not trusting her voice, not wanting to push her burden to another.

His hand skimmed her hair. "Ye hold back yer sorrow." His brow wrinkled. "Do ye feel I'll think less of ye if ye cry?"

"It would be foolish to cry. I've already mourned his loss." Traitorous tears blurred her vision.

"I dinna think ye have." He rested his chin on the top of her head and curled his body around her. "And I willna think less of ye for it."

His soft words were all the encouragement she needed. Her face pressed into the protection he offered, and she surrendered to the searing press inside her. Her heart bled out hot tears that dissolved against his leine.

She did not only weep for the father who never accepted her. She wept for the loss of Bernard and the grisly death he endured. She wept for the lies she'd been forced to tell to keep her people safe. She wept for the life her mother had been forced into and for the burden of shame they had both endured.

And there Brianna cried, taking comfort in the arms of a husband she had never wanted.

Colin braced his weight on his elbow and studied Brianna's profile. She had finally fallen asleep. Her eyes were swollen from tears too long pent-up, and red still tinged her nose and cheeks. His chest tightened.

Burying her father had been difficult for her, more so than she realized.

He rubbed a tense area at the base of his neck. Now that Brianna was calmed, he had another issue to sort through—Lindsay's public accusation of murder.

Colin absently massaged the knot from his muscle and let his head fall back against the wall.

Bitter men with little to lose and everything to gain were the most dangerous, especially ones who held Parliament's ear. And men like Reginald Lindsay had a way of winning favor.

The guards stationed around the castle would need to be doubled for a while to keep vigilant for suspicious activity. While Colin was innocent, he was not sure what loose ends Brianna may have inadvertently left behind. Her uncle would latch onto anything he could find and use it to his advantage.

Colin knew men like Lindsay. He would not be caught off-guard by underhanded tricks.

Brianna curled her legs against her chest with a soft sigh. An unfamiliar warmth heated Colin's stomach and a smile rose on his lips. Her nose rounded slightly at the tip, the sensual shape of her plump lips tempting him even in slumber. Careful not to wake her, he stretched a hand toward her and stroked the velvety softness of her cheek.

They had only been married for a few days, yet he found himself thinking of her more frequently than he thought possible.

A delicate line appeared on her brow, the line that always seemed present. The line that indicated she worked too hard.

The last months of her father's illness must have been difficult. She'd had to do the work of a man, and those efforts exacted a heavy toll.

Her worry needed to be eased and her burden lifted. She

needed his strength to see Edzell to right after her ordeal, to ensure all remained safe. His fingertip skimmed the delicate crease on her brow. He knew how to clear the troubles from her mind, and how to prove himself worthy to his family as well.

His father would need proof Colin could manage an estate, keep its people happy, and see the taxes paid and the villagers flourish. All things he knew he could accomplish successfully.

Renewed vigor pumped through him. Tomorrow would bring a new day and a new beginning. A chance at a life he was otherwise denied.

Tomorrow, Colin would claim full duty as laird and free Brianna of her obligations.

Chapter Twenty-One

Brianna stole down the halls, each footstep chased by the overloud swish of her velvet skirts. Clouds hung heavy outside, and a resigned gray sagged over Edzell Castle.

Colin had not been there when she woke, nor was he practicing with the men outside. Truth be told, she was eager to see him. He'd been a steady foothold in her turbulent world of chaos the previous day, like one of Camelot's chivalrous knights protecting his fair lady.

She rounded the corner and stopped abruptly. The door to her solar stood ajar.

Alarm tingled at the base of her neck.

Had someone entered without permission?

The shushed whisper of a page being turned floated from the room. A gentle rustle of parchment, as if it were being flipped through.

She clamped her fingers to her lips to squelch the cry that threatened to tear from her throat. Was someone going through her documents? Had someone broken into her home and her private solar to uncover her affairs?

The contents in her stomach roiled. Her uncle's men, perhaps?

She should call the guards and order the grounds swept for any other intruders. However, by then the person may have already left.

Her pulse raced frantically in her temples. She crept closer and peered through the narrow crack between the door and its frame. Her pounding heart ceased and dropped into her stomach.

Colin sat at her desk, in her chair, surrounded by the ledgers in which she had so carefully noted every purchase, every payment of tax, every rent received.

Her shaky indrawn breath was so loud, she thought surely he might hear. Alas, he was too busy poring over countless hours of her painstaking labor.

His finger traced down the page and his eyebrows rose. The quill perched in his hand scratched over the parchment beside him.

What a fool she had been to think he was different from her other suitors. Yet here he sat, reviewing his fortune, prying open the very core of her life without having ever asked permission.

Part of her wanted to run from the discovery, to find solace in the comfort of her mother's tiny reading room. But there was another part of her, a greater part, that demanded an explanation.

She pressed her palm against the door and pushed it open. "I see you've been busy this morning."

His head jerked up and a wide smile lit his face. "Ah, my bonny wife."

Her gaze deliberately fell on the ledgers surrounding him, silently demanding justification. He rose from the chair, oblivious, and stretched his arms back behind him with a yawn.

The book on the desk lay opened to the very page she had written when he became her Captain of the Guard, the paltry income scribed next to the position in tall, ornate numbers.

"Ye slept so well, I dinna care to wake ye." He made his way toward her with a proud tilt to his jaw.

Captain of the Guard.

The title churned in her mind. Colin had insisted on the position, yet he was a laird's son. He had no need of the income or the title.

Her cheeks burned beneath the frantic tap of her heart.

He'd used his place as a servant to encourage her affection and persuade her lust with graceful fingers and skilled words.

Ignorant to her thoughts, he leaned over her, his intent apparent in the way he angled his mouth toward hers. She turned her head to the side and presented her cheek for his kiss rather than her lips.

He had lied to her about who he was because he had intended to woo her all along. Where other men had failed, he succeeded, because he was far more clever.

And she was the fool.

His lips pressed to her cheek after a brief pause.

She looked behind him to where the desk lay scattered with private matters and notes of accounts she had taken upon herself to see guarded. All the work and time of a full year bared to the mercy of his ravenous eyes. No matter what charming words he would attempt to wrap the scene in, she saw it for what it was.

The inspection of his newfound wealth.

* * *

The thundering silence coupled with the sharp glint in Brianna's eye cautioned Colin from naming a paltry excuse for his presence in the solar.

He did not have to turn around to know what she saw. Ledgers had been pulled from their respective shelves and laid on the desk. His efforts to understand where the accounts stood before assuming his place as laird would not be seen as innocent.

The tight lines around her eyes and mouth told him this. The cheek she'd presented him with confirmed it.

"Ye're tired." His words were justification to himself as much as explanation to her. "I'll have someone fetch ye some broth and Magda can tuck ye back into bed—where ye need to be."

"And let you handle all my accounts?" Her arms folded over her chest.

"I mean to help ye. Ye've taken on too much for too long. Ye dinna have a choice, I know. But this is men's work, the work of a husband, and I intend to take care of all of it. Ye need no ever worry about anything again."

Her eyes flashed with something he couldn't name, not that

he needed a name to know what it meant. He was in trouble.

"You'll take care of everything?" Her voice was harsh, grinding out the words as if it were physically painful to do so. "And what of me? Do you expect me to sit in a room, pregnant, while I sew pretty tapestries?"

Answering yes would be a bad idea.

He rubbed the back of his neck. That damned spot had drawn tight again. "Ye dinna have to sew if ye dinna want to. Ye can do whatever pleases ye."

Her lips thinned and locked all words from his ears.

Colin reached for her arm. "I'm just trying to help ye."

She jerked away from him. "By going through my ledgers," she surmised. "I don't need your help." Her chin raised in a show of defiance. "I don't need *you*."

Colin tried to ignore the way her barb caught at his chest, the way her frosted gaze cut through him. "Ye've taken on too much and canna expect to do everything without help." He shook his head. "Even a laird has a steward and a wife to split the burden ye've assumed."

She pulled something from the folds of her dress. A flash of gold winked between her fingers before she drew her arm back and threw it at him. A heavy ring bounced harmlessly off his shoulder and clattered to the ground.

"Take your ring of office, *laird*. You've earned it." She backed toward the door. "I only request that rather than follow me, you stay with your ledgers and see how wealthy you've made yourself."

She spun into the hallway in a swirl of gold velvet and slammed the door shut behind her.

Colin lifted the ring from the ground. The Lindsay checkered crest was set in grooves upon its wide surface. He looked up and stared at the bolted door where Brianna had stood only seconds before, her words stuck in his heart like a thorn.

The land he sought came at a higher cost than anticipated.

* * *

Brianna stalked the narrow length of her room. The overcast skies left crowded shadows stretching across the walls and floors. Moisture swelled in the air and stuck in her chest. Was this how it started? The very hell she had sought all her adult life to avoid.

She glared at their door in silent challenge. Heaven help Colin if he ignored her warning and followed her into the room.

When the door did not open, a flicker of disappointment only served to fuel her rage.

He'd stripped her of her authority, banished her to a lifetime of women's work. He crushed the light from her soul the same as her father had done to her mother.

What would Colin do next? Intercept her correspondence and burn it?

An image of smoldering letters ripped through her mind, wax seals melting upon the hearth like thick pools of blood. Her mother's fingers clawed, outstretched toward the curling parchment despite their ruined state. The glint of satisfaction in her father's gaze while his soldiers held her back.

Brianna's fist pressed into her flat abdomen. Would Colin restrict her visits with their children? Punish her before them so that they might learn a lesson from her disobedience? A ragged gasp choked from her throat.

She could not allow her child to endure what she had.

A merciful breeze stirred the curtains and carried in the comforting scent of roses, a sweet balm to the pain in her heart.

Brianna made her way to the window, where the flowers climbed the lattice and bloomed against the castle walls. A heavy blossom grew beside her windowsill, vibrant red in the gray light. She cupped her hand beneath its weight. The petals were like fine silk against her fingertips.

What would her mother say if she were here now? Would she lend courage? Incite further rebellion?

Brianna caressed a petal with the pad of her thumb. Her mother's words echoed in her head, the very ones she'd recited to Brianna again and again through her childhood.

Wield knowledge and you can never be disarmed.

What knowledge would aid Brianna now? What must she

learn to better her life? To prevent her enslavement to marriage?

Determination straightened her spine. There was a way to reclaim her freedom. It just had to be found.

Chapter Twenty-Two

The wooden door was heavily banded with iron. More so than all the other doors in the castle, Colin noticed. A door meant to be locked were it not for the twisted mass of metal where a keyhole had once been.

"Are you sure this is it?" he asked Magda.

She squinted at the door. "It is." Her fingers twisted against one another. "I only show you this because I know you intend to help her."

"Thank ye, Magda. I give ye my word that I willna read her correspondence."

Her soft blue eyes met his. "I trust you."

She pushed against the door and it opened with a low, haunting groan, revealing a walled enclosure that could hardly be described as a chamber.

Colin entered the small room, its plain stone walls devoid of the elaborate paint of others. The space was barely large enough to contain the narrow desk and several book shelves. A large, inset window occupied the eastern wall and provided a cushioned bench so one might sit and stare outside. There was no latch. The paned glass could not be opened.

"Why would she stay in here?" he asked.

"This was her mother's study. It isn't much, but the countess did not have many pleasures allow—" Magda pursed her lips and folded her hands together at her waist. "Your wife now spends her time here."

He glanced at the partially filled parchment on the desk. It appeared to be a letter of some sort. "Does she do business here as well?"

"No, she typically uses it for her studies and reading." Brianna's nurse turned toward him. "But if there is a missing ledger, this would be the only place it might be."

What he sought must contain the most recent statement of accounts, as none were uncovered in his assessment of the property, and its standing.

"Thank ye, Magda. Ye've been most helpful."

The lines across her brow deepened. "I'm afraid that is not always the case."

He opened his mouth to protest when her dry fingers settled atop his. "You will always be there for her, to protect her. Knowing she will be safe gives me great comfort." A wistful smile touched her lips. "You're a good man, Colin MacKinnon." Her hand slipped from his. "Summon me if you need anything further."

"Aye, I will. Thank ye, Magda."

He stepped behind the serviceable chair at the desk and glanced around the miserably small room once more. A book lay on the padded seat of the windowsill, the spine soft with age and use.

The Faerie Queene.

The cover fell open like an eager lover. The print was smeared in places and puckered spots showed on the parchment beneath, as if the page had been wet and long ago dried.

He brushed the book closed and left it where it lay. His gaze wandered over a stack of books piled neatly on the desk. He needed to stop wasting time and find the ledger lest Brianna seek him out. If she found him in this room, he knew there would be no undoing the damage.

As it was, he already feared the hurt he'd caused.

He pulled two of the books from the pile and reached for the third when a voice interrupted him. "Are you lost?"

His head jerked up at the sound. Magda stared at him, her usually kind face cold and suspicious, her blue eyes filmy.

"I was looking for—"

"Evidence," she finished for him. "You were looking for evidence against the countess."

Color rose in her thin cheeks, and her eyes flashed with an anger Colin didn't realize she was capable of.

"Magda, ye brought—"

"Don't feed me your excuses and your lies. I've heard them from others before you." She stepped closer, intent obvious in the tension of her slender body. "I know you mean to report what you find to the laird, but mark my words, if you bring anything to his attention about my ward, I'll make sure you live to regret it."

The strength of the old woman's love for Brianna remained the sharpest thing about her.

"I promise ye I'll no ever implicate the lass," he said earnestly.

Visible relief eased the tension from Magda's tired face. "Thank you." She smoothed the front of her dress with trembling hands, much like he'd seen Brianna do on several occasions. "She is an innocent child, a very good child."

She began to turn away and paused, her gaze hesitant as she regarded him once more. "You have kind eyes. I feel like I can trust you."

He smiled, hoping to set her at ease. "Of course ye can."

She edged closer and lowered her voice to a whisper. "Please don't report what you find of the countess's letters." Her gaze slid to her feet. "The punishment she receives far surpasses the offense."

Before Colin could ask for clarification of her disturbing words, the old woman fled from the room, and the partially finished letter floated from its place on the desk.

He knelt low and caught it between his fingers before it landed on the floor, a victory short-lived when his head connected painfully with the underside of the desk. He sat back with a loud curse. His free hand covered the stinging spot of his scalp, probing for blood. He glared up at the offending piece of furniture.

A discolored patch of wood caught his eye. He blinked several times to clear his vision and craned his neck beneath the desk. The lighter colored wood had not been imagined after all.

The surface was flush under his fingertips and shifted with the slightest pressure. He narrowed his eyes to keep the dust out and slid away the detachable piece. The slender hole was almost too small to accommodate his large, clumsy hands, but with a little patience, he managed to pry the treasure from its confines.

Stacks of brittle, yellowed parchment came free from where it'd obviously been stuffed many years ago. A quick glance confirmed the handwriting was not Brianna's.

Quickly, he slipped the desk piece back into place. He'd look at the parchment later. Right now, he needed to speak to Brianna before supper began and he lost his chance.

* * *

Brianna succumbed to the shadows stretching toward her. She lay atop the bed, too resigned to pull the coverlet over her.

The door latch clicked open, but she did not turn toward the sound. For all she knew, it was a servant coming to inform her the evening meal was to be served. Not that she possessed an appetite.

But it was not a servant in the room. Brianna did not need to turn to realize this. She could feel the imposing size of him, sense the direction of his footsteps despite his silence. She curled tighter into herself, her back facing him.

The aroma of Colin's soap teased her nostrils, a scent that once offered comfort and now left her frantic for air to breathe. The mattress moved beneath her to accommodate his weight. She stiffened against a touch that never came.

"Her angels face," his voice was gentle, smooth.

Her brow furrowed at his words.

"As the great eye of heaven shined bright..."

Recognition penetrated her soul. She squeezed her eyes shut and mouthed the remaining words as he recited them.

"...and made a sunshine in the shady place."

Her curiosity nicked the ache of his offense. "You quote Edmund Spenser. Why?" She opened her eyes, but did not turn toward him.

"I can relate to the despair of his characters." Still he did not move closer.

"Oh?" Had he read *The Faerie Queene?*

"I can understand the fear Scudamour must have felt when Amoret was taken on their wedding night. To know she was in the hands of such cruelty and he so helpless to stop it."

He paused, and silence lulled between them.

"To see the delicate flesh of her face turn white with an absence of life," he said. "To fear no ever feeling the heat of her silken flesh, the pain of no ever seeing her smile again." He drew a deep breath. "The shadow of imagining a world without her laughter. Tis a death of hope and joy I couldna bear."

Brianna mentally combed through her books of poetry. Did he know of a poet she had yet to read? "I do not recognize the author," she whispered.

"There is no author," he said, his voice tense. "This is what I felt when I saw ye laid out on the bed of the summer home and I thought—"

This time she turned toward his silence and found his jaw clenched tight, his face lined with a vulnerable sadness she had not before witnessed.

His eyes searched hers. "Ye make a sunshine in my shady place, Brianna. I dinna want a life without ye."

"Colin." She turned over and sat up. "I don't—"

His finger pressed against her lips. "Nay, I want ye to listen, aye?"

She nodded and his finger fell away. "When we wed, I promised to protect ye. This doesna only mean against the cruelty of men. This also means I keep ye from *all* harm."

He stroked her cheek and she did not move away. Such beautiful poetry earned him an explanation at the very least.

"Ye are tired, lass. Worn out with the weight of yer father's death, frightened by the accusations of yer uncle, and buried under the obligations that belong on the shoulders of yer husband. What kind of man would I be to allow ye sleepless nights while I turn my back to ye and train the soldiers?"

Concern shone in his warm green eyes. "I am no asking ye

to give up yer books or yer writing. I'm asking ye to share with me what is my right and let me carry some of yer burden." His thumb circled against her palm, and a ball of warmth pooled low in her belly.

"Let me fulfill my promise to protect ye, aye?" His fingers threaded through hers.

If what he said was true, he meant only to see her happy and healthy. A noble desire for any husband.

Perhaps his intentions to become her Captain of the Guard were as noble, encouraged by the death of Bernard. She thought back to the bitter accusation she'd hurled at him, and her heart crumpled.

She had been cruel.

Her body longed for the security of his embrace. She wanted the heat of his arms surrounding her, making her feel safe and cared for, she wanted his breath stirring the hair along the nape of her neck and his scent filling her with a comfort only he could provide.

And if the sacrifice of sharing her burden was needed, it had become a price she was willing to pay.

"Will ye let me help ye, wife?" he asked.

"Yes," she said softly. "I will let you help me."

He eased closer and pulled her into his arms. She turned with greedy affection toward the spicy lure of his breath.

"Thank ye." His lips brushed hers and ignited the spark of mutual desire.

• • •

Colin strained to see in the flickering candlelight. The stack of brittle letters was laid flat atop the solar desk. Though the hour was late, he found he could not sleep. Not with the mystery of the letters racing through his mind. A letter quivered within his hands.

Damn. It was all in French. The parchment was important enough to be kept hidden from view. What did it say? He knew he could ask Brianna to translate, but was uncertain if the content would cause her further distress.

Fortunately, he knew someone who spoke French, someone who would also be helpful with obtaining information from Lord Lindsay's household without appearing obvious.

A wide smile spread over his face.

Edzell Castle would soon receive a visit from Marie D'Aubigne.

Chapter Twenty-Three

The red-painted walls of the solar had once appeared so luxurious to Colin. Now they were too dark, too aesthetically cloying. They absorbed sunlight and choked the air.

The clash of swords and the rowdy banter of the guards wafted through the window like a cool breeze on a hot day.

He gripped the quill in his fist and leaned against the hard-backed chair. Every part of him ached from lack of movement, from the protesting muscles of his neck, to the creaking of his spine and the stiffness of his knees.

A cheer met his ears followed by hearty laughs. What could possibly be so damn humorous? He turned a page in the ledger and bumped a vial at his side. Black ink poured from the tipped glass and bled out onto the parchment he'd been writing on.

An hour's worth of work—gone. He wanted to throw the desk across the room.

Alec's voice carried through the window, challenging the men. It was a lure Colin could not ignore, especially on a day where the sun rose high in a cloudless sky.

He shoved himself from the hard chair and stalked through the black corridors within Edzell's bowels. The doors ahead of him were propped open to let in the fresh summer air. He quickened his pace toward the temptation of freedom and stepped out of the castle and into the courtyard.

Blinding spots of sunlight danced before his vision, and a gentle breeze rustled his kilt against his knees. How could he have been indoors on a day such as this?

He made his way toward the side of the courtyard and found Alec standing before the men, arms crossed, legs braced wide. A leader's stance, fitting for Edzell's new Captain of the Guard—a role Alec had taken on with ease.

One slight nod from him and the soldiers flew into a battle of dulled blades, their movements graceful and skilled. The earthy scent of sun-warmed grass caught at Colin's awareness and set his heart pounding. After two long weeks sitting prone in a stiff chair, his muscles burned with the need to stretch, and his hands ached to wrap around the hilt of the sword.

He leaned against the wall of the castle and waited for the action to cease before speaking. "Well done, men." He nodded his approval. "Ye've far surpassed my expectations and have turned into a formidable force. I'm proud of ye."

Backs straightened and chests puffed out. As well they should, they'd gotten damn good.

"Ach, through no effort of yers." Alec threw his arm around Colin's shoulders and squeezed.

Colin grimaced. "Ye needn't remind me. I've been away too long."

Two weeks might as well have been a lifetime. Colin missed directing the men, watching their progress, feeling the sun burn his back and warm his hair. Every day he told himself he would show for the morning training session, and every day he found time too sparse to allow such a feat.

Alec shrugged a shoulder. "A laird stays busy."

"Never too busy for my old friend." Colin clapped Alec on the back, and the heavy Lindsay ring shone bright in the sun. All the authority of Edzell and the wealth of its lands were housed within that ring.

But the piece of gold meant more to Colin than authority—it signaled the accomplishment of a goal. He could now prove to his father he was a strong leader. One worthy of ruling MacKinnon land.

Alec turned his back to the men and faced Colin, his face lined with his usual stern expression. "I intended to speak with ye this morning. There is some news I wish to discuss."

Something in the wariness of Alec's eye caught Colin's attention and sent a tense ribbon of alarm coiling in his gut.

"Are the men done at practice?" he asked.

"Aye, do ye want to speak in yer solar?"

A breeze swept in and sent the trees rustling. It was all Colin could do to keep from closing his eyes and reveling in nature's sweet caress once more. The last thing he wanted to do was return to the gloomy, sequestered room and sit in that rigid chair again. "I'd rather speak out here if it suits ye."

"Outside always suits me," Alec said. "Lindsay's men are coming around here more frequently than they were before."

This did not come as a surprise to Colin. In fact, he'd expected it. "Have the men not been following orders?" he asked. All the guards had been given clear instructions to keep Lindsay's men from coming onto the land. If someone ignored these orders, he would need to be reprimanded and made into an example.

"The soldiers are following their orders fine," Alec said. "But Lindsay is getting sly. He's hired men to follow anyone who leaves the castle in an attempt to get someone to talk. Last night, there was another attempt on the grave."

Colin frowned. He did not have to ask which grave. Lindsay's relentless efforts to uncover a nonexistent truth left discontent sloshing in his gut. "Have any of the servants talked to his men?"

Alec's dark hair rippled over his face with an unexpected gust. He shoved it off his brow with an impatient grimace. "I dinna believe so, but that only makes Lindsay all the more suspicious, aye?" Again, he glanced around them. "That's no all I wanted to discuss with ye."

Colin arched an eyebrow and waited for Alec to continue.

"They're asking about Lady MacKinnon too."

A flash of ice froze in Colin's veins. "Brianna? Why?"

A lone guard walked past them and gave a friendly nod. Alec watched the man with sharp eyes, waiting until he was out of earshot before continuing. "They've been asking how distraught she was over his death. If anyone noticed her acting strangely before ye even arrived. If there were bloodied sheets or freshly turned earth."

Colin uttered a low curse and rubbed the back of his neck. Having his own life in danger was a threat he could handle, but the thought of Brianna being in danger was more than he could bear.

"Marie cannot get here fast enough," he muttered.

Alec's brows shot up. "Marie? Marie D'Aubigne?"

"Aye, I asked her to come when I first took charge of Edzell. She should be arriving any day now."

Alec lowered his head and kept his eyes on Colin. "Do ye really think that's wise to have Marie come here?"

"Of course it is. I found a document that needs to be translated, and she can help." Colin's gaze skimmed the grass, brilliant green beneath the sun's glow. For all the work sitting on his desk, he was loathe to go back to the solar. "I figure Marie can also be of assistance in helping us understand what is going on with Lindsay."

Alec grunted.

Colin studied his friend. "Ye dinna think it's a good idea."

Alec smirked and shook his head. "We'll find out."

* * *

The point of the needle pierced Brianna's flesh.

Again.

She popped the injured finger into her mouth and pressed her tongue to it. While it did not stop the ache, the action somehow made her feel better.

She settled back against the alcove in her mother's study and looked down at the half-finished leine in her hands. The sharp needle to her thumb and the dulling labor to her mind were worth the row of neat, even stitches. Now that Colin was laird, he would need a saffron-dyed leine as befitted his station. He had yet to see one made, and so Brianna had taken the task upon herself.

The gold-colored material was soft beneath her fingertips, and her stitches came out perfectly, a testament to the skill she seldom put to use. Were it not for the constant jabs at her fingers, she would be doing quite well. Thus far, her greatest challenge was keeping blood from dotting the costly fabric.

She imagined the look on his face when she presented it to him, and the surprise when he learned she had been the seamstress. A burst of giddy excitement bubbled within her.

Her labor of affection was the least she could do in gratitude for all he had accomplished. Thomas had been right; Colin was a good laird to her people. He was well-received by all and spent long hours in the solar. Though she had only glanced a time or two when he was detained, the accounts all appeared to be well documented.

"My lady, to see you thus reminds me of your mother." Magda's voice floated in from the hallway.

Brianna looked up and found Magda stepping into the room. "My mother? Sewing?" The thought was unimaginable.

"Only for a small period of time that I remember." She stroked Brianna's cheek with a cool hand. "When she was expecting the sweetest bairn in all of Christendom."

Magda lifted the shirt from Brianna's lap and studied the stitching with the eye of a craftswoman. "I see you have her skill. It will serve you well when you have your own children."

A rock settled in the pit of Brianna's stomach. There would be no children. She had seen to that.

Not with whore's tricks. Not when such tactics could be misconstrued as witchcraft. She was too educated to fall back on base concepts that centered more on myth than fact.

She had researched pregnancy. Extensively.

Her studies indicated a man's seed grew potent through abstinence. Scholars recommended a week or two of chastity prior to copulation for the highest chance of conceiving.

She and Colin had not gone a day without relations. Her cheeks heated, and the telltale rush of moisture warmed between her thighs.

Granted, the frequent coupling was done through desire more than her intended prevention, but the end result was still the same. His seed would remain weak and her womb empty.

Magda's hand curled around Brianna's and pulled her away

from musings that would otherwise lead to an interruption in Colin's work. "My lady, you will be a wonderful mother. The kind of mother yours would have been were she allowed."

Guilt robbed Brianna's words of strength, and her voice came out in a weak whisper. "Thank you, Magda."

Perhaps Colin would not subject their offspring to the same unhappiness of her own childhood. Thus far, nothing in their marriage had been the same as her parents' union.

But an innocent child was not something she was willing to risk.

So long as she could keep Colin's interest at night, such a curiosity would never be realized. And that was for the best.

* * *

The movements of the servants throughout the castle had long since ceased, yet still Brianna lay awake in bed. Awake and alone.

Had the mattress always been so large when she'd slept in it by herself? Had the room always been so disturbingly quiet?

She shifted for the countless time, the warmth of her arousal long since cooled with her unease. Colin had missed supper with no word to her of his absence.

Bitterness rose in the back of her throat, and the heavy meat pie eaten earlier roiled in her stomach.

Something kept her husband from their bed.

Chapter Twenty-Four

Colin settled in beside Brianna's sleeping form, his movements slow lest he wake her. The silver light of the moon shone through partially open shutters and lit her porcelain skin.

He wanted to pull her into his arms and let the warmth of her sleeping body ease the late-night chill from his flesh. But he dared not, not when he reeked of Marie's perfume. She always wore more than necessary no matter how many times he had chastised her for it. The French and their heavy scents.

He lay stiffly beside his wife and smiled into the darkness. Marie was still as he remembered. Vivacious. Young. Impetuous.

Her tinkling laugh had filled the room upon her arrival, and her flashing blue eyes sparkled like sapphires.

Several years had passed since he'd last seen her, and most of the night was spent making up for lost time. When he finally mentioned the letters, he knew Brianna would be well asleep. Surely the additional hour or two would cause no harm. Seeing his wife asleep beside him confirmed his assumption.

The smile faded from his lips at the thought of those letters.

Code. The whole damn set was written in some kind of code.

Together, he and Marie had pieced together half of the first page. A love letter of some sort. Certainly nothing that would assist Colin in his cause to thwart Lindsay's investigation.

Brianna shifted in her sleep and rolled toward him. She nuzzled the pillow, and her soft sigh whispered across his shoulder.

Guilt fell heavy over Colin. He should have been in the room to see her to bed as he had every night before. At the very least, he could have sent word to let her know he would be late.

Tomorrow he would make a concerted effort to send Marie away earlier, to ensure he was home with Brianna before she drifted off to sleep.

* * *

Brianna nibbled the inside of her lower lip and stared at several bolts of brightly colored fabric. Jonathan stood protectively between her and Magda in the shade of the luckenbooth, hand poised over the hilt of the blade at his side.

The merchant leaned across the smooth counter of his opened booth, and his voice rose above the bustle of the marketplace. "The lady would look lovely in this shade of pale pink." His creamy white fingers trailed over the layers of fabric in front of her.

"Ah, or perhaps this." He lifted a bundle of shimmering russet silk. Several bolts of fabric toppled into its empty slot. "This would complement the lovely golds in your hair, Lady MacKinnon."

Lady MacKinnon.

The source of her discontent. The reason for her frivolous purchase.

A fortnight had passed since her husband had ceased to love her to sleep, since he had bothered to come to bed with her, since he sought to woo her as he once had.

Jonathan's eyes flicked across the crowd. He was tense. She could feel his unease as surely as she could see it lining his eyes. He did not wish to be here and did not like her lingering so long, only he was too respectful to state such.

"I'll take the red," she decided.

The merchant's eyes lit up, proof she had indeed spent a tidy sum.

The coin was hers from the start, earned through a life beneath the earl's fist. She may spend it how she pleased, and presently its weight fell heavy in the purse at her side.

Magda collected the bundled fabric in preparation to leave,

but still Jonathan's stiff posture did not ease.

Brianna placed several coins on the wooden counter and thanked the merchant before turning away from the building. Her metal pattens clanked against the dirt-spattered cobblestones, and her mind drifted toward Colin once more.

He did not come to their bed as she went to sleep each night, nor was he there when she awoke the next day, but proof existed that he slept beside her. The way the rumpled blanket was pulled back, the dent against his pillow.

Perhaps she had been similarly distracted when she ran Edzell. Was it possible she could so easily forget?

But she was no longer in charge of Edzell. She had relinquished her freedom for honeyed words that melted away all too quickly. And why wouldn't they? Colin had what he wanted.

A woman swept from one of the luckenbooths across the street, the brilliant red of her gown a startling contrast to the milky white of her skin. Her blonde hair hung in silken waves down her back and shimmered like rays of sunshine.

Her head lifted with an air of entitlement and peasants scuttled out of her path, their wide eyes feasting upon her ethereal beauty.

She was a Venus among mortals. The kind of beauty who made women with plain brown hair and muddy-colored eyes slip into the background.

The kind of beauty who wore the same costly russet silk with more finesse than would ever be possible for someone like Brianna.

"Who is that?" Brianna asked, her gaze never leaving the exquisite woman who made her way down the street.

Jonathan cleared his throat, obviously not unaffected himself. "Marie D'Aubigne."

"I've not seen her before," Brianna murmured. There was a sway to the woman's hips that bordered on vulgar. Certainly not the gait of a lady. "How is it I have not yet met her?"

Jonathan shifted from one foot to the other. "She has only recently arrived."

Brianna turned to face him. His flushed cheeks and averted

gaze told her more than he was saying. Her stomach curled into a hard knot.

"How did she come to arrive?" she asked. Her mouth was so dry it was a wonder any words came out at all.

Jonathan's throat bobbed. He looked across the street, in the opposite direction of the woman. "At your husband's insistence, my lady."

The breath sucked from her lungs and left her wounded heart at the mercy of her next question. "And when did she arrive?"

Time dragged in slow painful seconds that lasted lifetimes. Poor Jonathan pulled in a steadying breath. "A fortnight ago, my lady."

Chapter Twenty-Five

Brianna's face smeared in a distorted reflection within the Venetian looking glass. Her hands braced against either side of her washbasin table. Finally she was alone.

Tears stung her eyes, and her stomach wavered with a nausea that threatened to spill from her lips. If she possessed the energy to walk three steps, she would throw her body upon the mattress and sink into its comforting embrace.

All her power had been spent in her forced stroll from the marketplace. Supper had been torture, a brutal charade where the food turned to dust on her tongue and the flavors soured in her belly.

Colin knew something vexed her, she could see evidence of such in his wary gaze. Her nails dug into the smooth washbasin until her knuckles stretched taut over bone.

Did he compare her to that woman on the street?

A ragged gasp tore from Brianna's throat.

She could never compete with such beauty. What a pathetic fool she had been to have thought to keep her husband's affection. To fall for his sugared lies.

If only this were a figment of mischief summoned by Morgan le Fay, like when Sir Gawain had encountered his deal with the Greene Knight. But Brianna's wayward husband did not bear a green silk girdle of shame as Gawain had in the *Greene Knight*—instead his shame scorched her cheeks and scalded her poor heart.

The low groan of her door opening shot through her frazzled control, and her tense muscles jerked her body forward. The ewer clattered against the basin, betraying the awkward reaction.

"Brianna?"

She squeezed her eyes shut. Not him. Anyone but him.

The air froze in her chest. She refused to breathe. To do so would inadvertently take in the scent of him and summon forth memories scarred upon her soul. Marks of her humiliation, denoting the time she had fallen prey to pretty words like some silly courtier. She had never been a silly courtier. She had always been clever. Intelligent. Educated.

Her eyes opened to the looking glass, and disgust lashed at her withering pride. The elegant hairstyle Magda had fashioned that morning fell in limp strands around her flushed face.

A movement in the glass caught her attention, and a wave of trapped panic surged through her.

He moved closer.

"Brianna?"

She did not want him here in her room. His presence burned a hole in the shield of her privacy and lay bare an intimate part of her life she no longer wished to share.

Her heart slammed in her chest, preparing for a battle she did not know how to fight.

She spun around to face him, but the bitter words she'd intended wilted on the tip of her tongue.

Was he always so tall? So imposing?

He took a slow step toward her, his face unreadable. Her face, she knew, was an open display of emotion.

Another disadvantage.

He lowered his head, his eyes intent on hers, as if seeking a connection.

She severed any chance of that by wrenching her gaze away to stare out the window, into the graying light of dusk.

His hands caught her icy fingers. The same hands that had once stroked her flesh into submission. The same hands that caressed his blonde whore. Fury and humiliation flared to life.

Brianna snatched her fingers from his and shot him a look that left her hatred and anger unveiled.

He regarded her for a moment, his eyes devoid of emotion

as he searched her face. Was he glad for her distance? Relieved?

"Ye're no happy with me."

Not happy didn't properly encompass the rage smoldering within her, the splintering disgrace in her heart.

Brianna crossed her arms tightly over her chest, ensuring he could not grab her hands again, hoping he would go away.

Instead, he pulled the chair from beside the washbasin and slowly sat down.

"I have been gone often," he said softly. "My absence has upset ye. I wanted to tell ye—"

"I already know." Brianna's muscles tightened once more.

Surprise lifted his brows and his lips parted. Lips she had once thought sensual. Delicious.

"I dinna understand. How did ye find out?" His eyes narrowed. "Did someone tell ye?"

"No one needed to tell me." Her words quivered and she hated her weakness. "I saw her."

"Her?" His brow furrowed for the briefest of moments. "Ye mean Marie?" A wide grin split his face.

A grin!

She lunged forward and thrust her finger to his chest. "You offend me with her presence, but do not insult me with your mirth."

He tilted his head and gave her a boyish smile. The one that used to make her melt. "Brianna, I dinna mean it like that. Ye dinna understand—"

"No," she hissed. "I understand just fine." Each word was punctuated with another jab into his granite hard chest. Was every part of him so impenetrable?

"I didn't want this marriage," she ground out. "I did it to save you." Her vision clouded with traitorous tears, and her hand fell away from his body. "I can't do this any longer. In the morning, I will travel to the Commissary Court in Edinburgh to petition for a divorce."

The obnoxious grin on his face wavered. "Divorce?" He unfolded his large body from the chair and once again towered over her. "Ye dinna understand. If ye would let me explain—"

"No!" The word flew from her mouth like a whip. "*You* don't understand. You don't know the effects of infidelity like I do, nor how the children suffer. I was a bastard, Colin. I *know*. My father believed my mother was unfaithful and discounted me as illegitimate."

Colin's eyebrows flinched, his face displaying an expression she had seen too many times on others before. Pity.

She should stop talking, cease her tale before it was too late to rescind. But the painful truth fell from her lips with abandon. "He never loved me as his daughter because he never believed I *was* his daughter." Her words grew thick. "And he never let me forget."

"Is that why ye kept his death a secret?" Colin asked quietly.

Brianna turned away, unable to look at him any longer. "Because a bastard cannot inherit the property of an earl. Yes, that is exactly why I kept his death a secret." She forced the knot of emotion down with a hard swallow.

Colin stepped closer to her. "Ye canna divorce me, lass."

She jerked her chin up, fire once more kindling in the hole of her despair. "I certainly can."

"Ye certainly canna. I have four reasons why this isna possible." He tugged his right thumb with his left hand. "First, if what ye told me is true, ye hold no power and so ye have no choice but to stay with me." He waggled his eyebrows, and ire sizzled in Brianna's blood.

His forefinger joined the thumb thrust in the air. "Second, if ye dinna have my nobility tied to ye, Edzell would end up in yer uncle's hands."

He grabbed her hand before she could dart away. She tried to tug herself free, but he held her too tightly.

"You force me to stay with you through politics?" One hard wrench and she would be free of his burning touch.

He wrapped his arm around her shoulders and pulled her against him, close to the heat of his body.

A poisoned blade to the heart would be more comforting.

"The third reason ye canna divorce me," his voice was husky in her ear, a sound that made her body react with an effect she wished to ignore. "Marie and I are no lovers. We have never been and will never be, aye?"

Hope flickered to life, but she snuffed it out. She would not lose her heart to mere words again.

"And fourth." He leaned back and grinned down at her. Her heart skipped a beat, and the pleasant warmth of anticipation shot through her before she could stop it.

How did he do that to her? She gritted her teeth against her all too familiar response.

"The fourth is what I like to think of as the main reason ye willna divorce me," he said.

Curiosity drove the words from her mouth. "And what is the fourth reason, pray tell?"

The heat of his hands slid down her back the way he used to, the way that left her knees weak and her breath heavy.

His emerald gaze met hers. "Ye stay with me because ye want to. Because ye like me." A twinkle showed in his eye. "Because my kisses make ye do that noise in yer throat that makes my cock stand hard."

Brianna gasped at his audacity and found a smile breaking through her hurt.

"*Ja swiss dessolay*," he said, his expression earnest.

She paused, unsure if she had heard correctly. "If that was French, your pronunciation is, well, it's not good."

His shoulders lifted in a shrug. "That's what Marie says as well. She is a friend from when I was a lad. I asked her to come so she could teach me French."

Brianna frowned. "I could have taught you French."

His grin turned sheepish. "I was learning it to impress ye. I thought it might be verra romantic."

"That was sweet of you." She slid closer into his arms.

He let her relax against him and cradled the sweet lavender warmth of her body against him. Getting her to believe the partial lie was far easier than he had expected. He wanted to tell her the true reason he'd been meeting up with Marie in the middle of the night, the hours they'd spent poring over those love letters from the French marquis to Brianna's mother.

Now that he realized how truly important the contents of those missives might be to Brianna, he could not allow her to know of their existence. Not until all had been decoded and translated. Not when the letters were written with such florid confessions of love and adoration. Reading them would only serve to cause her hurt.

He stroked her delicate cheek, hating her tears against his fingertips. "I would do anything for ye, wife." Truer words were never spoken. He would do anything for her, even keep the truth hidden from her lest it cause injury.

She rested her chin against his chest and looked up at him. "I'm beginning to understand that, husband." Something shone in her eyes, something hard and shrewd.

She did not believe him.

Chapter Twenty-Six

The too sweet fragrance of roses lingered in the hall and alerted Colin that Marie was in his solar. Sinister shadows of night hid the tapestries and decorative wall hangings. It was so damn late, even the rush nips had burned out.

He scrubbed a hand over his face and yawned. Brianna still slept in their bed, unaware of his departure. The solar door was slightly ajar, a soft light beckoning him in the darkness. He pushed into the room and found Marie standing by his desk, her blue silk back facing him. "You're late." She spoke without turning.

Colin closed the door behind him. "Brianna saw ye at the market today."

Marie glanced over her shoulder with a smirk. "I'm sure that went well for you."

He pressed his ear to the door and listened for a moment to ensure he had not been followed. Silence.

He turned the key, locking them in before approaching the desk. Several letters spread across the glossy surface.

"I hope it went better than I think it did," he said.

Her small hand settled on a piece of parchment. "I've been working while I waited for you to arrive." She glanced up at him. "My contacts in France have found information on this Marquis de Condorcet, but I'm afraid the information is quite dated. He moved to Italy over ten years ago, and if anyone has heard from him, they are not speaking."

Colin gave an irritated sigh. "I told ye to let that go, Marie. We dinna need the man, just what is in the letters."

"If the marquis is still alive, it seems knowing his

whereabouts could prove beneficial for your wife." She arched her eyebrow. "Lindsay grows suspicious. I'm not sure how much longer I can sneak away."

Her brilliant blue gaze caught his eye, unguarded, the way it always was when they were alone. He studied her heart-shaped face and upturned nose. His chest squeezed with a familiar ache. She still looked a great deal like the hopeless child he had met so many years ago.

"Ye need to leave Lindsay to my men if ye believe yerself to be in danger," he said.

A coy smile flitted across her lips. "Are you worried about me?"

He frowned. "Ye know I am. I dinna want to see ye hurt."

She patted his hand with the pads of her fingertips, an act that would be condescending with anyone other than Marie. "I'm safe for now, but I don't know how often I can make excuses to leave from his manor to my rented room in the middle of the night. The guard waited longer than usual before leaving this time."

Colin studied Marie's face, searching for something she might not be saying. "This will be the last time we meet then. I believe I have enough of our previous work to piece together the last of the letters. I'll send ye the French words through one of my men and ye can translate it, aye?"

She cast him a dubious look. "With your spelling?" Her chest swelled with a dramatic sigh. "It will have to do. I cannot resign myself from Lindsay's confidence. Not now."

"Why? What have ye heard?" He leaned close enough to see the layer of powder she'd brushed across her smooth cheeks.

"Lindsay's men are certain they found someone they can get to talk. I don't know who it is yet," Marie whispered.

Colin balled his hand in a fist and squeezed it to keep from slamming the table. He pressed a tight knuckle to his lips.

"How the hell can they even make a crime that doesna exist?" Another breath hissed between his teeth. "And who the hell is talking?"

"*Je ne sais pas.*" Her lower lip thrust out in a sympathetic pout. "But I will find out."

* * *

Sunrise broke through the dusk and poured into the darkened solar, announcing a completed night where Colin had not slept. A feat more easily handled when he was younger.

Exhaustion numbed his mind and left his movements automatic and thoughtless.

Marie sat slumped in the great chair, her lips soundlessly reading through their decoded parchments.

"These are all more of the same as we've read before." She flipped through the pages. The rustle of the aged parchment was loud in the otherwise silent room. "The marquis begs her to leave her husband and return to France where he will care for her. He is so persistent." Her smile turned wistful. "So eloquent. Any other woman would not be able to resist such a beautifully composed offer. Especially when proposed as many times."

She hugged the pages to her chest and her eyes swept closed. "He loved her."

"But she did not love him," Colin surmised.

Marie's eyes flew open. "You are such a man. So Scottish." Her paper-stuffed hands fell to her sides. "She kept the letters, didn't she? Despite the danger in doing so, she kept the letters and she replied." Her finger tapped the stiff page. "Every one of these save the first is in reply to one *she* sent him."

A creak of someone's foot upon the stairs below interrupted them. Jonathan, no doubt. It was time for him to show.

"Anything that could prove Brianna's legitimacy?" Colin asked quickly.

If Brianna knew Marie had been told of her illegitimacy, she would be furious. Unfortunately, Marie was the only person who could help him discover for certain. Proof would do nothing to secure the property to Brianna, but he knew such knowledge would set her mind at peace.

Marie tucked her lip into her mouth and shook her head. Fatigue lined her eyes. He had kept her here too long. She was exhausted.

He rested a hand on her elbow. "Thank ye for doing this

and for seeking answers from Lindsay."

Her gaze trailed to his hand and her cheeks colored. "You know I would do anything for you," she said, her voice low and throaty. Her eyes met his, almost pleading. "Anything."

He drew his hand back lest the action be construed as something other than friendship. "Then stay safe," he instructed.

A single rap upon the door indicated Jonathan's arrival to take Marie home.

Colin swallowed his concern and let her walk away. She was determined, overeager to please.

Hopefully she would trust her instinct and flee if she sensed danger.

"I'll contact you," she said.

Of that Colin had little doubt.

• • •

Anxiety danced a frantic tattoo in Brianna's chest. The late morning buzz and bustle of the market hummed behind her. She tugged the hood of her cloak more securely over her face. A respectable woman did not stand before the door of rented rooms as she did now.

Whether real or imagined, she felt the weight of eyes boring into her. She clenched her hands in front of her in an effort to keep herself from picking at her cuticles. Magda always fussed when she did that.

Still the door did not open. Her courage faltered.

She tugged at her hood again, pulling at fabric that could give no more, and turned to leave. The low squeak of an old key grating against an old lock stilled her movement, and the door cracked open to reveal the Venus from the day before.

Brianna's confidence slithered into a ball of self-consciousness. The Frenchwoman's face was alabaster white and her hair gleamed like spun gold. The brilliant blue shift she wore made her eyes look like a cloudless sky.

She stared at Brianna with candid curiosity. "Lady MacKinnon, you took longer to approach me than most wives."

A gentle French purr laced the English words into a blend of husky seduction.

"You expected me sooner?" Brianna asked.

Full, red lips curled up in a humorless smile. "All the wives seek me out eventually."

Something burned in Brianna's chest, despite all her mental preparations. She glanced around them and switched to French to prevent eavesdropping. "I think you'll find I'm approaching you for a different reason."

Marie's head tilted, and she replied in her native tongue. "Your French is perfect."

"I would be disappointed otherwise, considering the length of time I studied," Brianna said. A final scan of the empty walkway confirmed no one listened. "May I come in?"

"If you wish." Marie stepped back and pulled her door open in invitation. The scent of fine perfume wafted from the woman's private room and curled around Brianna with an enticement she knew most men would not resist.

She crossed the threshold in her curiosity and idly wondered if she would smell thus upon her exit. Her stomach knotted. Would Colin recognize the scent?

Marie's rented room was small, but richly decorated in swaths of red, orange, and dark blue velvets that mirrored the sensuality of its tenant.

Gauzy crimson curtains lined the windows and blotted the brilliant summer sun to a red glow of ambient light.

"I know you are Marie D'Aubigne." Brianna slipped the mud-spattered pattens from her shoes and placed them on a straw mat beside Marie's. "But that is all I know."

The woman walked around Brianna and settled back against an arrangement of garnet and gold silk pillows. Her eyes trailed over Brianna with slow purpose.

"What is it you wish to discuss?" Marie asked after her thorough inspection. She did not appear intimidated by what she saw.

Brianna lifted her head, refusing to cower before her rival. "I came to seek your…talents."

Marie stretched out on the cushions and draped her arm across the voluptuous swell of her hip. The sleeve of her thin satin dress shifted and exposed a milky white shoulder. "If you wish to use my...talents," she said the word as Brianna had, but slightly mockingly, "...toward your husband, you are wasting your time. He has made it clear he is not interested." Her gaze cut into Brianna. "I confess I do not understand. I have lured men from women far more beautiful than you."

Brianna ignored the insult. "I do not seek your company for my husband, but for myself."

"Oh?" The corner of her lips quirked up in an amused smile. "You are full of surprises, aren't you?" Her stare slid down Brianna's body once more, this time with renewed interest.

"You mistake me still." Brianna took a step closer. "I've seen you from a distance, and somehow you call attention with the sway of your hips, the lift of your chin. You are the kind of woman who can get what she wants with just a glance. Up close, you are exquisite and move with grace—"

"Are you certain I mistake your intent?" Marie asked. The pad of her middle finger swept back and forth across her lower lip.

"I am a student," Brianna declared. "I study many subjects, and when I do not understand something, I do my best to learn more. You possess knowledge I am lacking." She tore her stare from the path of Marie's finger. "Teach me to behave like you. Teach me to wield my body."

"You are a nobleman's daughter recently plucked," Marie scoffed. "You are far too prudent to appreciate what I would say."

Brianna narrowed her eyes at the woman, refusing to accept her mirth. "You underestimate me." Coins clinked within the heavy velvet purse Brianna set upon the table. "I am willing to pay handsomely for your instruction and believe you will find me an apt pupil. If I am too resistant, you may the keep the purse and ask me to leave."

Marie rose with the sleek grace of a feline and hefted the purse into her hands. "When would you like to begin?"

There was a palpable shift in power, and Brianna intended

to use it to her advantage. "As soon as you've told me what business you have with my husband, and what the two of you have been doing in the middle of the night."

Chapter Twenty-Seven

Marie set the purse on the table and made her way to the pillow-strewn settee once more. She motioned to the plush chair at her side. "Please have a seat."

With trembling legs and a straight back, Brianna complied with Marie's request and settled back against the overstuffed cushions.

Marie's gaze followed Brianna, her expression shrewd. "You have a natural grace that will aid you in what I teach." One long leg slid onto the settee, revealing a slender ankle and part of her calf. "But that is not what you want to hear right now." She rested an elbow on her knee and leaned her chin on the back of her hand. "What is Colin to me?"

Colin.

She referred to his given name, her tone intimate. Too intimate.

Brianna pressed her knees against one another to keep from squirming. The glint in the Frenchwoman's eye confirmed she did nothing by accident, and she was enjoying every second of her teasing.

"He's a protector," she said finally. "A benefactor."

A benefactor?

Brianna's heart crumpled with a force she wished she could ignore. Men paid for the living expenses of women like Marie for one reason.

"Not in the way you think." Marie smiled and her sharp white teeth glinted in the softly lit room. "You needn't worry, little scholar. We were never lovers."

The clopping of a horse sounded outside. She glanced out

the window beside her, her gaze following something Brianna could not see. "I was a girl of twelve when I first met Colin. He was hardly more than a boy himself at that time, an adolescent who thought himself a man. Given his height, I mistook him for such."

Her finger traced an invisible circle across the top of her thigh. "When I first saw him, he wore a green velvet doublet and a costly sword at his side. He had money and I—" Her focus turned toward Brianna. "I was a prostitute."

Brianna pressed her thumbnail into her finger to keep from gasping. Not that she was surprised Marie had been a prostitute. But at such a young age—it was deplorable.

The tightness around Marie's eyes softened, as did her stare, and Brianna realized her lack of response passed some sort of an unspoken test.

"I waited until he was alone," Marie continued. "The way most men prefer to be approached." The mask she wore faltered, and for a flash of a moment, her crystal blue gaze reflected a startling vulnerability. "He smiled down at me, and at first I thought he would agree to my proposition. Then he asked my age."

The veil slid over her emotions once more. "I lied and he knew it." Marie's smooth mask did not crack again. "Rather than shun me, he paid for an apartment. He made sure I had food to eat, fine clothes to wear. He paid for an education I would never have received." She broke eye contact to study the lazy movement of her finger across her leg. "And he expected nothing of me in return except that I pay attention to my tutors. Even when I was old enough to repay him with what I'd tried to sell him so long ago."

Her finger stilled. "But you are only a year or two older than I, yet he still sees me as a child." She drew her palm across the curve of her exposed calf. "I'm a woman in my own right, one who has taken lovers of her own choosing, one experienced in the art of pleasure and desire, but it will never matter to him. He will never want me as I want him." Her averted gaze did not hide the chill of her stare. "He will never want me as he wants you."

The squeeze of Brianna's chest seemed to lessen, and the breath flowed into her lungs with more ease. For all of her incredible beauty, Colin did not lust after Marie.

Brianna eyed her self-professed adversary with suspicion. "You confess you desire my husband, yet you agree to help me. Why?" She glanced around the sumptuous room. "I don't think you need the coin."

Marie flicked a golden tassel dangling from the corner of a pillow. "A woman always needs coin. Besides," she said, her gaze sliding across Brianna's face and down her stiff body. "I think teaching you will prove fun."

Brianna's cheeks scalded with the force of her blush, and a prickle of unease wobbled her hold on the power she thought she held. Power she would see reclaimed.

"If you are not my husband's lover, what is it you do at night that keeps him from my bed?"

Marie's fingertips hovered over her lips like a child was wont to do when she'd been naughty. "Oh, I should not tell you that." Her eyes danced.

"I think you want to tell me."

"Perhaps you are right." Her chin tilted in a coquettish fashion that showed the sharp line of her jaw. "Your husband found some old letters to your mother. Colin preferred them to be translated without your knowledge, and I have other matters that require me during the earlier parts of the day."

"Letters?" Brianna asked. "What kind of letters?"

Something creased Marie's brows. "Letters to your mother from a French marquis."

The pungent aroma of perfume pulsed in Brianna's head and made the room blur. She knew what those letters meant. And so did Colin.

She focused on maintaining a steady voice. "How has it taken over two weeks?"

"They were all written in code." Marie examined her fingernails with a slight frown. "We didn't finish yet, so I can't tell you much about them."

Letters from a French marquis written in code.

"You want those letters, don't you?" Marie asked.

Brianna looked toward her once more, but did not bother to reply. The Frenchwoman already knew the answer.

Marie leaned forward on the settee so the tops of her breasts squeezed over her gown. "Now, let's teach you how to get what you want."

* * *

Colin stalked away from his desk where Alec stood, his muscles burning. The solar walls closed in around him and darkness chased away the dying light. The hour was late and Brianna was missing.

He jerked his head up at Alec, his face tense.

"When did she say she was meeting with the cook?" Colin asked.

"This morning, yet the servants say the cook went to market at midday." His dark brows drew together.

"And ye just tell me this now?" His fist connected with the solid wood desk. "Did ye no think that was important to tell me when ye found out?"

Alec's lips tightened, the way they did when he felt strongly about something. The way they did when he was about to fight. "I dinna see anything out of the ordinary. I dinna know she would be gone the entire day. We have too few guards to worry themselves about what every person at Edzell does or doesna do."

Alec spoke true. No matter how good the soldiers, no matter how well trained, Colin could not turn the number of men into more than what actually existed.

He swallowed the bitter taste of a fear he wouldn't allow himself to think on. "Have the castle searched again for Brianna or the cook. Magda too for that matter." Colin turned toward the window. His eyes settled on the pristine garden below, half expecting to see Brianna sitting at her usual spot beside the roses. "Notify the men to contact me immediately when she arrives. She's been gone too long, and it's far more dangerous out there than she realizes." He squeezed his fist. "And for God's sake, hire some more damn guards."

An hour later, Colin climbed the twisting stairs to the room he and Brianna shared. One foot in front of the other, resisting the urge to take three steps at a time. No, he needed the extra time to cool off.

His hand wrapped around the cold iron handle and squeezed in a final attempt to drain some of his rage. He tugged the door open, stepped into the softly lit room, and stilled.

Brianna stood beside their bed wearing an unbelted robe of white satin, her taut nipples standing out like pearls against the sheen of the fabric. Her hair fell in riotous waves down her back, and her eyes were lit with excitement. Mischief. As if she intended to do something wicked.

The anger pumping through his veins turned molten, pounding. A low growl sounded deep in his chest. His cock pulsed to life with a hardness so sudden and intense, it left his breathing tight.

And she knew it.

"You may want to close the door." Her lips curled in a slow smile, and the robe slipped from her shoulders.

Chapter Twenty-Eight

The warm air of their chamber caressed Brianna's skin, though it was cool in comparison to the burn of Colin's stare. Her hair rested against her naked back, raising bumps of anxious excitement over her flesh.

She sauntered toward him, her hips loose and suggestive. The way she had seen Marie walk. The way she'd practiced in front of the looking glass before the shuffle of Colin's footsteps sounded in the hall.

"Are you going to close the door?" she asked.

Colin kicked his leg behind him and the door slammed shut. His eyes restlessly skimmed her body, lingering on intimate places she longed to shield with her hands. She resisted the pull of modesty. Men liked a woman with confidence, according to Marie.

"I'm mad at ye." Colin's voice was tense even as his eyes caressed her breasts.

Nervousness fluttered in the pit of her stomach. How would Marie respond?

When she reached him, Brianna drew her fingertip across his bottom lip. "I know," she purred. No explanation. No detailed apology.

She placed her hands on his chest and tilted her head up, teasing him with a kiss she would never deliver. "I'm sure you'll forgive me when the night is done."

He groaned and leaned forward to kiss her, but she stepped away with a coquettish smile. She shook her head and wagged her finger playfully in front of his chest. "No touching."

A muscle ticked in his jaw. "Ye canna stand naked before me and tell me I canna touch ye." His gaze turned fraught, desperate.

Brianna gave a soft, throaty laugh. "Yes, I can." She openly admired him with the same intensity he'd gazed upon her. "And I will."

She walked around him, inspecting him, keeping her eyes locked on his until she could do so no longer.

Marie had said to flatter.

"I like to watch you without your leine on." Brianna winced at the awkwardness of her shallow attempt.

She was a reader of poetry and possessed the skills of language and expression. She could do better.

"I love how the sun touches the lines of your body, so hard and masculine." She stopped in front of him and let her fingertips stroke the leine over his torso. "So strong." Her hand closed around the soft fabric and slowly plucked his leine from his kilt. Colin needed no further encouragement. He yanked it over his head and tossed it aside.

Brianna arched forward so her nipples scraped his naked chest. Pleasure needled through the sensitive buds. "I love to caress your carved body, solid granite beneath the softness of my hands." She stroked his powerful torso, gliding over the muscular planes of his chest. "I love the tightness of your stomach." Her fingertips trailed across the ridges of his abdomen. "And the way you suck in your breath when I dip my hand lower." She followed the narrow strip of hair below his navel and let her finger curl inside the waistline of his kilt.

He drew a sharp breath.

Colin's hands balled to tight fists at his side, but he did not touch her. His heart raced beneath her hand, his breathing deep and heavy. The hardness of his lance jutted out with need.

"Ye torture me, wife." He stared down at her with a wild gaze.

Her heart sped in anticipation of her next action. She could not allow her nerves to show. She would be brave. Seductive. "I've only just begun." Her weak knees gratefully folded to the floor before him, her face directly in front of his kilt.

With hands that trembled more than she liked, she reached for his belt and tried to shove aside her shy anxiety.

* * *

Colin's body clenched tight, his cock near bursting with Brianna's teasing words and touch. God's teeth, had it been over two weeks since he'd loved her?

It felt like a whole damn year.

Brianna's fingers tangled with his belt, her mouth so deliciously close to the source of his desire, it was all he could do to stay his hands. She tugged the leather once, twice. Her eyes narrowed and her teeth sank into her lower lip. She gripped the belt with two hands and jerked.

He braced his weight with both feet and a grin of endearment broke on his face. For all the part of a seductress she played, her actions were still those of the wife he had come to care for so dearly.

He covered her hands with his, offering the assistance her reddening cheeks begged for. The soft pop of the leather sounded and the belt slipped free from the buckle. Dutifully, he moved his hands back to his sides and waited.

Brianna's fingers were graceful, caressing the leather in a way that made him long for her delicate touch. A longing that was apparent when the kilt slid from his hips, a longing that pointed directly toward Brianna's sensual mouth.

Her fingertips slid up the base of his cock and his body lurched.

"I've missed you." Her warm breath bathed his rigid flesh. Teasing.

His fists squeezed tighter.

The tip of her forefinger brushed his swollen head, and pleasure blazed through him.

She looked up at him from her position. Her knees were spread, her breasts full and round, parting her long unbound hair. Her lips were so damn close.

"I know what you've been doing at night." She gave him a coy smile.

A soft note of alarm tapped in the back of his mind.

Her fingers continued to explore his aching cock. His body

was hot, pounding. So hard.

She wrapped her hands around him and slid her fist up his length. He flexed forward, into the warmth of her maddening embrace. Sweat prickled his brow.

"You have something I want." Her voice was husky.

She wanted this as much as he did.

She leaned forward and every muscle in his body tensed. Her lips were a hair's breadth from the head of his cock. "I want the letters."

Her whispered words skimmed across his flesh, stoking the flame of his desire.

Letters?

Her lips parted.

"I said I want the letters."

Warm breath.

Her mouth would be hot. Moist.

"My mother's letters."

Damn.

He threw his head back in frustration. "I canna."

"You can." Her sultry tone pulled his attention back down to her. "They are of great importance to me."

Her tongue brushed the plump head of his cock. Reason slid away and stole his speech.

"I know how to decipher them," she continued.

He grunted, his gaze fixed on her mouth. Waiting. Hoping.

Her lips spread wide, and she moved her mouth over him, not touching, not closing. A mockery of what he longed for.

She pulled her head back, away from him, her gaze searing into his. "The letters are mine."

The warm summer air was cold against his cock compared to the heated grip her mouth promised.

She brushed the underside of his cock with her tongue, just beneath the tip, and his mind went blank.

"Say yes," she purred. Like a siren.

Another flick of her tongue.

"Yes," she coaxed.

She gripped him in her hands and looked up at him. Poised.

Ready to take him in her mouth.

"Yes," he groaned.

Victory flashed in her eyes and the warmth of her lips wrapped around his cock. The breath dragged from Colin's lungs in a strangled cry. The muscles along his arms and back burned with the cost of barely held control. Bliss tangled through his veins, boiling his blood and singeing all thoughts from his head.

She pulled him in, sucking him back against her throat. His buttocks flexed and his breathing went harsh and ragged.

Her tongue trailed along the underside of his cock as she pulled her head back, only to take him deep once more.

He couldn't keep from touching her any longer. His fingers threaded through her silky hair and cradled her head while she pleasured him. He stared down at her full lips, watching his cock disappear between them.

One of her hands slid from the base of his shaft to the cleft between her legs. Her fingers curled in a slow, languid stroke. Sparkling brown eyes hooded, and a moan vibrated against his cock.

Her fingers slid deeper, and her breathing grew as erratic as his own.

His balls tightened with impending release. He wanted her. Not just her mouth—her.

He wanted his fingers where hers were, soaking in the moistness of her passion. He wanted his tongue caressing the tang of her arousal. He wanted his cock plunging into her tight, wet sheath. He wanted to take what he'd gone too long without.

His hands tightened in her hair, stilling her efforts. He'd let her toy with him long enough.

Brianna stared up at Colin, suddenly unsure of her lascivious actions. Had she scraped him with her teeth? She'd been careful.

His gaze settled on her hand between her legs, and her cheeks burned. Marie had told her men enjoyed watching a woman pleasure herself. Perhaps Colin's tastes were different.

Her hand dropped away and reached for his length once more, shame glistening against her fingertips. She'd been reluctant to the idea of having him in her mouth. But his hard heat against her tongue, the slide of his silky flesh there, it was enticing and erotic.

Delicious.

She opened her mouth to take him once more, hungry for his groans of pleasure and the incredible surge of power she knew she could wield.

"No." His hands tightened further against her scalp before releasing her hair. He clasped her shoulders and helped her to a standing position.

Desire burned dark in his eyes, and his naked chest rose and fell with his deep breath. He gripped her behind the neck, locking her in his grasp before his lips crushed against hers.

There was no coy teasing, only raw, hungry strength behind his kiss. The stroke of his hand against her thigh eased her murmur of protest.

His fingers spread where her own had been only moments before, his thumb administering slow, maddening circles. She ground her hips against his hand, eager to feel him filling her, eager for the promise of release already drawing close.

His tongue swept into her mouth and caught her hungry cry. She caressed the muscular contours of his back, his skin slick against her fingertips with the sweat of his restraint. He was powerful. Beautiful.

His hand pulled away from her legs and cupped her bottom. He stepped forward, urging her back in a sensual, awkward dance until the cool painted wall pressed against her back.

He caught her left leg under the knee and swept it up, pinning her into place. She was open for him, waiting, ready for the thrust that would stretch her and bring her to the climax she so impatiently sought.

Instead he dropped to his knees and covered her sex with his mouth. Her standing leg lost its strength, and she would have sagged to the ground had he not grasped her thigh and held her in place. His tongue found the source of pleasure his thumb had abandoned and carefully, slowly stroked again and again and again. Heat tingled through her body and hardened her nipples.

"Yes," she moaned.

He sucked her bud into his mouth and flicked his tongue against its peak until stars danced in front of her and whimpers of her release filled her ears.

She looked down at where Colin knelt between her legs. "I want you," she said breathlessly.

He got to his feet and pushed his hard body against her. "I've been wanting ye."

His nose nuzzled her neck and tickled the sensitive skin there with a long, slow, indrawn breath followed by a low growling exhale. "On the floor and on the bed." The length of him nudged between her legs. She arched her hips, trying to draw him within her. "Against the wall."

He pushed inside her and slanted his lips over hers. He caught the knee of her standing leg, lifting her, so her legs draped over his massive arms and her body was pressed between him and the wall.

His thrusts were deep and long, driven by a pent-up longing that brought them both to a fevered passion. He groaned against her lips, his hard breathing matching her own.

The tightening of another climax caught Brianna in its decadent clutches. Colin's teeth nipped her lower lip. "Come with me, Brianna." He plunged into her. "Come with me."

He swelled within her, and her body clenched tightly against him with the force of her incredible release. Her back pressed into the wall, thrusting forward to catch the full force of Colin's narrow hips between her legs. He leaned his head back and gave a low groan. The lapping waves of her pleasure coincided with his final jerking pumps until they both gasped for air.

Colin lowered her trembling legs to the ground and rested his forehead against hers. "Ye never stop surprising me, wife."

Brianna closed her eyes and waited for her heart to stop racing.

Would he be so complimentary when he realized he'd promised her the letters?

• • •

Colin lay in the embrace of his bed with his wife beside him, her body gloriously naked in the first dark shades of night. Her long hair draped across her back and tickled the side of his arm.

The tension had eased from his back, drained away with the release of his frustration. His fingers laced through the silky strands of her hair in slow, languid rakes, and a contented smile lifted the corners of her lips.

"Are you still mad at me, husband?"

He chuckled and shook his head. The lass knew how to placate a man. "I'm no happy with ye being gone so long, but I'm no angry with ye." He studied the delicate lines of her face, the softness of her lips in the fading light. "I was worried about ye."

"You? Worried?" Brianna propped herself up on her elbow and stared down at him. "I didn't think you ever worried about anything."

He caressed the velvety softness of her cheek. "Ach, I do when it comes to ye. I dinna realize meeting with the cook would take a whole day, nor did I realize he would be going to market." He flipped a lock of hair from her brow. "Ye should have had a guard with ye."

"I didn't go see the cook." Her cheeks went pink and she turned her eyes away from him. "I went to see Marie."

Relaxed muscles knotted once more. "Marie?"

Brianna's eyebrows rose. "Where do you think I learned everything I did tonight?"

"I thought ye'd located another wee pamphlet." He sighed and leaned his head back on the pillow.

"Where do you think I discovered you had the letters?" she asked.

Letters?

The memory of her luring request slammed into his mind. Damn it!

A frown pulled at his lips. "I dinna want ye to find out about those."

Brianna sat up and clutched the sheet to her breasts. "How could you keep them a secret? Don't you realize what they mean to me?"

Colin rose to a sitting position beside her and met her hurt glare. "I dinna know what they'd say, Brianna. Ye had too much ye worried over already. How could I hand ye something that might add to that burden?" He rubbed his fingers over his chin. "And then ye told me about yer mother and her alleged infidelity." He shook his head. "I wanted to make sure those letters dinna have anything that might hurt ye."

"I still want them," she said stubbornly.

Colin was old enough to know when he was defeated, and his wife was an unyielding opponent. "Then ye can have them."

"Thank you. And now that I know about the letters, I can help you in place of Marie." She chewed her lower lip before opening her mouth to speak again. "And you can come to bed with me at night again, yes?"

Wide brown eyes met his with such innocent hope, he could not help but grin. "Aye, lass. I'll be joining ye in bed again."

She lay back, her gaze still trained on his. "And you'll be here when I wake?"

He eased himself to the mattress and pulled her warm body against him. "Aye, I'll be here when ye wake."

She laid her head on his chest and nuzzled against him. "Please don't lie anymore, Colin. Be honest with me."

He ran his fingertips over her smooth back and she made a soft little hum of pleasure. "I'll be honest with ye, wife."

His body was sated and his wife was safe in his arms. Sleep pulled at him, luring him into the unconscious darkness of its embrace. A low chuckle rumbled in his chest as a sudden thought occurred to him.

"What did Magda think of Marie's instruction?" he asked.

"Magda?" Brianna asked, her voice thick with the edge of sleep. "I didn't bring Magda."

The blanket of exhaustion fell away. "Ye dinna bring her?"

He felt her smile against his chest. "Of course not."

A seed of worry planted itself in the forefront of his mind. If Magda hadn't been with Brianna, then where was she?

. . .

Colin's night of fitful sleep came to an abrupt end somewhere between the rasp of the blanket against his bare legs and the layer of sweat chilling his skin. Brianna slept soundly beside him, her breathing deep, even and suggesting she would not wake soon.

If Magda had not gone with Brianna to Marie's, where then had she gone? Had she returned to Edzell? The not knowing sank thick knots into his already tense shoulders.

He shifted in the bed to see if Brianna reacted to the movement. She did not stir. Perhaps he could leave to ensure Magda slept soundly in her own room and return before Brianna roused.

He sat up and hesitated.

If Brianna woke and found him gone again, he knew she would be greatly displeased. He grimaced at the thought.

She'd be more than greatly displeased.

And yet, if she knew of her nurse's disappearance, she would forgive him for breaking his promise.

He knew what he had to do. Quickly, quietly, he slipped from bed and dressed. One quick kiss against her warm forehead and he eased out the door.

The thump of hastened footsteps met his ears, footsteps headed in his direction. Colin took the stairs two at a time, the worry in his mind pounding with each step drawing nearer until he all but ran into Jonathan.

"I was just coming to wake ye," Jonathan said, his tone quiet. Ominous.

Something was wrong.

Jonathan drew a steadying breath, his cheeks flushed with exertion.

"Magda?" Colin surmised.

Jonathan nodded and turned to head back down the hall. "We've found her. She's waiting in your solar and is very upset."

Together, Colin and the young soldier sprinted down the quiet halls, through the sleeping household until they reached the solar. Colin pushed open the door to find four soldiers surrounding Magda's hunched form. Alec held out a steaming mug toward her, his jaw clenched tight.

Jonathan spoke behind Colin. "We found her wandering outside and believe she may have gotten lost. She's very upse—"

"I wasn't lost." Magda protested. She turned toward Colin with tear-filled eyes. "I wasn't lost. I was taken."

Chapter Twenty-Nine

Rush nips lit the dark solar and cast heavy shadows across the crowded room. Magda broke away from the circle of soldiers and ran to Colin.

"I was taken," she whispered again. Her slender body trembled.

Colin turned his attention to his men. "Go back to yer stations. Dinna let anyone in the castle without my permission."

Jonathan nodded and herded the others from the room. Alec stayed behind, arms stubbornly crossed over his chest. "I'm no leaving," he said when everyone had left. His gaze settled on Magda. "I promised her I wouldna leave her."

Colin helped Magda into a seat then lifted the warm mug and pressed it into her hands. "Who took ye, lass?"

Strands of silver hair fell around her face, her neat bun listing to the side. "I don't know. A black carriage. I didn't know the men."

Her head bent forward and a tear fell into her lap. "They asked so many questions. I got so confused, I couldn't even remember my own name."

"Did they harm ye?" Alec asked.

She shook her head. "I don't know. I don't think so. I'm so tired and I get so forgetful." She clutched the mug. "I think I said something they wanted because they let me go."

Colin's gut tightened. He squatted in front of the old woman, pried a hand from her mug and held it. The heated cup left her fingers hot to the touch. "Do ye remember what ye may have said?"

Her sharp eyes were heavy with exhaustion. "I told them

Laird Lindsay's room stood empty before your arrival." She cast an uneasy glance at Alec. "And I told them about the woman from the market and how I've seen her leaving the castle at odd hours," she whispered. "That's when they let me go."

Colin's body froze, numbing and tingling, the way it had when he'd jumped into a loch in the middle of winter once. If they thought the earl was dead before Colin arrived, Brianna could be tried for her father's murder. He took a long, slow, painful breath. Marie was in incredible danger.

They all were.

A harsh sob tore from Magda's throat. Her hand slipped from his to cradle her face. He got to his feet and eased a hand over her back in comfort. She shook beneath his palm, her small body at the mercy of her tears. His gaze drifted to the graying darkness outside the open window.

Alec's voice interrupted his thoughts. "That's enough now, aye? She needs sleep."

Colin nodded with reluctance. He wanted more answers, but one look at her face told him he would most likely not find what he sought. She was too fatigued, too frightened. She would not remember the details he needed. "Ye're right," he said. "Alec, see her to her room, aye?"

He turned to Magda and forced a gentle smile. "Thank ye for yer help."

Magda's lips thinned. She glanced away and allowed Alec to lead her from the room.

God willing, her mind would sweep away her memories after some much needed rest.

He returned his attention to the window once more, to where the sun was beginning to peek across the distant hills. Marie had said Brianna's uncle found an informant, but Colin had not suspected they referred to his wife's own nurse.

The cruelty of forcing Magda to offer information against her own ward was more than he could bear. He would see Lindsay defeated for reasons other than the threat against his wife. Once this was over, Lindsay would never hurt another person again.

But first, he had to warn Marie.

* * *

The marketplace crowded with merchants preparing for their day, but Colin hardly noticed them. His gaze assessed Marie's rented room and the darkness of the windows. She'd slept late since he'd known her, but there was something unnatural about how tightly the windows were shuttered against the warm air. He drew closer, and the prickle of unease gave way to alarm.

Her door stood ajar.

He pushed his way in and was hit with a wall of thick perfume, stronger then he'd ever smelled. The bright glow of the morning sun behind him touched the room with gold, lighting the decadent pillows and silks strewn across the floor, the costly jars and bottles tipped on the table. An oily residue streaked the floor, blue shards of broken glass resting in the thick fluid. Marie's perfume.

All of it confirmed what he already knew.

Marie was not there.

She had put up a valiant fight from what he could see, but her efforts had been in vain.

First Magda, now Marie. Was Lindsay so close to striking?

A lone scarf lay upon the ground. Colin pinched the red silky fabric between his fingers and balled it in his fist. He would find Marie.

And he had a damn good idea where to start looking.

The low groan of wood creaked beneath someone's feet. Colin whipped his blade from its sheath between his shoulders and spun around.

A boy no taller than Colin's waist stood in the doorway, his wide ears framed by the light outside. He pulled his bottom lip in his mouth and studied Colin with a wary brown gaze.

"Are you looking for the French lady?"

Colin nodded. "I am."

The boy's stare dropped to where he rubbed the scuffed toes of his shoes against one another. "I saw someone pull her into a carriage this morning."

Just as Colin had suspected. "Can ye tell me what happened?"

The lad sucked in a deep breath, and the lower lip he kept tucking into his mouth quivered. "I heard her scream, but I couldn't help." His head bent low. "I was too afraid."

He approached the boy and knelt in front of him. "I think ye were verra brave in coming here this morning."

Large eyes rose to meet his. "I wanted to help."

"Ye still can. Did ye see the carriage?"

The boy nodded.

"Glossy black?" Colin surmised.

The boy shook his head so hard, his smooth blond hair moved with the action. "No, this was a rented carriage. The kind I've seen before on the street."

A rented carriage? Why would Lindsay have paid for a rented carriage when he had access to his own?

"They weren't the usual men either." The small voice cut through Colin's thoughts.

"The usual men?"

"Yeah, the guys that pick her up during the day. These men were different."

Had Lindsay sent other men? "Different how?"

The boy's shoulders lifted. "They spoke with words I didn't know. Words like the pretty lady uses sometimes."

French. Colin's head ached like it was being squeezed in a vise. If Lindsay's men had not abducted Marie, who had?

"Is there anything else ye can think of that might help me find her?" Colin asked.

The boy's mouth twisted to the side, and he looked up toward the ceiling in concentrated thought. "No." His shoulders sagged. "I guess I wasn't much help."

"Ye've told me more information than I would've found on my own, lad." Colin pulled the dirk from the side of his belt. The dagger was basic, plain steel with a leather wrapped handle, but its weight was solid and the blade sharp. "No warrior should be without a weapon, aye?"

The boy reached slowly toward the gift, his eyes wide with the disbelief of a boy who couldn't believe his luck.

"Be careful with it, lad, it's verra sharp." He waited for the boy to tuck it into the waistline of his pants before speaking again. "If anyone else comes here, dinna speak with them and tell no one of seeing me."

Colin's request was met with a vigorous nod.

"If ye see anything else or happen to learn anything, please come to me with the information. Ye can find me at Edzell Castle."

Widened eyes grew larger. "Edzell Castle? Are you—"

Colin grinned and ruffled the boy's hair.

The little head bowed reverently. "Yes, laird, you have my word."

Hopefully the boy could uncover important information. Colin would need all the help he could get in finding Marie.

And he *would* find her.

Chapter Thirty

Colin pressed his shoulder to the door of the chamber he shared with Brianna and eased it open. Perhaps she still slept and had not noticed his absence.

He stepped into the room and found his wife sitting in the middle of the bed. Sheets tangled at her waist and legs, leaving her bare torso rising from their bed like a goddess from a cresting wave. Tousled brown waves fell around her, wild and beautiful. She curled her hand around, shielding her naked breasts.

She stared at him, imploring, wounded. "You weren't here."

Her gaze followed his approach to the bed and her hand tightened against her arm.

"I'd hoped to still find ye sleeping." He smiled down at her, though he knew not a lick of it would do any good. "I'm sorry, lass. I couldna sleep." He sat on the edge of the stuffed mattress and turned to her. The warmth of her body beckoned him, tempted him to curl into bed beside her.

"Has something happened?"

Colin hesitated. He wanted to reply in the usual fashion, to reassure her everything was fine, to placate her until the issue had been resolved. Until Marie had been safely recovered.

Brianna peered over the mattress to Colin's boots. "You've been in town," she said softly. "The mud there is a lighter color than at Edzell."

"I dinna want to tell ye, but ye've made it clear ye want the truth."

Her legs shifted beneath the sheets and she sat up straighter. "Please tell me, Colin."

He rubbed his brow where a line of tension stretched taut

through his head. "Marie has been taken. By Frenchmen, from what I've been informed."

Brianna gasped behind her hand. "Why would someone take her?"

Colin shook his head. "That's what I canna figure out." Alec was already in town, asking questions. Hopefully he would get an idea of who the men were and where they had taken Marie.

Brianna's fingers remained pressed to her lips. "Why would you not wish to tell me something like this?" Her hand fell away. "I don't understand."

He looked down at the palms of his widespread hands, at the hard-won calluses slowly beginning to fade. "I know I can find Marie and have her safely returned. Telling ye would only give ye cause to worry." His ink-spattered hands balled into fists, hiding away proof of too much time behind a desk. "I dinna keep information a secret to hurt ye, I do it to protect ye. I would rather problems be found and corrected before ye know they exist." He looked up at Brianna. "That's how I prefer it."

Her lips were pursed in concentration. "Like my letters?"

"Aye, like yer letters." And like Magda's abduction. If Brianna realized what her nurse had been through, she would be horrified. Magda was already safe at home, and hopefully her memory had cleared itself of the terror she'd experienced. Brianna had no need to be informed. This would be the last secret he would keep from her.

Brianna's cheeks flushed pink. "I still found a way to get my letters from you."

Colin chuckled. "Aye, that ye did."

Her expression grew serious. "I do not want to have to always resort to trickery to get what should have already been shared with me."

"I would strongly encourage ye to employ the use of your trickery." He pulled off his boots and grinned at her over his shoulder. "Any time ye want."

His boots thunked to the floor. He crawled across the bed and slid his arms around Brianna's naked back. Her warmth, her sweet scent, all of it eased the unrest in his mind and soothed some of his stress.

He nuzzled her ear and caught her earlobe in his mouth. "I happen to enjoy trickery."

She leaned into him. "You're not using trickery on me, are you?"

He ran his lips down her neck. God, her skin was so damn soft. He brushed the sheet away from her breasts, and desire rose hard and thick between them.

She leaned away from him. "Colin, what about Marie?" Concern showed in her doe-eyed gaze.

Marie. Colin clenched his jaw. He didn't want to think of Marie or her abduction or what Magda's confession held. Right now he wanted to lose himself in his wife's silky embrace and revel in the comfort of knowing she was safe.

He pulled her toward him and kissed his way down her neck to the round swell of her right breast. "Alec is looking for Marie. Nothing more we can do, but wait."

Brianna's heart raced beneath his mouth. "I still want my letters," she gasped.

His tongue found the peak of her nipple and circled it. "Ye'll get yer letters." He teased the tender bud with his lips as he spoke. "But first I need more trickery to persuade me."

She gently pushed his chest and gave him a shy, ducking look. "Then you should lie down, husband, for there is more I have not shown you."

He lay back on the bed and pulled her with him. The letters would be the perfect distraction to keep her busy while Alec was in town.

Letters that would still be there after a bit of sport.

* * *

The parchment was smooth against Brianna's fingertips. Smooth and brittle. She would have to handle it with great care.

She settled against the seated window in her mother's study and craned her neck over the page.

The words were vaguely familiar. Something she had

seen before.

The memory slid into place and a nostalgic grin spread over her lips. Her mother had taught her the complex blend of Greek and French when she was a girl. That Marie and Colin were able to piece together as much as they had was impressive.

Brianna angled the page toward the glow of sunlight streaming through the lead-cased window and read.

My Elizabeth,

Not a day goes by that I do not think of your beauty, that I do not relive the enlightening conversations we shared. I know I should not be writing to you, yet I cannot bring myself to stay my hand.

The words lanced her heart, and any hope she had of her mother's innocence bled out from the wound.

The weight of Colin's stare lay heavy on Brianna's face. She flipped another page to the back.

"Ye read them quickly," he said from where he sat on the window seat across from her.

Her eyes were quick across the page, as if the faster-paced reading would make the contents carry less impact. But every endearing, incriminating word blazed itself in her mind. "The marquis was flattering," she murmured. "Very, very flattering."

No, not flattering—doting. Insistent. All but demanding Brianna's mother flee her home and return to him.

"They are but love letters, nothing more." Brianna forced strength into her dry throat lest Colin regret his decision.

He gently pulled the papers from her hands. "Ye wished they were something more?"

She shifted her gaze across the room to where a chipped flagstone called her attention.

"Brianna."

The fight slid out of her. "I thought I would find proof of her innocence, that she hadn't-that she'd been as honorable as I remember." She stared at the damaged wall. It'd been broken when she was a girl.

The earl paced the room, the air humming with his agitation. "You're a pathetic excuse of a mother, Whore. Teaching the girl words your lover wrote to you."

He hefted a marble ball from the desk, the one they used as Jupiter in their lessons, and sent it soaring through the air. The sphere slammed into the wall in an explosion of dust and rubble. A sliver of stone fell away and bounced on the hard floor. His face turned red. "Do you see what you've made me do, Elizabeth?"

Her mother's sobs echoed in Brianna's mind. "The earl didn't deserve her loyalty," she said in a wooden voice. "But I never expected anything less of her regardless."

The earl, *Brianna's father.*

The words soured in her thoughts. Was it possible someone else had fathered her? She looked down at the letters and her heart crushed into her stomach. Could she have had a father who loved her? Who cared for her, respected her?

Why had her mother stayed? Why had they not started the life the marquis promised her?

The swell of emotion in her throat warned of looming tears. Tears she would not have Colin see. She forced the darkness of her thoughts deep into her mind to mull over later. When she was alone.

She rose from the seat and tucked the letters into a drawer in her desk. "Enough of the letters for now."

Colin's eyes followed her hands. "I hope this hasna been too difficult for ye."

Brianna forced a smile. "It is the past, and the past cannot be changed. Let us look toward the future instead."

She reached into the drawer, lifted out the saffron-dyed leine and tucked it behind her back. The final stitch had been completed just before she'd discovered Marie in the market. Her fingers squeezed the fabric she had pored over for painstaking accuracy, suddenly grateful she had not thrown it in the fire as temptation had demanded.

She approached Colin, and a sudden wave of nervousness fluttered through her. Would he like it? Would it fit?

Brianna approached the sunny cushioned windowsill where Colin sat and kept her hands tucked behind her back, the leine hidden from view. "I made something for you."

He pulled back in surprise. "Ye made something for me?"

A grin lit his face.

She mentally measured the length of his arms. Had she miscalculated? Would he even be able to get it over his head?

She brought the leine from behind her back and held it out to him.

He lifted the fabric from her hands. "Ye sewed this?" He looked up at her, his gaze earnest. "For me?"

Brianna nodded. "Every Highland laird has a saffron shirt. Angus isn't the Highlands, but I figured you'd need one all the same."

He tugged his plain, white leine off and cast it aside, his muscles flexing with each subtle shift of his body. The golden fabric slipped over his head and Brianna held her breath. Would it fit?

Colin thrust his arms through sleeves that reached his wrists perfectly. He laughed and rubbed his hand along the front of the shirt, his eyes gleaming. "This is the finest leine I've ever owned. Made all the finer by my bonny wife's own hand."

The rich gold-yellow highlighted the striking auburn of his hair and drew her attention to his intensely green eyes. As much as she hated sewing, the shirt had come out exactly as she'd envisioned.

Colin's strong hands caught her waist and drew her to him. "Ye sew beautifully, Brianna."

Her cheeks warmed with pleasure. "Don't tell anyone lest they expect it of me more often."

"Yer secret's safe with me." He winked down at her and bent her backward. His strong hands braced the center of her back and gave her the confidence to know he wouldn't drop her.

"Thank ye, wife," he said earnestly. "I know what this cost ye."

His warm lips swept against hers, and the trepidation firing through her veins thrummed to the eager pulse of desire.

Someone cleared their throat in the doorway, interrupting the intimate moment. "Laird?"

Jonathan stood just outside the room, his gaze averted toward the floor.

"What is it, Jonathan?"

"Alec just rode in. You said you wanted to be notified immediately of his return."

Brianna touched Colin's chest. "Marie."

Colin nodded. "Forgive me. I must go."

She caught his hand. "Take all the time you need."

He nodded and disappeared from the room with a shadow of regret lingering in his gaze.

Alec asking around town after Marie's whereabouts would get nowhere, not while he wore a kilt. No Lowlander would soften beneath the hardness of his stare.

Brianna, however, knew several merchants she met with regularly who might offer assistance. The cost of running Edzell was substantial, and being a frequent customer would ensure their cooperation.

The guards had been difficult to trick the previous day. She knew they would not fall for the story about working with the cook again. In light of Marie's abduction, they would be all the more suspicious. Fortunately for her, she knew the hidden door through the bathhouse. The guards would not dare follow her in, and she would be able to slip away.

While Colin and Alec were busy with questions leading nowhere, she would conduct her own investigation.

Marie would be found.

* * *

One look at Alec's flushed face and Colin knew his old friend did not carry good news. He quickened his pace to where Alec stalked out of the stables.

"What did ye learn?" Colin asked.

Alec raked his hand through his black hair and did not slow as Colin fell into step beside him. "I learned the people in the village are as daft as they are unhelpful."

Damn. "So ye found nothing to help us then?"

"Did I no just say that?" He glared at several soldiers who strode past at a leisurely pace. Their backs snapped straight and their steps hastened.

Doubtless, he had displayed the same level of patience and warmth with the townsfolk. Colin pinched his whiskered chin between his fingers. Perhaps sending Alec to town had been a poor choice.

"Did ye no find anything else in her room?" Colin led the way into the castle and toward his solar, a path more routine than he cared to admit.

"I dinna get much of a chance. Lindsay's carriage came as I started to look around."

Colin's heart quickened. "Did the men get out?" He'd secured the room before leaving, but he had not set it to rights.

"Aye, they went in and came out with worried looks on their faces. Ye already knew it wasna Lindsay's men who took Marie. Their reactions confirm that." His large shoulders lifted in a shrug. "It isna more than ye already know. But dinna worry—we'll find her."

"Of course we will," Colin said. He didn't sound any more confident than he felt, a feeling wholly uncommon and unsettling.

At least Brianna was safe.

* * *

The alley between two filthy buildings stretched before Brianna in cluttered chaos. Sunlight did not dare touch the soiled ground and left piles of refuse shrouded in darkness.

A woman emerged from an unseen door, her hood pulled low over her head. She paused and slid a small green bottle into the folds of a dress that held the glossy sheen of expensive silk.

She turned in the opposite direction and departed, her steps hurried. The alley was empty. Now was Brianna's chance.

She darted around haphazard stacks of rubbish, her feet slipping and sucking in the muck. The hem of her dress was heavy with stains of the soiled streets. This would mark the last time she forgot her pattens.

The doorknob was hot in her hands, and an unnamed

odor clogged her nostrils. She forced her breath through her mouth and pulled at the heavy door. After the second attempt, it opened into black nothingness.

Brianna plunged into the unknown, her heartbeat erratic against her ribs. The door slammed shut behind her.

Perhaps not black nothingness. A single candle flickered its feeble light throughout the small space. The cheap tallow sputtered thick, acrid smoke that settled around the room in a noxious fog. The meager flame reflected off shelves of bottles, like a wall of distorted mirrors.

"Another fine lady." The words rasped through the darkness, taking her aback.

A man edged into the dim light, his black hair and smooth skin marking a distinct difference from his aged voice. His lips pulled back in a grin stretched to ghoulish proportions by the shadows. "Do you want someone to fall in love with you?" The smile did not leave his lips as his eyes widened. "Or is there a baby you wish to rid yourself of?"

Brianna lifted her chin. She would not allow this man to sense her fear. "Neither. I seek information on men recently arrived in town. Frenchmen."

His hand glided palm-up toward the stocked shelves. One fingernail was long and filed to a sharp point. "As you can see, I sell dreams. I do not provide information."

The response was not unexpected. She lifted a small purse between them. "Perhaps you do today."

His sharpened nail dragged across his chin and filled the silence with the hollow scrape of it upon his flesh. "Perhaps I do indeed."

She pulled the purse out of his reach. "The other merchants said you know of all people who enter and leave."

His gaze did not follow the coin as expected, but bore down upon her, pressing her soul. Her spine tingled with a cold chill.

"The Frenchmen you seek are most unusual. I would caution my lady from approaching their master."

Doubt flitted through Brianna. If the man before her deemed the Frenchman unusual, what sort of man was he? She shoved aside her reservations and met his wild gaze. "I didn't ask your counsel, I seek information." She forced a note of defiance into her tone.

The pointed nail tapped against his chin. "Then perhaps I should caution him against you." His whooshing exhale bordered on a chuckle. "Very well, what is it you wish to know?"

• • •

Colin let the solar's solid door click shut behind him, a glorious sound that marked his freedom.

He could not spend another minute in that chamber. The odor of books and potted ink robbed him of air, of life. Of precious time he could use to find Marie.

Alec still combed the outskirts of town, but something in Colin's gut told him the efforts would be fruitless. If only Marie had left some sort of clue.

"Laird, a word if you please."

Colin turned to see the young pastor striding toward him.

"There's a boy outside who wishes to see you." Thomas said and extended his hand. "He bade me give you this."

Resting against his palm was the plain dagger with the leather handle. The gift he'd given the boy at Marie's flat.

"Where is he?" Colin demanded, grasping the dagger.

"At the front gate," Thomas said. "Shall I tell him you'll be down?"

"No need. I'll go myself. Thank ye, Thomas."

He sprinted from the castle to Edzell's entrance, where the boy stood staring open-mouthed around him. His eyes shone bright with excitement.

"Did ye find out more information?" Colin asked. He held the dagger out to the lad, returning what was his.

The boy tucked the blade into his belt and nodded. "I think I know where she is—a manor off the main street where they hold market."

Colin looked toward town. The castle was situated close enough that they could arrive in half an hour, significantly less than that if they ran. Assembling his horse and a team of men, however, would take too long. Marie's life was at stake and every moment was precious.

He ran his fingers across the hilt of his sword, reassurance for their protection. "Take me to her."

The boy took off down the road without further encouragement. Together they dashed down the narrow path and into the crowded streets.

"Just up ahead," the boy shouted over his shoulder and darted into one of the many alleys.

He was still several steps ahead. The smack of his bare feet in the mud echoed off either side of the stone buildings and kept Colin abreast of his location.

Alarm raised the hairs on Colin's arm. Something was wrong.

A hard object crashed into his side with a ferocity wholly unexpected. He clamped the hilt of his sword in his fist, but his actions were slow, clumsy. His head swam with pain.

He roared through it and turned toward a tall, thick man who evaded Colin's blade with awkward jerks. The heat of another body plastered against Colin's back, arms clinging to his neck.

He rolled his body forward, but the person held on and smothered his face with their hand. Something wet pressed to his nose. Noxious.

He shoved the hand away, but the odor remained.

Heavy. Everything felt heavy.

The boy crouched behind a pile of trash, his hand gripping the dagger.

No.

Colin's thick tongue prevented his cry.

The boy must flee.

Colin swiped a leaden hand.

Tired. So tired.

Couldn't call.

The alley darkened, and Colin's world went black.

Chapter Thirty-One

Murmuring voices faded in and out, twisting Colin's subconscious and conscious into a dizzying mix of unstable reality. The words grew louder. More rapid. Not English. He squinted an eye open and nausea rolled through him. His head sagged forward and forced his gaze on his own lap. He was sitting in a chair.

Yellow walls and polished hardwood floors spun through his vision. His stomach tightened. He was going to be sick on that hardwood floor.

The hurried talking hummed around him. Goading him. He clenched his hands to strengthen his stomach. His hands were behind his back, and something jutted into his armpits. Something hard.

He was a prisoner.

By the French?

Marie.

He shifted, keeping his movements slight to avoid drawing attention. Rope bound his wrists. He twisted his hand back and forth. Slack rope.

Who did they think they were dealing with?

Awareness tingled along the right side of his body, and a shadow obscured the slowly clearing haze. One quick jerk of Colin's hands and his fist was free. He threw a blind punch and connected with something soft that grunted and swore in French.

Colin pulled his left arm free from the back of the chair. Blood returned to his limbs with a stinging rush, as if he were being jabbed with a thousand needles. The man he'd punched lay on the ground with a purple face, hands cupping his genitals.

Colin grimaced and glanced behind him. There had been two voices.

The room stretched long and narrow and housed a table that ran the length of the floor. Aside from a wooden hutch and several dozen chairs, the room appeared empty. Had the other man left and he did not hear it?

He turned his attention to the man who now struggled to his knees. Colin might have crouched down beside him if the room would stop spinning.

"Ye have Marie D'Abigne," Colin said in his rough French.

The man's face crumpled in pain. "What?"

A slight scuff sounded behind him, like the whisper of a curtain against the floor. Colin's body tensed, but he turned too slowly.

Something caught him around the neck and shoved him backward. The left side of his face pressed hard against the wall and left him blind to his attacker.

"*You* are laird of Edzell Castle?" Disbelief laced the hiss of French.

If Colin weren't preoccupied with trying to live, he might have been offended by the Frenchman's implication.

Colin's hands shot out between them and shoved. The pressure released from his neck, and he was free. His captor staggered back in a clatter of shoes slipping across slick, hard floor. Colin's muscles fired with the need to fight back. He braced his feet and stared down at the alarmed gaze of his opponent.

The Frenchman pushed aside a curtain of long black curls and righted his frilly blue silk jacket. He did not move again to attack. "You are not what I was expecting," he said.

Colin rubbed the tender skin of his neck and eyed the man's thin frame. The hit had felt like it should have come from a man twice his size. "I was just thinking the same thing."

The man did not smile.

"I have your woman." His lips pulled back in a sneer. "Your spy. She is in this house. If I do not return within the hour, they will slit her throat. Do you understand?"

Before Colin could answer, the man's long fingers gripped

the back of a chair and tugged it free from the row. "Sit. I want to ask you questions."

Colin did not sit. Not until he got his own answers. "Where is the boy?"

"The boy wielding the Highland dagger too fine for his station? The boy who has been asking questions about my whereabouts? The boy thrust into a fight he is too young to understand?" The muscles of the Frenchmen's neck stood out from beneath his lace collar.

Guilt fueled the anger roaring through Colin. "I dinna ask for an upbraiding. I asked his location."

"Upstairs with your spy." He shook his head. "And you need an 'upbraiding' if you think a child is the right soldier to send into battle."

Colin clamped his teeth together so hard he thought they might shatter. He'd meant to encourage the lad, to make him feel brave. He certainly hadn't meant to place him in danger.

A white hand lined with unexpected calluses indicated the empty chair. "Now sit."

Colin bit back his argument. No matter what it took, he would see Marie and the boy safe. Even if it meant bending to the Frenchman's will. A little. He lowered himself to the hard seat.

"That's better. With your cooperation, everyone will be safely released." The Frenchman propped an elbow on his knee and leaned forward. "Tell me about your involvement with Signore Capra."

Colin blinked once. Twice. Whatever horrendous poison they'd shoved against his nose had obviously affected his hearing. Or maybe it was the two times he had taken a solid hit in one day. Regardless, none of it worked in his favor.

The man leaned even further forward until he practically lay across his own lap. His thick curls spilled over the seat of the chair and dangled toward the floor. "Signore Baldessar Capra." His gazed raked down Colin's face. "And Simon Marius."

Colin studied the hard glint in the man's eyes. Was he insane? If so, the impending fight would be all the more difficult. "Are these men Marie knows?" Colin asked.

The man jerked back and slapped his palm against the glossy side of the chair with a resounding smack. "Do not feign confusion with me. You are laird of Edzell. And like the laird who came before you, you are eager to see me ruined. After all these years, I find peace, happiness, and yet again the master of Edzell Castle seeks to strip me of my joy."

"I dinna kno—"

"I found out about your spy. I heard about her all the way in Italy. At first I wondered why a woman would question my whereabouts, but then they found your letter asking for her assistance. The broken seal was described to me and I recognized it."

Long, thin fingers wrapped around Colin's wrist and gripped him with the strength of a vise. The Lindsay signet ring shone bright in the soft light. "This seal," the Frenchman said.

He pushed Colin's hand away. "I know that seal. I spent years of my life hating that damn seal." The spark in the man's eyes drained to exhausted desperation. "That seal stole the sunshine from my life, robbed me of the essence of my youth." His hand tightened to a fist and reverently pressed to his breast. "Pulled the blood from my still beating heart."

Irritation crawled over Colin's already tense shoulders. "I dinna know the laird befo—"

"You know more than you say you do. It is the reason I left Italy to come here myself. I know the power you Lindsays wield." Energy fired to life in the man's tired face. He leapt to his feet and began an impatient stalking back and forth, back and forth, back and forth. The heels of his crisp leather shoes rang against the floor, each step marked by a harsh tap.

Colin's head pounded. Italy. Marie. There was something he was missing, something he couldn't focus on long enough to hold on to. He shook his head to clear it of the effects of the drug and found the Frenchman staring at him.

"You knew I secured my patronage for Signore Galileo Galilei. Just like you knew Capra intended to release that plagiarized version on the military compass." His finger jabbed into Colin's shoulder.

One more jab and Colin would see that finger broken. The man must have read Colin's thoughts because his hand dropped to his side and he bent over, bringing his face to eye level. Fine lines imprinted a face that had appeared young from a distance.

"Capra and Marius sought you out knowing the Earl of Lindsay's hatred for me." The wrinkles deepened. "To punish me."

Colin's tether of patience snapped. He leapt to his feet and grabbed the man's arm. It was surprisingly firm beneath his grip.

Weak or strong, mad or sane, the Frenchman would no longer dominate the spinning conversation of insanity.

"Ye make no sense." Colin's fingers curled around the man's neck.

The other Frenchman shifted, but Colin swung to face him with the well-dressed man in his grasp. "Come closer and I will crush his throat, aye?" The large man's eyes narrowed, but he did not move forward.

"The laird ye speak of is dead." Colin stared down at the man with long hair. "And I dinna know him when he was alive. What I do know is that ye came onto my land, kidnapped my guest, as well as an innocent boy, and then threatened their lives." He squeezed tighter, and a choking whine hissed from the Frenchman's lips. The larger man tensed and a frown creased his bald head. "After all that," Colin continued. "Ye dinna let me talk while ye accuse me of conspiring with people I've never heard of."

He drew a deep breath to keep from killing the man. "Let Marie and the lad go, and then we can talk like gentlemen, aye?"

The man gave a vigorous nod and Colin released him. His gasping cough filled the room, a thunderous sound that echoed off the yellow walls. A sound that did not mask the gentle click of the door behind Colin opening. The Frenchman looked over Colin's shoulder, and his jaw went slack.

Chapter Thirty-Two

The hardwood floor beneath Brianna's feet ran the length of the room, the sunshine yellow walls a contrast to the tension vibrating in the air.

She still gripped the handle of the door, as if the smooth, unyielding metal could lend her much-needed strength.

Two men stared back at her. A third stood several feet away, his back toward her, auburn hair bound in a leather thong against a golden-colored shirt.

Her stomach spiraled to the floor.

Colin.

Her gaze returned to the foreign men.

Who posed more of a threat? The large one standing several feet in front of Colin? The elaborately dressed man in light blue silk? Or her husband when he realized she'd defied his orders, left the safety of their home, and came to Marie's rescue without guards?

Brianna swallowed down the bitterness of her own trepidation.

"Elizabeth." The elaborately dressed man spoke, the word a haunted whisper on his pale lips. He took a step toward her, and a low creak sounded from the floor beneath his foot.

His bright blue eyes glazed with tears, his emotions laid bare for her to witness. The sadness, the longing, the raw desperation—all of it exposed.

Colin turned abruptly. "What are ye doing here?"

The man who called her by her mother's name took another step closer, but Colin grabbed his arm and jerked him back before shooting her an icy glare. "Get out of here, Brianna."

The sharp movement jarred the man's body. "Brianna," he said, more to himself than to anyone else. "Of course." A smile touched his lips and he shook his head.

"Did you find Marie?" she asked in a voice she wished was bigger. More certain.

Colin ignored her question and captured the man by the back of his neck. He ripped a dagger free from his boot and pressed to the man's exposed throat.

"My wife is none of yer concern." Colin's voice carried in the stark room, his snarl possessive. Primitive. It made the hair on her arms prickle.

"Wife?" The Frenchman's mouth fell open and a low chuckle sounded deep in his throat. "Of course." His slender hand patted Colin's forearm. "I thought you were the Earl of Lindsay's son. Release me, boy. I would embrace the daughter of the woman I loved."

The daughter of the woman he loved. The elaborate, expensive attire. The French-laced Gaelic.

Brianna's breath went shallow with her realization.

He was the French marquis.

Her insides flinched. Her mother's French marquis.

Colin's arms tightened. "Ye'll do nothing with my wife."

She darted forward and placed her hand on Colin's arm. His taut muscles slackened beneath her fingertips, but still he did not release the marquis. "Stop, please."

Colin's face darkened to a brilliant shade of red. "What are ye doing, Brianna? Did I no tell ye to leave? Get yerself from this house."

She shook her head. "You don't understand, this man is—"

"Get out of here now." The edge of his words cut into her. "Ye are my wife and when I speak, ye will obey."

Despite the conscious act of stiffening her back, Brianna felt herself shrink under his anger. His authority.

He put her in her place as the earl had done to her mother so many times before. Her heartbeat staggered to life and pounded in her trembling hands.

Before she could respond, the marquis shoved the dagger

away and spun around to face Colin. "Do not speak to her in such a manner." He moved in front of Brianna, an act of protection. Against her own husband.

* * *

Colin stared in shock at the Frenchman who blocked Brianna with his body. The whole damn world had gone mad.

The breath eased from Colin's throat in a low growl.

Brianna's voice sounded behind the man. "I'm not in danger." She stepped around him, her gaze darting to the man's face. Searching. "From either of you."

"Ye know this man?" Colin asked.

"No more than you do." Her gaze dragged from the Frenchman toward Colin. "He is the marquis from my mother's letters."

"She kept them?" The man's eyes glowed bright beneath his heavy black brows. He stared down at Brianna. "What she says is true. I am Percival de Caritat, Marquis de Condorcet. If I am thinking of the same letters you speak of, then yes, I am that man." He bowed low. "Forgive the misunderstanding and inconvenience, *monsieur*. I thought you were someone you were not and assumed a vindictive act where there was none."

Colin glanced around the room. The turn of events had transpired too quickly. Only a fool would allow himself to relax. "I want Marie and the boy released."

"Of course." A string of French flew from the marquis's mouth so quickly that Colin only caught a word or two. The large man gave a gruff nod and disappeared through the door.

"You must come to Edzell Castle," Brianna said, staring up at the marquis. "There is much I wish to discuss."

Her expression was doting. Irritation tightened Colin's muscles further still. "There is much I wish to discuss *before* ye come to my home," he said. "Like who is Capra, what do ye have to do with Galileo, and how the hell do ye know Gaelic?"

"The English king hates Gaelic," the marquis said with an airy toss of his long hair. "As I've already explained to you,

Baldessar Capra has plagiarized Galileo's work on the military compass, and I seek to bring him and Marius down for their theft. In regards to Galileo—I am his patron." His chest swelled and his chin lifted with a note of French pretension.

"Galileo?" Brianna asked, her eyes wide.

Footsteps sounded on the stairs outside the door and tugged Colin's attention from his wife's adoration of another man.

The dagger still rested against his palm.

He stared toward the only entrance to the room, more anxious than he cared to admit. The door creaked open and Marie sauntered in, her appearance as immaculate as ever. Her slender hand folded around the boy's, who followed behind her like a soldier with a love-sick grin on his face.

"Are ye well?" he asked, his eyes skimming Marie's neck for the mark of a blade.

She waved her hand. "Aside from being pulled from my room in the middle of the night, I'm fine." Her smile widened as she looked down at the boy. "George and I were just playing with a top Pierre brought."

"Pierre?"

A man with a blond mustache that curled upward appeared behind Marie. "*Bonjour.*"

The third man. The man who had forced the wet rag to Colin's nose. The one responsible for the pounding headache that left Colin less than enthusiastic to return pleasantries.

"Monsieur de Caritat will join us for supper," Brianna said. "We should leave soon if we wish to arrive in time."

The marquis inclined his head. "Please, call me Percival. I would not have the daughter of my Elizabeth refer to me so formally."

* * *

The moon bathed the garden in an ethereal silver light. Brianna tipped her face toward the caress of a cool breeze. She walked two steps ahead of Percival, her footsteps threaded with a giddiness that carried her faster than intended.

He'd promised to show her the star Galileo discovered so recently, the one that defied the heavens and stood beyond the moon.

Her nerves danced with excitement. Tonight she would see not only the bold star. She would have her questions answered.

They reached the bench she sought, the one sitting in a sea of roses, where the comforting rush of the fountain bathed the night air.

"This was Mother's favorite spot," Brianna said softly.

The marquis lowered himself to the bench and breathed deeply. A smile blossomed on his lips. "I can see Elizabeth sitting here." His gaze skimmed heavy flowers propped on their thin stems, the brilliant red now darkened by the night to a purple crimson. "She loved roses."

Brianna sat beside him and tried to keep her eyes from scanning his face again. After staring at him through supper, she had already committed to memory every dip and curve of his features, from the shadow below his high cheekbones to the prominence of his nose. She longed for a mirror to sit before, to measure the cut of her own cheekbones, the length of her own nose.

"You look so much like your mother." He tilted her chin with the tip of his middle finger. "There is very little of your father in you."

Perfume wafted from the sleeve of his jacket, floral and spicy. Her pulse tripped to life, daring the question to flee her lips lest she lose courage. "And who would that be?"

He dropped his hand. "Pardon?"

Brianna cleared her throat to keep from stumbling over the words she'd wished to ask since she met him. "Percival, are you my father?"

Chapter Thirty-Three

Brianna folded her hands in her lap to mask their tremor. A restless breeze shifted through the garden, stirring the wisps of hair along her neck and forehead.

Percival did not stiffen at her bold question of paternity, nor did his pensive features register offense.

"Your mother was enchanting. She was beautiful and graceful and highly intelligent. I wish I could say I acted the part of a gentleman when I was with her, but that would be a lie. I was young and in love." Percival shifted his gaze to the dark garden, toward the rose bushes. "For all my advances, your mother remained ever stoic in her loyalty to her husband." His eyes met hers. "Your father."

Brianna should have been elated at the declaration. It proved her legitimacy and proclaimed her mother's innocence. Yet it was an overwhelming disappointment that rocked her back like the force of a blow.

A sad smile jerked at the corner of his lips. "While I would be honored to have fathered such an educated, lovely woman, alas it is impossible that I ever lay claim to you as mine."

Unexpected tears filled her eyes. She'd wished too hard for a second chance at a father's love.

The fountain's steady trickle occupied the silence while Brianna gathered her composure. "You could have been my father," she said in a thick voice. "I would have called you such had my mother gone to you."

"I had no right to ask that of her." Percival's voice held an edge. "As I said before, I was young. Selfish."

She glanced at him and found the muscles of his jaw

strained. Her own desperation pulled at her heart and seeped into her words. "You wanted a better life for her. You said so in your letters."

He shook his head, and his heavy curls brushed against his lap. "Those letters only served to make her life more difficult." He propped an elbow on his leg and cradled his chin in his palm, looking very much a pensive scholar. "And yours. Because of those damned letters, your father thought your mother and I had been—" He slid a sidelong glance at Brianna, as if in apology. "Intimate. She was treated as prisoner in her own home, and you were taken from her to ensure she would never leave."

The painful childhood memories slammed into Brianna. The visits from her mother with a guard hovering in the distance. The fierceness of her mother's hugs, as if she couldn't bear to let Brianna go. The adoring way she would brush Brianna's hair as they spoke.

"She stayed because of me." Brianna choked on the realization.

"No," Percival said. "She stayed for you. Because she knew if she left you alone with him, your life would hold no joy." His long fingers slid over her clasped hands, drawing her from her memories. "Because she knew if she left without you, her life would hold no joy."

He squeezed her hands gently. "I did not understand such love. But seeing you now and knowing you are my Elizabeth's daughter." He paused and drew in a slow breath. "I can understand such love." His voice trembled and his eyes grew wet with unshed tears. "I wish you could have been my daughter."

A dagger of longing pierced Brianna's heart, into the dark spot she thought was buried deep enough to never again hurt. The ache of years repressed spread in a flood of sorrow and pent-up rage.

"No more than I wish it," she said. There was a passionate flare to her voice she could not temper. "I've known you only several hours, but already I know life with you would have been different than with the earl. Different and better. You would have encouraged my learning, applauded my accomplishments."

She balled her hands into fists. "You would have been proud of me."

"Despite his lack of praise, I do believe your father was proud of you." Percival laid a hand on her shoulder. "What father could not be with a daughter so rare and magnificent?" He patted her shoulder in a gentle, soothing way. As a father might have done to his daughter. "Sometimes one is blinded by his own failures and cannot bring himself to see the accomplishments in those he loves." He dabbed his eyes with a thin handkerchief pulled from his pocket. "I wish there were something I could do to erase the burden of your childhood."

But he couldn't. There was no way to erase those years of lonely degradation she'd suffered with her father's suspicions.

Or could he?

The weight in her heart lightened. "Perhaps there is something you can do for me."

* * *

Colin stared down into the garden from the window of the solar, his back toward Marie. Brianna sat on the same bench as the marquis, their heads bent together. Colin's fingers tightened against the hard stone windowsill.

The scene was far too intimate for his liking.

He should have the man thrown from Edzell, yet he knew if he did so Brianna would never forgive him.

Right now he needed to keep his focus on her. He knew all too well the hurt of a father's disappointment. Brianna needed the marquis in a way Colin could never provide. And he would have to accept that.

"You believe Magda is Lindsay's informant?" Marie asked from across the solar.

Colin turned away from the window. "Aye, Magda gave him all the information, voluntarily or no. I canna see anyone else speaking to Lindsay."

"*Merde.*"

He was grateful to have her returned and safe. Little George had already been sent home with a purse for his mother and a strict set of combat rules that mainly consisted of staying safe until danger passed.

Marie's head tilted thoughtfully. "I need to come up with an excuse to explain my absence. I need to get back—"

"No," Colin said in a stern voice. "I willna have ye going back to Lindsay. Magda inadvertently exposed yer involvement with us. Ye've risked yerself too much already with yer questions all over France about the marquis." His fear over her loss was still too sharp. Too recent. "When I saw ye were taken, I assumed Lindsay had realized from Magda's confessions that ye were spying for me. I couldna forgive myself if something happened to ye, Marie."

"I can handle myself." A glint shone in Marie's eyes, obstinate and hard.

"I willna have it. Ye willna risk yer safety anymore. My men can take care of Lindsay."

She held up her hand. "While I appreciate your concern, I will not have you making my decisions for me. You will not allow me to repay your kindnesses in any other fashion—please let me do this for you."

Colin shook his head. "I canna."

Her cheeks darkened, and he knew he had offended her.

"That's it?" she snapped. "You expect me to turn my back on you and your wife? To go home to France as if none of this ever happened?" Her voice turned shrill.

"That is exactly what I expect."

"You will regret this decision, Colin. You are too stubborn, too determined to complete something on your own." She snatched her purse off the desk. "I only hope your wife does not pay the price for your arrogance."

Before Colin could protest, Marie spun away in a flounce of perfumed silks. The door slammed shut behind her and left him in silence, to feast on sharp words that kept close company with those of his father.

Chapter Thirty-Four

The slanted streets of Edinburgh were slick with the effects of a recent rain, but Brianna did not see the dark clouds. She saw only the light that poured in through the long windows of her rented room and bathed her skirts in its sunny warmth.

Brianna was legitimate. Officially. Deemed such by the Commissary of Edinburgh and forever recorded in their massive ledger.

She ran her fingers over the thick parchment, careful not to smear the ink. Her mother's name could never be cleared from gossip, but Brianna knew the truth.

The only way her valiant success could be more perfect would be if Colin were at her side. Alas, she knew too well the draw of necessary tasks back at Edzell.

"You are pleased?" Percival asked from the doorway. The small traveling cases she'd brought with her were packed and ready to be loaded into the carriage once it arrived.

"Very," she breathed. "Thank you."

He inclined his head toward her. "May I enter?"

Brianna smoothed the parchment once more before wrapping it in a leather flap for protection. "Of course."

The click of his raised-heeled shoes fell silent as he strode over the thick carpet to where she stood beside the table. A slightly floral scent wafted from his hair, a scent she'd come to recognize as his.

"The carriages will be here shortly."

"Carriages?" she asked. "We are taking more than one?"

"*Oui*. One is to return to Edzell Castle, and one is to take me to the docks." His brows drew together in an apologetic expression. "I must return to Italy. I need to resume my efforts in aiding Galileo, and there is much that requires my assistance."

Brianna bit back her displeasure. Of course he had to go, he had his own life, his own pursuits. Had she expected him to stay in Scotland forever?

Her cheeks burned at her own foolishness. "Of course you must return," she said quickly. "I understand."

He stepped closer and cradled her chin with his slender hand. "You could come with me."

Nervous excitement flashed through her. "What?" Had she heard correctly?

He smiled down at her, the way she'd seen fathers do to the daughters they loved, the way she'd longed to be looked upon by the earl. Her heart swelled in the warmth of his gaze, and all at once she felt the paternal protection and adoration she'd spent a childhood without.

"*Mon petite*, I would never forgive myself for leaving you in a situation like I left Elizabeth. I was helpless then, but now I have power and wealth." His blue eyes searched hers. "You did not choose to wed your husband, and you do not have to stay with him. You have your legitimacy, but no reason to seek divorce. I am giving you the option to return with me to Italy where <u>you</u> may live the life of a free woman to come and go as you please."

Brianna pulled in a deep breath to still her spinning mind and gently broke away from his embrace. Leave Colin?

She leaned back against the sharp edge of the dressing table, away from the heat of the sunlight. It had grown too hot.

She'd never been given the freedom to make choices for herself, she had always decided based on what was right. Even running the estate when her father had been ill. True it had been enjoyable, but ultimately her efforts had been for the protection of the people, for financial security.

Never once had she been presented with the opportunity to make a choice dictated by her own desires.

Now two paths stretched before her, both uncertain. And whichever path she chose would be of her own volition.

Chapter Thirty-Five

Dust motes floated through a stream of sunlight, their movements delicate, carefree. A slight brush of Brianna's hand and they would dance in frenzied circles. She felt like one of those errant motes.

Percival studied her from across the sunbeam, his gaze soft, patient. "Leaving Scotland to come to Italy is an unexpected consideration, I know. A decision not easily made. Know that if you come to Italy, you will be treated as my daughter."

He continued with an excited spark in his eyes. "You could listen to lectures given by men of great learning, and you would, of course, meet Galileo. You could see firsthand his military compass and hear of his latest inventions."

His enthusiasm was contagious, and his words spun an image of a world so full of learning and incredible opportunity, it left her breathless.

Meeting Galileo, speaking with him on his inventions and discussing the movement of the stars. The very thought of being in his presence made her tremble.

The existence Percival painted seduced her with the promise of everything she had wanted. Everything she had never thought to have.

And now it stood at her fingertips. She only had to close her hand around the new life, and it would all be hers.

"It sounds so wonderful," she whispered.

His smile grew and the lines around his eyes creased.

Doubt flickered through her, calming the eager pounding of her heart. If she went to Italy, she would leave Edzell.

She would leave Colin.

His face surfaced in her mind. His rich auburn hair that made his emerald green eyes stand out, brilliant and clear. The way he always seemed to grin with a mischievous joy and lent him that carefree nature she found irresistible. The dimple in his cheek when he smiled, the warmth of his laughter and the giddy rush of knowing her wit had sparked such a reaction.

True, she had been forced to marry him, but he had been a good husband to her. He was faithful and considerate. He gave her the freedom to study and read as she pleased. It was he who had encouraged her to come to Edinburgh with Percival.

Her life without Colin had not been as happy, not even when she managed the estate. All this time she'd focused on Edzell and the unfairness of her life. Never had she focused on what she'd gained.

She had been imprudent.

Colin brought a pleasure she had never known, an eagerness to face each day to see what challenges arrived. He protected her and made her feel safe. His methods were heavy and overbearing at times, but his intentions were always well-meaning.

The crunch of gravel sounded outside the thin glass windows, accompanied by the hollow jostling of large wooden carriages. The time had come for her to make a decision.

A life of learning or a life of love.

Love.

The realization spread through her, warm and beautiful. For as hard as she'd fought Colin's affection, as much as she swore to guard her heart, she was in love with her husband.

And a more wonderful understanding had never been met.

Percival sauntered to the window and pulled the heavy green curtains back with the top of his cane. "The carriages have arrived, but you may take all the time you wish to make your decision. I understand I have sprung a large choice on you rather precipitously."

She shook her head. "No, I've made up my mind. I know what I wish to do. I appreciate what you've offered and confess to the pull of temptation. But I will go back home to Edzell." The smile blooming on her lips echoed in the swell of her heart.

"Back to my husband."

"You make an important statement with this pronouncement." Percival strode across the room toward her, the concentrated furrow on his brow now smooth. "Can this mean you love the man?"

"I do," she breathed. "I just didn't realize it until now." She laid a hand on his forearm. "Until I was left to choose on my own."

His dry fingers ran down her cheek in a tender caress. "If you have love, *mon petite*, then take it." A pained look flitted across his composed features. "I would give up my world to have your mother back. To have her to myself."

He pressed his lips to Brianna's forehead. "Know that you are always welcome in my home, and that I am always here for you." His arms came around her, the fine silk of his sleeves slippery against her dress. When he finally released her and stood back, welling tears glistened in his eyes.

He offered his arm, and she slid her hand in the warm crook of his elbow. "You will always be cherished by me as a daughter."

"Thank you," she said. "For legitimizing my birth." She lowered her gaze. "And for letting me realize what I have."

"To see you happy fills me with delight." His hand rested atop hers. "And thank you for allowing me to be a father, something I never dreamed to experience, nor enjoy, as much as I have."

Together they walked from Brianna's rented room, away from the fork of difficult decisions and toward the path she chose, the path that took her to Colin.

The path that took her to love.

• • •

Colin's shirt clung to his back with sweat, and the marble seat dug into the hard bone of his arse. He braced his elbows on his knees in an effort to find a more comfortable position, with no luck.

A fat bee bobbed through the air and dipped from one ready bloom to the other.

For the first time in his life, Colin did not know what to do. He'd sent Marie away, a decision he did not regret, but now he was left without an informant, and his own men had been unsuccessful in tracking Lindsay's activities. That did not mean the bastard had given up. Doubtless it meant the opposite.

The thunderous quiet before an attack.

Colin could feel it in his bones, that twitchy awareness. The one that had saved his life many times before.

The steady trickle of the fountain imbedded itself in his brain and drowned his thoughts.

He scowled at the marble fixture with its cascading water.

The bowl was too small to bathe in, and the damn thing made him have to urinate.

Brianna found peace in this garden, yet all he found was unbearable heat and a ready bladder.

Alec had reported earlier that Marie's room now stood empty, confirmation that she had indeed left as directed. She was safe.

Brianna had not yet returned from her trip to the Commissary Court in Edinburgh. She was safe.

Even Magda, who had taken ill after the ordeal that God had the mercy of striking from her memory, had left with Brianna for Edinburgh and was no longer in Edzell. She too was safe.

A shout went up behind him, from the towering walls of the castle. He turned, tense, ready for a battle he knew drew near.

"Men approach," the guard called from his position above.

Colin ran into the cool silence of the castle, raced up the steps and burst through the door leading to the roof. Sunlight turned his vision into a sea of yellow-white dots, and a stiff breeze tore at his clothing.

He shielded the glow of the sun with his hand and stared across the horizon to where a black carriage and an army of several dozen guards on horseback rode in their direction.

Colin's nerves hardened in preparation for a fight. A handful of his soldiers were in Edinburgh with Brianna, but the men who remained were all skilled. They could handle the army, even if they were outnumbered.

Colin faced the harrowing wind with confidence.

Some might consider his decision to fight impulsive, but he would see it met with success.

His conviction wavered.

Impulsive.

Brianna would never make such a rash decision.

He lowered his hand and stared down at the golden seal upon his finger, the seal he had gained through marriage and earned through the direction of Brianna's detailed notes and accounts. He was laird, and the people of the castle relied on him for safety.

There had been no time to prepare for this battle. No time to assemble more guards or recall the ones from Edinburgh. No time to secure a safe location for the women and children who served within Edzell. His small number of guards could defeat the force Lindsay brought, but at what cost?

If he lost, Edzell's people would be slaughtered or enslaved for his foolish attempt.

Colin leaned over the battlements and stared down to where his soldiers gathered below. The time had come to make a decision entirely foreign to him.

He turned to the guard beside him. "Get Alec and tell the men to return to their stations. I would see this handled as gentlemen rather than warriors."

This was a resolution a laird made. Colin's people would stand protected no matter what price he paid.

And perhaps his father would be proud.

* * *

Brianna leaned against the cushioned seat of the carriage and arched her back to relieve the ache of cramped muscles. Naught showed through the open shutters of their rolling coach save a steady line of trees, all identical to the one before. The ride had seemed longer returning to Edzell than leaving. Perhaps due to her eagerness to rediscover her husband, to face him with the newfound realization.

She loved him.

The high sandstone entrance came into view, and her pulse danced an excited beat through her veins. She shifted restlessly in the thinly cushioned seat.

The horses drawing the carriage moved too slowly.

Her anxiety bounced with her tapping leg. Seconds. She was mere seconds from seeing him.

Centuries passed before the carriage finally crawled to a halt. Brianna pitched onto her feet before the floor had stopped swaying and caught the fragile handle of the door. She could not wait for it to be opened for her. Not when she knew Colin would be waiting in the courtyard.

She pushed the door open and stepped from the stuffy carriage into a breeze that carried the welcoming scent of sun-warmed roses. Her footing wobbled against sturdy ground after two days in a jostling coach.

She ran on shaking legs through the archway, into the courtyard.

And froze.

All the joy, all the excitement, drained from her body and pooled into lead at her feet.

Her lungs couldn't draw breath.

Her heart couldn't beat.

No.

Chapter Thirty-Six

The cobblestone beneath Brianna's feet clutched her to its uneven surface. She was trapped, forced to watch an army of unknown guards swarm the center of the courtyard like restless ants. Forced to watch her husband's proud posture bow beneath the awkward angle of the manacles locking his wrists behind him.

Her uncle's dark head bent over the task of securing the lock at Colin's back.

Her uncle?

Disbelief jarred her mind. Confusion. Her body was numb, her eyes seeing but not registering.

Colin caught her gaze and his jaw tightened. His head shook, a subtle motion, one she would not catch were she not staring so intently at him.

Her legs pumped into action, moving on their own, racing the couple dozen feet toward her husband. "Stop!"

Her uncle's head snapped up and his black eyes met hers with indifference. The sun slid behind a cloud and a chill settled across her skin.

His puffy hands twisted the key in the manacle. "Your husband is under arrest."

"Under whose authority?" she demanded.

"Mine." He stepped toward her. "He is being arrested for your father's murder."

The chill she'd felt earlier froze her heart and cooled her blood. Countless eyes stared at her, but she did not care. "That is impossible."

Colin looked at her from over his shoulder. "Brianna—"

Her uncle slammed his elbow in Colin's back and sent him staggering forward. "Quiet, prisoner."

Brianna's stomach swam. "Stop this at once." Her voice carried over the crowded courtyard and echoed off the high castle walls. "He isn't a murderer. You don't understand."

"Don't I?" Her uncle sneered. "Your father lay dead prior to your marriage to this barbarian. What else is one to assume but murder?"

She straightened her back and faced her uncle with determination. If only she could breathe.

"The earl died—"

"Brianna, stop." Colin turned to face them. One cheek was red and swollen.

Her heart wrenched against her ribs. Smears of dirt streaked his saffron shirt. Footprints.

They had beaten him.

"I can't let you do this." She shook her head. "You didn't kill him. I can't let you take the blame when I—"

"You have nothing to do with this," he growled.

She opened her mouth to protest, but he cut her off once more. "This is my castle, my land. *I* will see it safe." A soldier moved forward to restrain him, but Colin shook him off with a gruff twist of his shoulders. "He cannot see me hanged without proof, and there cannot be proof when I am innocent."

Brianna stepped closer to him and suppressed the urge to wrap her arms around his solid body. She turned aside, refusing to see his battered face, refusing to let the image of his arms bound behind his back bring tears to her eyes. She would have herself appear as brave as him.

"You don't understand the power of his influence," she whispered.

"And ye don't understand how hard I've worked to get this land."

Her gaze snapped toward Colin's hard stare. Her heartbeat pounded in her temples. "What?"

"I've worked too damn hard to get this land to see it stripped from me." His eyes narrowed down at her. "Ye werena as easy to win over as I thought ye'd be."

Her corset strained against her indrawn breath. "Easy to win over?"

He widened his stance and the manacles clinked together. "The rumors all indicated ye'd be hard to sway toward marriage, but I knew if I approached ye looking for work, ye wouldna turn me away." A cocky grin lifted his lips. A grin that did not reach his eyes. No emotion did.

She shook her head emphatically. "That's not true. You came across Bernard. You helped me."

"Bernard was a fortunate encounter. Had it not been for him, I may not have found employment with ye."

The blade of his words twisted in her belly.

Fortunate encounter? She did not know how to reply to such a heartless statement.

Though he had spoken in low tones, the eyes of the soldiers fixed on her, witnessing her shame. Witnessing the tears burning hot in her eyes. She would not cry. She would not cry.

A telltale warmth burned against her lids, but she blinked them back.

"You wooed me," she said quietly. Why must everyone stare at them? Why must every ear strain to hear what they said?

"No." His gaze was unyielding. "I seduced ye."

Her heart stung beneath the slice of his words. "You are saying these things to protect me." The excuse felt feeble sliding off her tongue.

He looked above her head, no longer meeting her gaze. "I am saying these things because they are true, a confession should we never meet again. I have never cared for you, Brianna. I never will."

She staggered back, hating the weakness of her wretched heart, of her trembling knees.

Yet he did not look her in the eyes. He did not mean what he said.

And then his eyes locked on hers, as hard and cold as chips of emerald. "You were coin and title. An impossible conquest no other man could claim."

Her uncle stepped between them and shoved Colin back. "That's enough."

The soldiers closed around Colin, but she could still see the glow of his rich russet hair and the hard lines of his face through the press of bodies. She waited for a subtle grin, a playful wink perhaps to let her know she was in on his scheme. The men turned him from her, his fierce expression never smoothing. His gaze never returning to her.

The pleading in her heart warred with her stubborn mind. She wanted to approach her uncle to beg for Colin's release. He was innocent, and she could see it proven with her own confession.

A hand gripped her arm. Not with the malice of an enemy, but the warning of a friend.

"Be still, my lady."

Jonathan.

She did not reply, nor did she turn to him. She could not.

Instead, she watched Colin roughly hauled away in a clatter of chains dragging against the cobblestones. Past the Edzell guards who stood by with red faces, past Magda who covered her mouth with both hands, past Thomas who kept his head bent in reverent prayer, past her uncle's men.

The courtyard cleared of her uncle and his guards, and time slowed to nothing. The clinking of saddles and clopping of horses sailed over the castle walls, yet still the remaining people within Edzell remained frozen in place. A door slammed.

A key grated against aging steel. Hollow jostling sounds accompanied the crunch of a wheel turning over gravel. Brianna listened, waiting for all sounds to disappear.

She blinked her eyes open and found herself the center of everyone's attention. Her back screamed with the force of her proud stance, a pathetic defense to the harsh words they had all witnessed.

"Bring me Alec," she ordered. She would have her doubts quelled and her questions answered.

The men looked at each other, their discomfort evident.

"Alec is no longer here," Jonathan spoke from behind her.

"I'm sorry my lady."

Brianna crumbled inside. Without Alec, there would be only doubt and assumption. Without Alec to prove otherwise, Colin's words held a note of truth.

* * *

Brianna slumped against the large chair in the solar. She was dry-eyed and would remain thus. Tears were not warranted for the things Colin said.

They were lies. All of them.

Lies.

He merely sought to protect her in his own stubborn way.

A little voice in her mind argued the coincidence of his 'lies' matching her own suspicions, but she drowned it beneath a sea of excuses. He sought to save her, to ensure she wouldn't follow him. His own safety in forfeit of hers.

"My lady?"

Brianna lifted her head to find Magda in the doorway.

"Forgive me," she said. "You have a visitor. He said you would want to see him."

Hope shone through her dark thoughts. Had Alec returned? Was perhaps little George come with good news?

Her heart pounded to life.

"Please send him in."

Magda stepped aside, and Brianna's visitor entered the room. His leather boots were soundless against the floor, his fine clothing rumpled, the fashionable sword flapping at his side. "Greetings, cousin."

Her stomach clenched around nothing.

Robert.

Chapter Thirty-Seven

The solar that had once felt so large to Brianna was now too small. Too few feet separated her from Robert, and the desk before her was a sorry shield.

A smile pulled his face into an arrogant smirk. "Brianna Lindsay." He spoke her name in a sing-song tone. Mocking. He meant to intimidate.

"It's MacKinnon," she said. "Brianna MacKinnon."

He approached, his gaze locked on her.

His fists wrapped around the arms of the chair, locking her against the hard wood. She did not struggle against her entrapment. It was what he would want.

He squatted in front of her. The relaxed position did nothing to quell the unease tightening in her stomach.

"You will not be Brianna MacKinnon for long."

Her heart snagged against her ribcage.

Before she could respond, he released her wrist and roughly tightened his fingers around a fistful of her hair. Had she not been holding her breath, she might have cried out.

"Your barbarian will soon hang." He leaned closer and his leather boots creaked. His lips moved next to her ear. "When you are a widow, I will see you well cared for."

Her lungs burned for air.

The heat of his slimy tongue trailed across her neck and the breath shuddered from her chest.

The odor of his greased hair met her nostrils and curdled her stomach. She tried to force her face from his, to turn her nose away.

Robert shrieked suddenly and his body jerked backward. A

thin hand clutched the top of his head, clawed fingers gripping his dark hair.

"You will respect my mistress," Magda cried. "Do you understand?" A tug on his hair punctuated her question.

Brianna wrenched open the bottom drawer and prayed the earl's old dagger would still be there. With her attention fixed on Robert, her fingers blindly patted the smooth wood.

He writhed against Magda's grasp in an attempt to free himself.

Cold metal met Brianna's fingertips. A blade. She wrapped her hand around the hilt and ran to her nurse's defense.

Robert cocked his fist. Before he could land a blow on Magda, Brianna pressed the dagger to his neck.

"I have no fear of using this," she warned. Her hand shook with the force of her emotions. The fear, the hurt, the anger, the vehemence.

Robert's fist dropped and he went still beneath the threat of the blade.

"Magda, please advise the servants downstairs of our visitor's arrival." By servants, she knew Magda would realize she meant guards. Or at least she hoped.

Hesitation crossed her nurse's withered face. "My lady—"

"Please do as I ask." Brianna nodded to Magda. "You may release him now."

The older woman's hand opened and Robert jerked upright, his back locked straight. His dark hair jutted in all directions like a peacock with a broken tail.

The tap of Magda's shoes against the floor clicked from the room and echoed down the hall, her pace brisk.

Brianna waited for the footsteps to fade. "I should kill you." She lifted the hilt of the dagger. A simple push of the blade and it would sink into his neck.

He stared down at the weapon through lowered lids. "You would hang beside that barbarian for murder?"

She'd rather hang than have Robert's hand upon her. "You know he did not kill my father."

"I don't care if he did or not. I only know he stole

my wealth."

The same greedy gaze now slid over her body in a way that left her bare, as if his eyes had stripped her of clothing. "I know he stole you."

"He rescued me," she said. "From *you*."

The heat of Robert's glare pummeled her and tense silence shot through the room. "You were 'rescued' by a landless vagabond."

"Landless?" The word slipped out before she could stop it.

His eyebrows shot up. "You didn't know?" The sour expression on his face gave way to laughter. "And to think Father always praised your intelligence."

"Colin is the firstborn son of Laird MacKinnon."

Robert ducked back from the blade and maintained an arm's-length distance from her. "You know those Highland barbarians don't follow the laws of God."

She left the dagger raised between them, but did not pursue him. What he said was true. In the Highlands, the current laird chose his successor. Birth order was considered for *tanaiste*, but was not ultimately the deciding factor.

A cruel grin spread over Robert's lips. "Your husband's own father did not deem him worthy to run the land of his birth, and yet you've given him free reign of Edzell."

Blood rushed loudly in Brianna's ears. "You're lying."

The staggered pounding of dozens of footsteps sounded from the hall.

He shrugged. "Believe what you want—what I'm saying is the truth."

Guards poured through the door two at a time until the room crowded with armed men.

Robert ignored them. "He used you. And for all your knowledge and learning, you fell for it like a common, over-flattered courtier."

Brianna's stomach dropped.

Jonathan stepped from the ring of soldiers and grabbed Robert by the shirt. "You will be escorted out now." Jonathan's hand went to the hilt of the sword that now hung between his shoulder blades, the same as Colin and Alec. "Or I can drag you."

Robert's hands raised, palm up, and Jonathan released his shirt.

Robert may have surrendered, but he'd hit his mark in Brianna's doubt, and the spark in his eye told her he knew it.

* * *

Blades of grass tickled Brianna's ankles. She'd walked the length of the garden twice over, yet her mind still churned. All the while Thomas followed at her side, quiet in his support. Her fingers skimmed the sculpted detail making up the final panel of the Cardinal Virtues imbedded in the high wall. *Justitia.* Justice.

The carving of a balanced scale was rough beneath her fingertips. Jagged.

Brianna drew in a deep breath and let it slowly blow out between her lips. Her frenzied heartbeat ebbed. For now.

She needed to separate her own emotions from the facts. "Colin is innocent of the charges which he stands accused," she said. "But I do not know how to see him released."

Thomas's eyes followed her fingers as she traced the skillfully etched lines in the stone. "Will any of the surrounding lairds come to your aid?"

"He's a Highlander." She looked up at him and found his brow puckered with worry. It was an expression all too common among her people since Colin had been taken. Already two days had passed, and all letters begging for assistance had been ignored.

Frustration pulled at her squared shoulders.

Alec was still missing, and no one could give her any information on his whereabouts.

Brianna stared up at the cloudless blue sky and became lost in its endlessness. "While the other lairds like Colin, they do not trust him. My uncle, however, has great power and influence among them. He would sway the hand of any who sought to help."

She looked back to the carved panel once more and let her

hand fall away. "The court may not have proof to declare him guilty, yet I have no proof to vouch for his innocence."

Thomas clasped his hands behind his back. "Is he to be tried with the local Parliament? I may know someone who can help."

She shook her head. "I still haven't found where he will be tried, nor even where he's being held."

The letters from the local Parliament indicated Colin had not been declared a criminal with them. If her uncle planned to take Colin to Edinburgh to have him tried at the courts there, Brianna would have almost no influence.

She would not receive a response from Edinburgh for several days. Was he already en route there for his trial?

"He didn't mean it," Thomas said softly.

The eyes of the world seemed to settle on her, even though only she and Thomas stood in the quiet garden. She crossed her arms over her chest in a pathetic attempt to still the painful squeeze of her heart. "What?"

"He didn't mean what he said. It was a tactic to keep you safe. To keep you from placing yourself in danger to save him." Sympathy lined his eyes.

"Do not give me your pity."

"It is not pity I offer you, my lady. Only the truth. He wishes your safety no matter the cost—"

"Stop this." The words hissed from her tight throat. She gripped her skirt in her fists. "You overstep your role, Thomas. Leave me." Her voice was thick. Weak. She sounded as fragile as she felt.

Colin had confirmed her earlier suspicions with his public confession. He had come to Edzell to seek her hand.

Even in his admission, he had not been completely honest. He held no family wealth. He held no promise of land. He held only a name, and she now bore its weight.

She had suspected him many times of using her for her title and lands, but he had reassured. Comforted.

Seduced.

Her face scrunched against the tear of pain.

Whether Thomas stayed or left, Brianna did not know. She

was beyond the point of caring. All that mattered was the aching void in her breast where her heart had once been.

There was no way to save him.

There was no way to save herself.

* * *

Colin's cage was narrow, surrounded by walls that excreted the stench of fear and death. Aged mortar crumbled between stones, taunting him with the promise of what lay beyond. Trickles of water ran between the cracks and stained the wall with black slime. The sun shone brightly outside. Ethereal proof poured gold from a crevice and cut through the darkness like a noble blade of hope.

A door slammed in the distance, its echo loud in the harsh quiet. Colin shifted to a crouch from where he sat on the cold floor. His back groaned in protest and stiffened against the simple motion.

Footsteps.

Not the heavy, determined footsteps of a guard. No, they were the slow, steady shuffles of a man of great girth.

Shuffle, shuffle. Tap.

A man of great girth who used a cane to support his weight.

Colin rose to his feet, thighs burning with his measured movement in an effort to keep the manacles from announcing his preparation. He would not have Lindsay knowing he rose to greet him.

Nor would he face the bastard sitting down.

Shuffle, shuffle. Tap.

Colin eased forward and stopped inches away from the grated bars, its steel long since rusted with neglect.

Shuffle, shuffle. Tap.

A haunting light blossomed at his left and grew brighter with jerky sways and dips. Colin's head lifted with the pride of a MacKinnon.

Shuffle, shuffle.

The light of a candle burst into view and sliced through

Colin's eyes. Five days of darkness rendered the weak flame as brilliant as the sun. He narrowed his gaze in an effort to shield his instinctive wince.

Lindsay's stomach appeared before the rest of him. He lowered his cane.

Tap.

"You stand proud within your cage, barbarian."

Colin held his shoulders pulled back, his head lifted. "I stand proud with an innocence ye are well aware of."

"Innocence is subjective." Lindsay's gaze gleamed beneath the wavering shadows of candlelight.

Colin's eyes now welcomed the light and the ability to study his surroundings. He glanced over Lindsay's shoulder toward the vacated cell across from his, taking in the empty food trencher, the overturned cup. The filthy rushes spattered with dark stains.

Blood.

Colin exhaled through his nose, as if the act could expunge his nostrils of the odor clinging to the damp air.

"When will my trial take place?" He cast a look at his own trencher. The sour aftertaste of pasty gruel still lingered in the back of his throat. "Or will you see me starved to death before then?"

Lindsay leaned on his cane and a high-pitched whistle eased from his overworked chest. "I offer you something more important than a trial. I offer you a choice."

Chapter Thirty-Eight

The wet heat of an impending storm clung to Brianna's skin and muddled the reassuring scents of the garden. Her damp clothing stuck to her legs, her arms, her chest—slowly suffocating. A fire kindled inside her, fueled by thick air that refused to fill her lungs. The slow, whining buzz of an insect in the grass penetrated her skull and frayed her nerves.

Her garden no longer offered comfort.

She wanted to tear her clothes off to be free of their clutching weight. She wanted to stomp the grass until the insect fell silent beneath the crush of her heel. She wanted the whole world to stop so she could just think.

A rock caught her gaze, egg-shaped and white, nestled against the rose bed. *Where it did not belong.*

She swooped upon the hapless stone like a hawk. Etchings marred its smooth surface, carved to form perfectly shaped letters.

Brianna MacKinnon.

The proud K declared the writing as Colin's.

She turned the stone over and it clinked against her ring's gold band.

Colin MacKinnon.

The fire roaring inside her cooled with the significance cupped in her palm. Her fingers traced the carefully hewn lines. Deep grooves scored with a thin object, most likely the blade of a dagger. She pulled in a deep breath of sticky air.

He'd carved a marriage stone. A raindrop plopped against the top of her head and left a wet dot of hair pressed to her scalp.

Marriage stones were a Highland symbol of union that bespoke adoration for the intended bride and the love uniting them together. Thunder cracked overhead and another drop pelted her.

Perhaps Colin had cared for her. Her hands wrapped around the stone, and her heart staggered down the path of possibility once more.

One stone with two names opposite each other.

Wind whipped around her in a chaotic cyclone and left her staggering against the pull of its wrath. The pattering of wet footsteps sounded behind her.

"My lady, please come inside." Magda's words were weak against the storm's assault. "You'll catch your death."

Guilt propelled Brianna toward the castle more so than Magda's insistent tug. Her aging nurse shouldn't have to risk her own health to come into the downpour for Brianna's sake.

Together they ran through the rear door of the castle, into its dark shelter. The scuff of their feet across the floor echoed down empty halls. Though the shutters were thrown open, the storm allowed little light to grace the heart of the castle.

Where there was once warmth, there was now cold silence. Where there was once security and love, there was now blackness and uncertainty.

For six long days.

Nothing was the same without Colin's presence. Her hand hugged the stone.

She was lost between her head and her heart and didn't know which she needed to believe.

· · ·

The manacles of Colin's ankles were a weighty reminder of his captivity. He managed to make his way to Lindsay's solar with a wide-legged gait that stretched the binds of his confinement. The room was small, its shutters locked tight. A lived-in odor of halitosis and sweat permeated the dark furnishings.

Stacks of books lined the floor and crushed into the room. Colin narrowed his throat in an attempt to filter the offending air. Futile efforts against so vile an atmosphere.

Lindsay scuttled around his desk, his breathing labored. A rattle began in his chest then rasped from his throat into a foul hacking cough.

A grin lit Lindsay's paling lips. "You were…quite interesting…the way you walk…in chains."

His tortured breathing made Colin's chest burn for air. "Is that why ye escorted me with the guards then?"

Lindsay lifted a shoulder and dragged in another whining breath. "I had to…see the sight…for myself."

Colin kept his face impassive. "I see yer efforts paid off."

The grin fell from Lindsay's face. "You've got a smart tongue on you."

"I'll take that as a compliment." Colin grinned. He was goading a beast and enjoying every damn minute of it.

"It was not meant as such." Lindsay's palms pressed to the surface of the desk and he rolled to his feet. "I will see you punished. But first—"

He nodded once and an arm caught Colin around the throat. Blood pumped through him, hot and insistent, demanding he fight. But he was bound with steel and outnumbered by armed men. The odds were not in his favor.

Another hand grasped his wrist and roughly yanked on the signet ring. It slid loose, and his finger immediately mourned the loss of its weight. He stiffened and the hold around his neck tightened.

Lindsay's head tipped back in a show of satisfaction. He held his hand out, palm up, and received the gold seal for what it was—the greatest treasure Colin possessed. "Prisoners need no finery such as this."

Lindsay slid it over his fingertip and frowned. The ring could not slide past his fat knuckle.

Colin did not realize his body strained forward until the pressure around his throat increased.

Lindsay opened a long silver box at the edge of his desk and threw the gold seal inside before slamming the lid shut.

He did not lock it.

"A jeweler can fix that easily enough. Know that when you

hang, I will be wearing proof that I own Edzell."

The tension around Colin's neck eased and something smacked between his shoulder blades. He staggered forward and narrowly missed tripping over the length of chain between his feet.

Lindsay intended to make him appear weak, to strip away everything Colin possessed. To see him humiliated.

Colin's cheeks burned with Lindsay's success, but he'd be damned if he'd let the bastard see as much. "Ye're a coward if ye hang me without a trial."

Lindsay's face darkened from red to purple. "You are lucky it is you I have in chains and not your wife."

The manacles bit into Colin's wrists beneath his straining muscles. "Leave her out of this."

"Oh, but I can't leave her out. Not when she is the reason you are here." Lindsay pulled a ledger from a haphazard pile at his left and thumbed through the dingy pages. "Ah, yes."

The spine of the book gave a dry crack, and a folded parchment slid onto the desk. He unfolded it with the tips of his thumb and forefinger.

"I have here a confession from your wife's own nurse declaring my brother was dead long before your arrival to Edzell." Lindsay waved the letter in the air. "Do you care to read it yourself?"

Colin's stomach tightened.

He reached for the implicating evidence, the slight movement causing his chains to clink against one another. One of Lindsay's guards stepped forward and passed the parchment to Colin's outstretched fingers.

If he didn't cooperate, nothing would stand between Lindsay and Brianna. Colin turned his hard glare to the parchment and skimmed its contents.

The slanting letters wavered across the page, penned in a hand that trembled. The confession admitted to finding Laird Lindsay's room empty before Colin's arrival, to Brianna running the estate despite the laird's absence, and to her illegitimacy. It was signed with the same scrolling lettering.

Magda Swinton.

Colin's chest ached for the old woman and the pain it would cause her to know what her confused words conveyed.

No mention was made of suspected murder, but then none was needed. Too many assumptions would be made with the facts listed, and none pointed to innocence.

The guard snatched the parchment from him and passed it back to Lindsay.

"What do you intend to do with that?" Colin asked, his gaze never leaving the incriminating letter.

Lindsay folded the confession and tucked it into the breast of his heavy brocade jacket.

"I intend to give you a choice, barbarian. I thought I'd made that clear before."

Colin tore his stare from Lindsay's jacket. "What choice?"

Lindsay's fingertips steepled atop the desk and a smug grin sunk into his face once more. "You can either go quietly to your hanging and accept your fate as a murderer." He patted his hand over his chest where the letter had been concealed. "Or I send this evidence to Parliament, and Brianna will carry the guilt. No one will stand for you after that display of Catholic tradition at your wedding. Your gifting of a ring had the nobles in an uproar for over a week. But I digress."

Lindsay leaned forward and sucked in a whistling breath. "Would you see your wife accused of treason, or will you hang?"

Chapter Thirty-Nine

Brianna faced away from the bed she had shared with Colin and tried to ignore the way his scent clung to the curtains, the coverlet, the tapestries—everything.

"My lady, you must set this down." Magda's warm fingers wrapped around Brianna's hand, the one gripping the marriage stone. "Your sleeve will not go over your arm if you continue to hold it."

Brianna hesitated. The stone was solid, real. Proof that Colin held feelings for her. Proof that perhaps he had not used her.

A shiver slipped across her damp skin.

Magda tsked softly. "I don't know how you always manage to get yourself into such messes."

The stone dropped from Brianna's hand. "What?"

Magda nudged the sodden pile of Brianna's ruined gown with the toe of her shoe. "The fountain again?"

The old nurse's memory faltered with more frequency in Colin's absence.

"We were both in the rain," Brianna said. "You came to get me because I had foolishly stayed outside."

Magda waved her hand, and a crinkle of confusion showed at the corners of her rheumy eyes. "Oh pish. If that were the case, I would be soaked as well."

Brianna caught her lower lip between her teeth to keep the crush of helpless pain at bay. She'd insisted Magda change first, a decision she did not regret. The older woman was too frail to remain in such heavy, wet clothes for long.

Magda eased a dry satin sleeve over Brianna's hand and slid

it up her arm. "If your father finds out you've been floating rose petals in that fountain again." Her jaw tightened. "Well, never mind that. We'll make sure he never knows."

Magda paused to retrieve the stone from the floor. She studied it a moment, and a soft smile touched her mouth. "Where is your husband?" She traced the etchings with the same gentle care Brianna had. "You've been sad without him, and I know he must miss you."

"You mean Colin?" Brianna asked with surprise. "You remember him?"

Magda looked up. "Of course. How could I ever forget a man who looks at you in such way?"

"In such a way?" Hope chose her reckless words even as caution guarded her wounded heart. "How does he look at me?"

The unfastened dress sagged around Brianna's shoulders. "With all the love I've ever seen in a man's eyes, sweet child." She caressed Brianna's cheek. "With all the love you deserve."

Brianna could not speak, could not draw breath. She stood weighted to the floor by her own guilt and shame. Robert had twisted her with manipulation. And she had fallen prey.

She wrapped her arms around her slender nurse. "Thank you, Magda." Something crinkled in the older woman's bodice.

Brianna released her and both women looked down. Magda's fingers plunged into her gown and withdrew a crumpled parchment. Bewilderment lined her face. The bold seal of Edinburgh's Parliament imprinted the yellowed wax seal on the front.

"Where did you get that?" Brianna plucked the letter from the woman's limp grasp.

Magda shook her head. "I don't recall."

Brianna snapped the thick wax seal and ripped the letter open. The breath choked from her lungs. She read the missive once more. Edinburgh's Parliament had responded the same as the local authorities.

No criminal by the name of Colin MacKinnon stood accused. If he was not registered as a criminal, then where had her uncle taken him?

* * *

The light filtering through the crack in the wall had faded to dusky gold. Darkness squeezed Colin in a grip that would only tighten as night descended. His chest pressed against the slick wall, a squinted eye searching through the window of freedom, frantic to glimpse his last sunset.

To no avail.

Colin looked down at the hem of his once fine shirt, to where a pinprick of dried blood stained the golden yellow fabric. He did not need light to know there were two more against his back.

Brianna's blood. The efforts of her labor.

He had endured many injuries in his lifetime. Weapons and war had left marks peppering his body, yet none of them compared to the pain in his chest when he summoned the image of Brianna's face.

He longed to caress her silken hair, to tease her lips with his own, to see the trust burn bright in her eyes. But she would never gaze at him with trust again. He would never hold her again.

The spear of light now lost its golden tinge, and dusk began its quick descent upon his cell.

His goals had not yet come to fruition, and now they wilted beneath the drought of time.

Edzell was well-maintained and its people safe. He had sacrificed much to see it so, yet his father would never bear witness to his efforts. His father would never regard him with respect.

The land would pass to Brianna upon his death.

Colin's fists clenched with the knowledge of how Lindsay intended to use Magda's confession to persuade Brianna to marry his son.

Brianna.

She would never know how he felt about her. There would be no opportunity to apologize, to tell her he loved her.

The gray light of dusk yielded to the menacing pull of darkness, and his shoulders sagged beneath the shroud of black.

Tomorrow he would die.

* * *

Brianna ran through the courtyard. Steam from the drying cobblestones hissed against her skirts and clung to her hair. She paid little heed to any of it as she searched the faces of each roaming guard.

A shock of light blond hair caught her attention. Jonathan.

"Lady MacKinnon. What's happened?"

"Come," she gasped. "Please."

She led him into a guard room to the right of Edzell's entrance.

He stopped just inside and released her. "If possible, I would prefer to leave the door open lest rumors rise." His low voice echoed off the domed ceiling and stone walls.

Rumors?

She glanced around the dimly lit room. It lent a privacy lovers would seek.

Rumors didn't matter now, though his consideration was appreciated. She thrust the letter from Parliament toward Jonathan.

He snagged the missive in his hand. "What—"

"My uncle has not given Colin to the law."

His brows knit together. "If he's not awaiting trial, then where is he?"

"I can only assume he is within my uncle's manor."

The look on Jonathan's face, the flicker of horror and dread, indicated the other option she had not allowed herself to consider.

"We must go to him." Her words rang sharp with the force of her determination.

"We?" He shook his head. "I'll gather the men to take the manor. And you will wait here."

Brianna crossed her arms over her chest in the steadfast way she had seen Colin do so many times before. "No."

"The laird would not have you—"

"The laird would not have *you* sacrifice his guards for a mission that would end in naught but death. If you and I go alone, we can go under the cloak of deception. We can move quietly. We can escape without the sacrifice of lives."

His gaze turned appraising. "You sound as though you have a plan."

Perhaps he would consider her scheme after all. The weight in her heart eased. "Indeed I do."

If her uncle would go against the law to seize her husband, she would go against the law to see him saved.

Chapter Forty

Brianna pressed her back against the rough tree trunk and stared through the moonlit forest to where Jonathan stood. Her heart drummed so loudly, she suspected the guards surrounding her uncle's manor would hear.

She peered around the tree once more and squinted into the darkness. The guard stationed at the rear of the manor had not moved.

And his face did not appear familiar.

She swept off her cloak, revealing a bodice pulled too low and laced too tight. Jonathan's averted gaze confirmed her attire was anything but appropriate.

The attire worn by women who visited this manor at such an hour.

Marie's lessons would be well used tonight.

Brianna stepped onto the path toward the manor, into the glowing white light of the full moon. She masked her unraveling nerves with a loose-hipped saunter, the kind that offered the promise of greater things to come.

The guard's stare burned into her exposed flesh. He would be far too distracted to notice Jonathan creeping through the trees to his right.

She stopped before the man, but his eyes did not leave her breasts. "Which one are you here to see?" he asked.

Brianna took a deep breath, so her bosom swelled against the tight bodice. "Both."

The man stiffened and tore his gaze from her chest.

She held her breath in an attempt to keep her reaction from showing.

His suspicion melted into a wide grin, exposing a chipped front tooth. "Both, eh? You're an eager one." His stare rested on her breasts once more. "Think there might be some left for me when they've finished with you?"

"Perhaps if you are still awake when I leave." She forced the words from her mouth.

The guard cocked his head. "There's something about you I like." He looked up at her face. "Something familiar."

Jonathan crept up behind the guard, his feet silent.

Brianna shook her head, hoping Jonathan would realize the action was meant to stay his attack. "I don't believe we've met." She took a bold step closer to the guard and trailed a finger down his shirt. It was moist with sweat. "I know I'd remember if we had."

Jonathan paused.

The man's eyebrows rose with amusement. "I imagine you would."

Jonathan slipped back into the blanket of shadows.

The guard leaned toward her. "I do this suck and twirl thing with my tongue—you'd not forget."

Brianna swallowed a horrified gasp. "Perhaps you can show me later."

"Indeed I will." He pulled the door open and held it, his back facing the castle.

Her heart shrank from what she was about to do. Grotesque though it was, the act would save the guard's life and keep their presence unknown. Extra minutes could not be wasted on discovery. They were too valuable.

She leaned against him and pressed her lips to his. A gentle, teasing kiss that would have left Colin smiling against her mouth. One just long enough for Jonathan to slip into the manor behind the man.

"I'll see you at dawn," she said in a voice that passed for sultry.

"I look forward to it." His chest puffed out.

Brianna strolled around him. A muffled thwack popped across her bottom. Her eyes went wide with the realization that he'd just spanked her rump.

Moonlight filtered through the dirty lead-encased windows and cast twisted reflections down the hall. The scent of old wood and smoke pulled at memories buried deep, memories of her cousin's cruel pranks and heated arguments between her father and uncle.

Jonathan appeared at her side. His head craned toward her, his voice barely a whisper. "Did he just swat your—er—" he glanced back at her offended bottom.

Brianna held up a hand to still his tongue. "Don't."

"The laird would have preferred I kill the man."

"Your laird wouldn't have had to sneak in."

She eased forward on the balls of her feet. Distorted shadows clawed her deeper into their concealing embrace with each step.

First they would check the dungeon. Heaven help Colin if he were in there.

Together, she and Jonathan made fast, efficient work of threading through the complex weave of halls. Thus far without encounter.

Brianna layered her back against the stone wall and glanced around the corner toward the dungeon door. A man with cropped black hair leaned against a deep-set doorframe, his face relaxed.

She glanced at Jonathan and held up her forefinger, indicating she saw only one guard. The hard line of his lips reflected his regret of their previous agreement that she be allowed to address single guards without his aid. She saw it as a way to save lives. No doubt he saw it as a risk.

However, her success with the previous guard fueled her confidence and lent her courage. She gathered her skirts in her hands, exposing the tops of her ankles, and strode into the hallway lit with the warm glow of several rush nips.

The man eyed her from his station in front of the dungeon door, and a flicker of apprehension rippled through her.

She recognized this man. He had been with her uncle for some time now.

Of course, she did not appear as herself. Perhaps he would not know her.

"I'm lost," she said with a little pout.

He turned his body toward her. His shoulders were broad, his chest powerful. Truly every part of the man appeared enormous.

"Lost?" His face remained blank.

No recognition lit his eyes, and a wave of relief swept across her jagged nerves.

She brushed her fingers over the tops of her breasts, but his gaze did not follow. "I came in from the back door as instructed and got lost."

He nodded.

And said nothing.

Silence pressed upon her and made her hands clammy with unease.

"Perhaps you might point me in the right direction?" she prompted.

His arms folded over his chest. Massive arms. Arms that could rival tree trunks.

Arms that could rival Colin's.

She clasped her hands behind her back so her breasts thrust forward. His steady gaze still did not leave her eyes.

"Am I at least going the right way?" she asked.

"Girls don't come in through the rear entrance."

Her stomach flipped with a nervous lurch.

"As lost as I am, I can see why." She forced a lightness to her tone.

He stepped forward, towering over her. His gaze dipped to her bodice and his tongue ran across his lower lip. "They haven't had you yet?"

A trickle of ice raced down her spine and made the hair on her arms rise. "I'm lost, as I said."

His hand covered her breast and squeezed hard enough to elicit a needle of pain. "I charge a fee for directions." He shoved her backward, and her head smacked into the wall behind her. A squeak of surprise escaped her mouth, enough of a sound for Jonathan to hear.

Her balance swayed, and an insistent warning blared in her aching head. She was no longer in control.

The man covered her body with his, his excited breath stale where it rushed against her skin.

Where was Jonathan?

A whimper choked from her throat, an uncontrolled cry of weakness. She chanced a look down the hall to where he should be. No movement, no Jonathan. Nothing.

Her heart shriveled in her chest.

Had Jonathan been captured? If he had been, there would be no one to save her from this man.

"I don't think Lord Lindsay would like you—"

The man covered her mouth with his hand and jerked her head to the side.

Her vision swam with tears. Marie's lessons never covered such aggression.

Dread swirled thick in her stomach.

She was at the giant's mercy. And he had none.

She could cry out, but only her uncle's men would hear her.

The guard's breath was hot against her ear. "Perhaps we should make your husband watch." He grasped her arm painfully and shoved her toward the door.

Brianna fumbled in her skirts, seeking the dagger she should have had at the ready. Her trembling fingers sifted through yards of fabric with no end. Where was the slit of her pocket?

The man wrenched the door open and jerked her toward the darkened room. The silk-encased dagger bounced against her thigh, a tease of security she could not reach.

He pulled her deeper into the room where the soft light outside did not touch, her slippers skittering across pebbles and grit.

The door slammed behind them and plunged them into black. The man tensed at her side.

Someone else had seen it shut.

His breathing remained deep and even. He was not frightened.

The grip on her elbow loosened and released her into

tentative freedom. She stepped back while facing him. Her feet went nowhere certain, floating through a world she could not see.

Something hard pressed into her back and ceased her measured escape. Her hands danced behind her with slow, cautious pats. Steel bars met her curious exploration, hard and flaking with filth. And yet she gripped them as though they might somehow save her.

Silence descended, and the air crackled with the tension of impending death.

Ragged breathing filled the quiet. Hers.

She pressed a hand to her mouth to still the harsh sound. Her fingers stunk of soiled metal.

Footsteps shuffled across the ground and a rock screeched upon the hard floor. The soft thump of two bodies colliding. Grunts.

She should escape to search for Colin, she should locate her dagger. Yet coward that she was, all she could do was stand idly and tremble.

An unnatural tearing sound interrupted the scuffling fight. A choked gasp. Something dripped to the hard floor.

A copper odor seeped into the air and triggered a primitive reaction. Her body burned with the need to fight, an urge so powerful, it drowned her panic.

Her fingers moved of their own volition, past the paralyzing fear, and tore at her flimsy skirts. The offending pocket ripped in her desperation and freed the length of steel that would come between her and rape. Between her and death.

Footsteps sounded in the dark, moving in her direction.

Something gurgled. Wet with the defeat of death.

Her fingers tightened on the dagger. She would not die without a fight.

Chapter Forty-One

Brianna's eyes strained into the pressing black. The stench of blood was thick in the air, the metallic taste of it tinged every breath.

"My lady."

She leapt at the sound of the voice before recognizing its owner. Jonathan.

Her body sagged beneath her relief. She tried to say his name, but all that emerged was a shuddering exhale.

He squeezed her shoulders. "That was the last time I allow you to go forward without me. You are to drop your ruse at once, do you understand?" His grip softened. "My lady."

She knew he could not see her nod, yet her throat would not work to speak her agreement.

"And if you ever find yourself alone with a guard," he continued. "Please ensure his back is facing me so I don't have to travel to the other side of the hall to sneak up on him."

Her cheeks heated with shame. She had placed them both in danger with her lack of knowledge. For all the books she had read on war, nothing had truly prepared her for what she faced.

"There's another door through here," Jonathan said. "I saw it before I locked us in. I believe the dungeon lies on the other side."

Colin.

"It does." Her dry voice cracked.

"Are you all right?" Jonathan asked.

"Yes. Please—Colin."

His hand grasped hers, and together they stumbled through the penetrating darkness.

She felt his body jerk backward, and the groan of a heavy door tore into the silence. A decayed odor swept cold against her cheeks. They eased down unseen stairs and pressed deeper into the pit of fear.

Pray God they would find Colin.

Alive.

* * *

"Colin."

He stirred. A voice called him from the embrace of slumber. Reality skimmed the border of his conscious mind, stark and ugly. He did not want to be there.

His arms curled tighter around his torso in an attempt to cradle fleeting warmth.

"Colin."

Again the voice beckoned, dragging him toward something he did not want to face.

"Colin."

The voice caressed his ears, closer now. A delicate fragrance wafted above the stench of shit and decay. Lavender.

His eyes flew open. "Brianna?"

Only darkness met his desperate search. He would have thought himself dreaming were it not for the sweet warmth he sensed beside him. He sucked in a greedy lungful of her familiar scent.

"Colin." The tremble of her tone pulled at his aching heart.

Her arms came around him, and everything silky and soft he remembered collapsed against him. He buried his nose in her hair and breathed deeply. "My God, ye smell so good."

"I should have come sooner." Her voice muffled against his neck. "I didn't realize my uncle would—" She tightened her embrace. "Forgive me."

"Ye have nothing to apologize for, my love." He tugged her into his lap, grateful his manacles had been removed earlier, and held tight the curves of her body as he'd hungered to do, as even his most vivid dreams could not recreate. "I'm the one who must beg forgiveness, for hurting ye, for lying to ye for so long. Everything I said about my arrival to Edzell—it was all true." The confession caught in his throat.

He felt her pull back, but he tightened his hold, the way a drowning man might cling to a sturdy vessel.

"I know," she said. "You were denied your inheritance and you have no land. You sought me to gain all that your father would not grant you."

Her words slipped through his gut like a dagger.

"It was a purpose schemed before I met ye," he said. "Before I knew ye."

"Colin—"

"Ye came to say goodbye. Thank ye. I canna imagine having never had a chance to explain." He swallowed against his thickening words. "I dinna want to die without telling ye the truth, without telling ye it's no—"

"Colin, we are here to rescue you."

His mind scrambled to comprehend the most beautiful declaration ever spoken. "What?"

"We must leave now. Please, come. We can speak when we are home."

Home.

He pressed his head to her chest and felt the pounding of her heart beneath the bosom of her low cut bodice. Of her extremely low cut bodice. The satiny sleeves of her dress curled around his head, drawing him closer.

He nuzzled the pillowy warmth of her bosom. "Mmmm…I like yer dress verra much."

"You cannot see my dress, husband." Her tone held a smile he could picture in his mind.

"I dinna have to see it to appreciate it." His chest filled with one final breath of her sweet perfume before he allowed her to pull him to his feet.

His legs tingled with disuse and his muscles fired with the need to run. He wanted Brianna as far from this hell as possible.

* * *

Brianna's hand was tucked in the safety of Colin's fingers, and Jonathan moved silently at her side. The darkness had lost its edge.

Colin navigated them down an unseen path with his usual confidence, his footsteps never faltering.

His thumb brushed the inside of her wrist, as if confirming she was indeed there. The same way she'd continued to tighten her grip on his hand. A delicate shiver trickled down her spine.

The stench of spilled blood swam thick in the air. They were near the guard Jonathan had killed. Brianna squeezed her eyes shut and tried to focus on the positive.

The man's body meant they were near the door leading them from the dungeon.

She opened her eyes at the gentle creak of a door opening. Light spilled into the room, yet Brianna kept her stare fixed straight ahead. She did not want to witness the unseen nightmares in the darkness behind her.

The three of them eased into the empty hall. Silence.

Brianna glanced up at Colin. Purple showed beneath his eyes and dirt streaked his skin. He had lost weight in the five days he'd been in captivity.

Aside from the yellowed bruise healing on his cheek, he was unharmed.

His gaze darted down the hall, opposite the way she and Jonathan had come.

"We must go," Brianna said.

Colin's jaw clenched. "No yet."

She glanced to the other end of the hall where Jonathan scouted for guards. He nodded, signaling they were clear to escape.

She turned back to Colin. "Please, we must go."

He looked down at her, and his gaze lingered over her face. "Ye're so verra bonny." The dimple in his cheek showed at the lazy lift of his lips. "Ye go on ahead. I'll be just a moment." He winked down at her and turned away.

Her mouth fell open, but before she could protest, he released her hand and slid down the hallway, turning right instead of left. The warm imprint where his fingers clasped her palm cooled too quickly.

She could not let him go, not now. Not so soon after having finally been reunited.

She waved toward Jonathan, signaling her intent before turning down the hall and following Colin's careful steps. Her fingertips pressed to her mouth as if the motion could keep her movements all the more silent.

Jonathan followed at the same comfortable pace they'd kept when navigating the halls earlier.

The manor had been too quiet for far too long. An unsettling flutter churned in the pit of her stomach.

Colin slipped around the corner and disappeared from view.

Still no sound, save the deafening pumping of her heart.

They should be in the forest by now, on their way back to Edzell. Not creeping deeper into the bowels of danger.

She hugged the stone corner of the wall and tried to keep up with Colin.

Her uncle hired too many mercenaries. Surely they walked throughout the entire manor repeatedly. A chill raised the hair on her arms. Surely they had to notice the dungeon's missing guard.

Colin moved ahead of her still, making his way toward a door with the same simple wood and metal-banded style as all the others. Yet this one was different. This one was barred from her as a child. It held a note of mystery bathed in dark secrets. And apparently it held interest for her husband as well.

Colin gripped the handle and cracked open the door to her uncle's solar.

Chapter Forty-Two

Colin's muscles burned hot with the strain of his slow, quiet movements. The banded metal door stood between him and the signet ring, between him and everything he had fought for.

The door swung open without a sound.

Unlocked as it had been before.

A low fire pulsed in the hearth, adding heat to a room where none was needed. Red embers tinged the subtle light and sparkled against the silver box. Colin's pulse thrummed with his triumph.

The matted carpet beneath his feet masked his quickened steps. He covered the domed top of the box with his hand and pulled back the lid.

The gold signet ring glittered victoriously against the stained velvet lining. He slipped its weight from the box and onto his finger. Where it belonged. Unlike everything hot and sweltering in the room, the metal band was cool, comforting.

"Colin, someone comes." Brianna's low whisper slashed through his thoughts.

He spun around to find both her and Jonathan in the room. How the hell had he not heard them following him? And why the hell did they not leave as he instructed?

Colin blocked Brianna's body with his own and reached for the hilt of his sword. His fingers met the naked fabric of his leine. The scabbard he always wore draped across his back was still at Edzell, left upon his arrest.

He had no weapon.

The steps drew closer. His pulse raced and spun in his skull. His vision blurred. He'd gone too long without a proper meal.

The sounds were just outside the door. His body tensed

and his stance widened in preparation for hand-to-hand combat. The flat of a blade pressed into his palm. Brianna's warm body against his back broke through the haze of his light-headedness.

Her hand closed over his, forcing him to curl his fingers around the hilt. Forcing him to accept her means of protection.

The door slammed open and reverberated against the stone wall.

Three of Lindsay's hired guards barreled into the room, blades raised for attack. Jonathan's sword hissed from its scabbard. He lunged in front of the first man and blocked his path toward Colin and Brianna. His opponent whipped his blade with a careless swipe, which Jonathan evaded with a low dip before popping up to deliver his own attack.

The other two guards charged at Colin. Their movements matched one another in perfect unison. Together their swords lifted, and together they fell.

Colin knocked the first blade aside with Brianna's slender dagger. The second man's strike nicked his shoulder. A flesh wound that would bleed little.

Colin's fist slammed into the elbow of the second man and sent the guard's sword clattering to the floor.

The first man drove forward, the cut of his blade aggressive. Colin jerked to the right and buried Brianna's dagger into the man's neck.

Pain exploded in the back of Colin's head, and the room swam in a dizzying rush of pulsing embers and glinting metal.

He turned toward the guard, ready to attack. The floor wavered beneath him, and a heavy sweat broke out on his brow. He swallowed a mouthful of saliva, but the unsteadiness did not pass. Muscles that had once fired with energy now slackened with exhaustion.

Damn it, he was weaker than he realized. A wild look shone in his opponent's eyes.

Bile scalded the back of Colin's throat with the threat of vomit.

For the first time since he was a lad, he did not know if he could win a fight.

* * *

Brianna's fists pressed against her mouth in her effort to keep from screaming. The guard Colin had stabbed lay face down on the foul carpet. A puddle of blood swelled beneath his torso and crept toward her. No bubbles rippled the surface of the smooth, crimson puddle.

Oh God.

He was dead.

The open hearth spit hot breath against the back of her legs, preventing her from taking another step away. There was nowhere to go.

A panting breath heaved in the room. Not from the body. Of course, not from the body.

Her mind fogged with horror.

Something clattered to the floor. Not a sword. Smaller.

A dagger.

Colin.

She tore her gaze from the body and watched Colin tip toward the floor in a slow, steady lean.

Her stomach plummeted. The man he fought lifted a thick club over his head.

Brianna's pulse raced to life. Her eyes scanned the crowded room for anything that she could use to help her husband. A long pole rested beside the fireplace, like a spear absent its blade.

Consequences did not matter. There was no panic, only action. She grabbed the pole and raced toward the guard, her weapon lowered before her like a lance.

Aim toward the center of the chest.

She adjusted the tip's path.

Jab with arms only.

She shifted her hold.

Keep the torso flat.

Her shoulders squared.

The dull end of the pole caught the guard in the chest and thrust him back against the wall. His head snapped with an unnerving crack and he melted to the floor. The rise and fall of his hunched back indicated he still lived, yet he did not rise.

She spun around to where Colin knelt beside the desk, his eyes squinted with confusion. Jonathan stood unharmed beside him, mouth hanging open.

Only then did she realize what she'd actually done.

A rush of pride swelled her chest. "I told you I read Di Grassi."

Truth be told, she'd fantasized about applying the methods of defense after reading his book, but she never thought to actually put them to use.

She pursed her lips to suppress a cocky smile.

Colin pitched forward, and all vestiges of humor fled. Blood soaked the back of his leine and turned his golden auburn hair a deep red.

The pole slipped from her fingers and fell to the floor with a wooden clatter.

There was so much blood.

Before she could run to him, he staggered to his knees and planted his hand on the corner of the desk.

Jonathan grabbed Colin under the arm and helped pull him to his feet. "Laird, are you well?"

Colin grunted in an ornery, Alec-like way. "Fine." The word dragged from his mouth, slow and slurred.

As if to prove his point, Colin straightened upright and held his hands out, palms up in demonstration. He took a step forward, his footing sure. Relief eased the tension from Brianna's shoulders.

But then he stopped. His body wavered like a drunkard, and he crashed to the floor once more.

This time, he did not rise.

Chapter Forty-Three

Brianna shifted the position of Colin's arm across her back, but the action did little to ease the steady burn between her shoulder blades. If Jonathan weren't assisting, she would not have been able to move.

Colin's feet staggered with slow, halting steps. The effort did little to ease his burden. "Where are we?" He winced and his head sagged forward.

She made a quiet shushing sound in an effort to keep his slurring protests from ringing out again. Blood glistened against his hair and dotted the floor, trailing their path. They did not need him drawing further attention to their escape.

The door to the exit stood in sight.

Together, she and Jonathan eased Colin's weight from their shoulders and propped him against a wall. Jonathan's dagger slid free from his boot with a menacing gleam, and he nodded sharply at Brianna before opening the door.

She crouched in front of Colin, her own dagger locked against her palm.

She would kill for her husband.

Her ears strained in the silence to hear over her own racing heart. There was no sound of struggle outside, no grunt of battle or gurgle of death.

Jonathan appeared through the door, his jaw tight. "We need to go. Now."

"What happened?"

"No one was there."

The hair along the back of her neck prickled. "What?"

Jonathan hefted Colin's weight across his back, shouldering the burden on his own. "They know."

Something soft and warm moved beneath Colin. His body swayed, rocked. Started to fall.

His hands tightened around the thick threads tangling his fingers. He squinted his eyes open and found the moon shining down on him with all the brilliance of the sun. So bright it sent daggers through his skull.

Something furry pressed against his cheek. A musty scent hit his nose. Horse?

His left leg dangled into nothing, and his torso tilted sideways.

"Jonathan, he's slipping from his horse." A woman's hushed voice rose with concern.

No, not just a woman's. Colin's lips quirked up in a whisper of a smile. Brianna's.

The world dipped and rose around him, and his teeth clacked in time with each wild sway. His weight shifted off something.

Where was he?

A low curse sounded from somewhere. "I knew we shouldn't have let him ride on his own."

That wasn't Brianna. Where was she?

Nausea churned in his stomach and left cold sweat prickling his brow.

Where the hell was he?

He wanted to see Brianna. Feel her. Smell her. Lay his head in her lap and sleep.

Sleep would be nice. His eyes closed against the overly bright moon.

Everything stopped moving. Lavender surrounded him. He was warm.

* * *

Brianna sat in a sea of heart-shaped leaves layering the forest floor. Mist hovered over the ground like fine gauze and tangled in the branches overhead. The moon shone full and bright through a veil of clouds.

The romantic in her recognized the setting as a place where lovers met for moonlit trysts.

She looked into her lap where Colin had collapsed, his face pale, his lips locked tight. This was no romantic interlude.

Her lover lay dying.

Her fingers were slick with his blood, and the metallic scent of it clung to the moist air. His chest rose and fell with even breath. He was alive. For now.

The baying of a dog stalked them from a distance, the same howl that had haunted them for the last several minutes.

Colin blinked up at her, his gaze bleary, confused. "Brianna."

She silenced him with the slightest pressure of her fingertip against his soft lips.

"My lady, we must go." Urgency hummed around them, yet Jonathan's voice was calm as he spoke.

Brianna nodded. There was no time, yet there was so much she wanted to say. Colin's eyes fluttered closed. Even if she could speak around the lump in her throat, he would not be able to hear her. She nuzzled close to his face and reveled in the scrape of his whiskers against her cheek. "I love you, Colin."

He gave a soft groan, and his breathing drew slow and steady once more. He was asleep, or unconscious. Either way, his lack of awareness was necessary if her plan was going to work.

"I'm not strong enough to hold him as we ride." She looked up at Jonathan's shadowed face. "You'll have to take him on your horse."

As expected, Jonathan did not disagree with Brianna's suggestion. She waited until both he and Colin were on the horse before advancing with the second part of her plan. "You ride ahead, and I'll lead the guards on a chase through the woods."

The drumming of horses' hooves sounded in the distance.

"I can't allow that, my lady."

She glanced over her shoulder to ensure her uncle's men were not already breaking the tree line. "You are weighted down with Colin and I am a fast rider. I'll meet you at Edzell later." Her gaze returned to Jonathan, and she gave him a smile she hoped appeared more certain than it felt. "I'll be fine."

The dog's howl was close this time. So close, it sent fear skittering across her nerves.

"Go," she hissed with urgency. She gazed one last time at Colin's handsome face, relaxed now in slumber. In that one glance, she committed every line, every sweet curve to memory. "Please. Save him."

Reluctance crossed Jonathan's young features even as he gathered his arms beneath Colin's slumping chest. "I will see you at Edzell."

She knew his words were validation for himself more than for her. She knew he questioned her intent, and with good reason.

He snapped the reins and his horse galloped into the cover of the forest. Into the protection of darkness.

She swung up on her horse and eased toward the edge of the forest, where her uncle's men would see her and give chase.

They drew near. Their presence vibrated the air with the excitement of a hunt and stirred the languid mist.

The flanks of Brianna's horse flexed and flicked with uncertainty. She ran a soothing hand down his strong neck.

The clatter of armor and weapons assaulted the eerie silence, and her heart slammed in unsteady beats.

Her sacrifice would not be in vain.

Jonathan would escape safely to Edzell, and her people would be warned of the possibility of battle. Pray God the healer could aid Colin.

Her horse pranced with anxious energy beneath her.

"I see one of them!" The shout came from the opposite end of the glen.

Her horse did not need the snap of the reins. He darted forward and wound his way through the trees, his movements sharp, determined.

No matter how hard the poor beast fought for their freedom, they would be captured. Their defeat in sacrifice for the safety of those she loved.

The guards pressed closer. Their exerted breath hissed behind her, the musk of their sweaty horses tainting the air.

There was no escape.

And that was exactly what she wanted.

* * *

Brianna had thought she would feel more panicked. Her heartbeat was steady and her palms dry. Even her breathing was normal.

Colin was safe.

Her hands were bound in front of her with manacles similar to those he had worn. The great entryway to her uncle's manor opened wide above her, as if intending to swallow her up.

Her chin lifted with the pride of a queen. She would not buckle beneath the press of intimidation. She was a MacKinnon.

Her uncle waddled down the hallway, his gait slow in the absence of his cane. "For all that I trusted her, it is my niece who betrays me."

Despite the late hour, he did not appear to have been roused from bed. His stiff jacket still creased across his midsection, and his hair was perfectly slicked back.

He staggered toward her, and the scent of overly sweet perfume and alcohol compressed around her in a dizzying fog.

His forefinger pointed in her direction and waggled. "You have disappointed me." The breath whooshed from his chest like a great wind through a narrow tunnel.

Brianna did not bow beneath his criticism. Her heart was calloused to his disappointment, hardened by years of resentment and bitterness. If anything, his words fed her contempt. She had nothing to lose. "You arrested my husband with no regard for Scottish law. If anything, *I* am disappointed in *you*."

His flushed face deepened to a shade of purple, and a slow sigh rattled from his gaping lips.

The whisper of silk sounded behind him.

"What do we have here?" The feminine voice was rich, warm, and laced with a French purr.

Brianna went stiff, and her steady heartbeat bounced inside her chest.

She knew that voice.

Marie D'Aubigne.

Chapter Forty-Five

Brianna froze, her manacled hands held in front of her. "Marie?"

The Frenchwoman stepped forward, and her indifferent gaze swung to Brianna. "It would appear you've caught yourself a mouse," Marie said.

Colin had been betrayed.

Brianna's hands flexed and fisted until the heavy iron cuffs chaffed the skin of her wrists. She welcomed the pain. Anything to distract her from the sting of Marie's treachery.

Her uncle's disdainful glare settled on Brianna. "Either I have underestimated your bravery or overestimated your intelligence." His words slurred slightly. "I'm inclined to go with the latter. Interesting-I had never assumed you to be so naïve."

Brianna stared hard at Marie. "How could you do this to Colin? You betrayed us." She was no longer cool and emotionless. "He was down in the dungeon, sleeping on filthy rushes in the dark." Her lip curled with disdain. "You slept above him while he suffered."

A dark look shot through the Frenchwoman's eyes, hard and mean. "You'll get your punishment soon enough, little scholar. And then Edzell will be seeking a new mistress."

Brianna bit her tongue to keep from asking what they intended to do with her. Her sacrifice had afforded Colin a chance at life where he would otherwise die. She focused on that thought, clung to it.

Marie leaned toward Brianna's uncle. "I think we deserve a victory drink."

His gaze slithered down the Frenchwoman's body, in full view of Brianna and all the guards. "I'd prefer to go to bed."

Brianna winced in revulsion, but Marie's expression did not lose its sultry welcome.

"One more drink." Her voice was low, enticing.

Brianna's uncle swayed where he stood, as if he were adjusting to the rock of a boat. She knew him well enough to know he could not handle one more drink. And she was willing to bet Marie knew that as well.

"Very well," he slurred. "But just one more." He glanced back at Brianna, and a smug grin pulled at his jowls. "In celebration."

Marie slipped her hand into the crook of his arm and together they disappeared, leaving Brianna in the company of armed guards and her impending fate.

• • •

Brianna had expected a dungeon for her captivity.

Heavy silk lined the walls of her chamber. A bed sat in the small room, un-extraordinary in any other sense than it covered almost the entire floor and scraped Brianna's ankles as she tried to pass.

She hadn't slept through the remainder of the night, nor during the day. She edged past the foot of the bed to the window, if the slender arrow-loop could be called such. The narrow gap in the wall was meant for shooting at enemies, not providing light.

The moon rose bright against the inky night outside, and her eyes felt fat with exhaustion.

Colin had been so still in her arms when she held him in the glen. Too still. His breathing unnaturally deep. There had been too much blood. The underside of her fingernails still bore the stains.

She'd been given a fresh gown with her midday meal, and the previously soiled dress now lay in a pile beside the bed. The food she had not touched, but the dress had been a welcome comfort in an otherwise futile predicament.

The house had long since gone still, and the settling creaks and groans of age blew cold beneath her door. Such sounds had frightened her as a child, the petty angst of a girl who did not yet understand true fear.

A key turned in the lock. Brianna's head snapped toward the sound to find Marie slipping through the door. The Frenchwoman's face trained toward the hallway before she quietly locked them in together.

She motioned for Brianna to approach.

Brianna did not move.

"Quickly, come." Marie's voice was so soft, Brianna had to strain to hear it. "Do you want to stay here?"

She eyed Marie, uncertain. "I don't understand."

"Lower your voice, please." The woman paused and pressed her ear to the door. "I am not with your uncle, I've been spying on *him* for Colin."

Questions piled in Brianna's mind faster than she could assemble them. Her mouth opened, but Marie shook her head. "There's no time, I'll explain later. Come, we must hurry."

Still Brianna did not move. Her mind sped through reasons why Marie would be conspiring with her uncle and why she might actually be helping Colin. Fatigue weighed at Brianna and scattered her thoughts in all directions. "I don't trust you." She shook her head to clear it. "Why did you not rescue Colin?"

"A room in the manor is easier to get a key to than the dungeon." Marie pulled her shoulders back. "Were I in your situation, I would give pause as well." She stepped toward Brianna, and her face became visible in the scant moonlight. "I'm asking you to trust me as you did before. If not for yourself, please do this for the babe."

Brianna's weakened knees propelled her onto the window seat behind her. "What?"

Something distant banged in the hallway. Marie jumped slightly and eyed the door, her body locked in place.

"The servants said you were ill this morning," she said without turning toward Brianna.

"People get ill."

"You look exhausted."

Exasperation swelled. Marie's anxious energy picked at

Brianna's nerves. "I haven't slept."

Marie gave an annoyed tsk and shot Brianna a sharp stare. "If you want your freedom, then come. I do not risk my life to argue all damn night."

Brianna's body stood before her mind decided to.

She had to trust Marie.

What other choice did she have?

* * *

Once again, Brianna found herself creeping along the dank halls of her uncle's manor, every careful footstep made with the same silence as before. One hand covered the flat of her stomach. Whether she was truly pregnant or not, the heat of her palm brought a level of comfort.

Doubt niggled at the back of her thoughts. Had Marie been right? Brianna applied light pressure to her stomach. It felt no different.

Marie jerked to a halt ahead and turned back to Brianna, her eyes wide. "Someone's coming," she mouthed.

Footsteps followed her warning, hard and insistent upon the stone floor.

The hall had an alcove several feet back, yet when the women returned to it, Brianna realized it was little more than a shallow dip that would barely accommodate them.

They pressed their bodies against the stone so they faced one another. "Find safety," Brianna breathed. "They will think I escaped on my own."

Marie clasped Brianna's hand in a delicate fist of ice. "I won't leave you."

The footsteps turned down their hallway, silencing both women.

Brianna pushed against the stone, wishing she could force the wall to sink in, to make their sanctuary deeper.

"Marie, you naughty girl." Robert's voice echoed down the hallway.

Marie's pulse raced beneath Brianna's fingertips.

"I see your gown peeking from the wall." Robert's tone held the lofty air of confident flirtation. "Are you hiding from me, or do you offer pleasure in the shadows?" His speech grew louder as he drew nearer.

Marie dropped Brianna's hand and stepped away from the safe façade of their alcove. "Robert, what a pleasant surprise."

Marie's hands clasped behind her back, the way she had shown Brianna, to make her bosom thrust forward in invitation. The way she easily concealed the dagger glinting between her fingers.

"I have yet to be alone with you."

"And what would you do with me if we were alone together?" The hem of Marie's gown snagged against stone as she stepped forward.

A thick silence descended, and Brianna did not have to see his face to know the look Robert gave Marie. She could *feel* it.

"Things I've imagined doing time and again. Things my father could never do." The possessive edge rang sharp in his words.

"Then you'll have to come closer," Marie taunted.

Brianna pressed deeper into the alcove. Marie's impending attack stretched taut in the air.

A hollow punching sound filled Brianna's ears, followed by a slow, wet suck. A low groan.

No more could she hide like a coward. She swung out into the hall, expecting to see Robert dead upon the floor.

He was not.

He stood before Marie, his hand pressed to his chest, eyes wide with shock. His hand peeled away, bright and slick with blood.

"Guards!" He staggered toward Marie. "Guards!"

Her shoulders rose and fell with exaggerated breath, but she did not move.

Brianna stepped forward and found Marie's glassy stare fixed on the quickly spreading stain on Robert's chest.

"We have to run." Brianna grabbed Marie's slender arm.

The woman's body flinched, and her eyes ripped away from

Robert's sagging form.

"Brianna." The word gargled from his mouth, expelled in a splash of black blood.

She jerked her head away. She could not look at him lest she lose her courage. Instead, she tugged at Marie, and together they ran down the hall with feet that stumbled in clumsy shock beneath them.

No clattering of weapons echoed down the hall, nor was there the heavy sound of footsteps. The door to their freedom stood several dozen feet away. Brianna could almost feel the cool night air in her lungs.

A door swung open beside Marie, and a startled scream escaped her throat. A wet, tearing sound filled Brianna's ears, like what she had heard in the dungeon when Jonathan killed the guard. Her stomach twisted, and a wave of nausea sapped the strength from her legs. She knew that sound too well.

Chapter Forty-Five

There was no time for Brianna to go to Marie's aid. The woman's weight crashed into her and threw them both to the narrow floor of the hall.

Their landing was an awkward tangle of skirts and limbs. Nothing they could escape, not with five guards standing around them with swords at the ready.

Brianna struggled to a sitting position. Marie did not.

She lay on her back with one hand draped limply over her upper abdomen. Blood glistened beneath her fingers.

Brianna's body went numb, and her heart squeezed beneath the press of a thousand daggers.

"No," she said, her head shaking. "Marie, no."

"NO!" The cry echoing down the hall was ragged, rough with emotion before it strangled into a heart-rending sob.

Footsteps shuffled toward them with haste.

She turned away from the dark hall. She did not want to see her uncle's face as he approached. For all the cruelty he had inflicted upon her, she could not bring herself to see the grief etched on his face.

She gazed down at Marie. The woman's eyes fluttered several times before focusing on Brianna. "Take care of Colin." She swallowed thickly, a choked sound that stabbed deep into Brianna's soul. "For both of us."

Brianna could not draw breath through the tightness of her throat. "Marie—"

"Damn you," her uncle roared. The two guards in front of Brianna were shoved aside, and her uncle appeared between them.

His face was white, his hair flying in all directions, his body draped in a black dressing gown. He looked like the devil himself.

Brianna couldn't move, couldn't speak.

He caught Marie by the throat and lifted her with an unnatural strength. "You killed my son."

Her limbs flailed in weak defense, but still he did not release her. A knife glinted in the low light. Marie's own dagger.

His fist jerked across her throat, and the paleness of her chest splashed red with a river of blood.

Brianna found her breath. It came in frantic spurts and bounced against the ragged stone walls.

Her uncle released Marie's neck, and she fell to the ground like a discarded doll. Blood continued to seep slowly from the wound.

He stepped toward Brianna, but she could not tear her gaze from Marie. The woman once so full of vitality now lay prone and lifeless.

She had sacrificed her life protecting Brianna.

A bloodied dagger broke through Brianna's gaze, its point merciless where it prodded against the tender flesh of her throat.

"I should kill you," her uncle snarled. "I could do it as easily as I killed that whore."

Brianna's pulse raced, spurred by the metallic scent of Marie's blood. Tears burned her eyes, and she had to fight the urge to wrap her arms around her belly.

The blade's pressure increased, and a warmth trickled down her throat.

"Killing you would be too gracious." He relaxed the blade's pressure. "I've worked too hard to see you fall so quickly. I spent months convincing your father of your illegitimacy while you grew in your mother's womb. I spent years convincing him to keep you from marriage."

He leaned closer until his black stare blended with the dim hall. "I spent decades waiting for him to die."

His chest deflated with a hissing breath. "Do you know your old nurse signed the confession implicating your guilt?" He stared without blinking. "Do you?" His shouted words flew into her face.

Brianna's heart withered beneath the scorching wrath of his words. Magda, dear sweet Magda, doubtless the woman knew not what she had done.

He drew a deep breath with flaring nostrils. "I have enough men to take Edzell by force." Another exaggerated inhale. "And I will." Inhale. "Tomorrow night." Inhale. "And your husband will die by my blade."

Her strength waned. "How could you?" The words slipped from her mouth, between lips that did not move.

Such a paltry question did not begin to encompass the betrayal and pain coiling through her.

"Your father was weak. He let Edzell's potential slide away. He could have pushed harder, generated more wealth."

He looked over her shoulder and his gaze grew distant. "My son would have been a good laird had you but given in to his fancy to marry you." His eyes glittered with something dark and wild. "But now he's dead. And you will pay the price."

An arm clamped around her waist, and she felt herself pulled backward. Away from her uncle's glare, away from Marie's lifeless body. Away from the door that led to freedom.

* * *

Colin's body lay immobile on the stiff mattress, his limbs heavy with exhaustion. He groaned with the effort of movement, and a throbbing pain erupted in the back of his skull.

Maybe he could sleep just a few minutes longer.

"Laird?"

Damn.

He blinked his eyes open to the dark room. "Why are ye in my room in the middle of the night?"

"It's early morning." Jonathan's face came into view. "With all due respect, laird, you keep asking that same question, and I keep telling you that we've blocked out the sun from your room. You said it split your head."

Confusion furrowed Colin's brows. "Keep asking ye?"

Jonathan's watchful gaze did not leave Colin's face. "Aye, you've been like this now for two days."

Flashes of images came back. The scent of herbs as the healer worked over him, the sun shredding into his skull when he opened his eyes, the jarring horse beneath him, the awkward tilt of his ankles where his feet dragged along the floor of an empty hall.

Brianna.

"Where is my wife?"

Jonathan's looked down at his clasped hands. "At Lindsay's manor."

Colin pulled himself to a sitting position and gritted his teeth against the throb in his head. "For two days?"

Jonathan nodded. "She was captured in our escape, laird."

The breath punched from Colin's chest.

"Why? How?"

The lad shook his head. "She said she could outrun them. She said she would meet us back at Edzell." His thin shoulders sagged. "I think she knew she wouldn't be returning. I should have known."

Memories washed over Colin's mind like vinegar splashing a wound. The darkness of the dungeon, the way Brianna had risked everything to free him, the battle between the guards who had discovered them.

She had saved his life and now remained in his place.

He stared down at the signet ring on his hand. It did not glint in the cover of his darkened room.

They would have escaped had he not returned to reclaim the damned ring. The guards attacked them in the solar, where he'd received the knock to the back of the head that rendered him unable to function.

His heart shied away from the memory, but he forced himself to continue. Brianna and Jonathan, both significantly smaller than he, had carried him through the halls toward safety.

Brianna had sacrificed herself to save him. She was captured because of his actions. Impulsive actions.

The pain swelling within his chest made breathing difficult.

His father was right, and now Brianna paid the price.

"Is she—" Colin swallowed, unsure if he could even form the bitter words. "Is she locked within the dungeon?"

To imagine Brianna, all delicate scents and light and love, curled on that stone floor, surrounded by the stink of despair, tore at his heart.

"I don't know, laird." Jonathan's soft voice indicated his assumption. And it sliced through Colin's soul.

"Why have you not attempted to rescue her?"

"We have scouted the perimeter. Lindsay has too many men. He has fortified his manor in expectation that we would come to her aid. Rescue attempts have been—" His lips drew tight. "Rescue attempts have been impossible."

Colin dragged his legs over the edge of the bed. "There must be a way." Determination pumped through him and elevated above his pulsing skull. "I would rather die than allow her to spend another day in that dungeon."

He rose to a standing position, and the room rocked beneath his feet. His hand braced against the stone wall, but the swaying did not cease.

"She will not be there after today," Jonathan said. "Lindsay intends to have her sent to Edinburgh with a note implicating her in her father's murder."

"Edinburgh?" Colin asked.

Jonathan averted his gaze, but not before Colin saw the flash of angry hurt. "Yes, Edinburgh. To be hanged."

Colin's chamber was too dark, the air too still and hot. He turned away from Jonathan and squeezed his eyes shut. The ground rolled again and everything spun together. He locked his knees and pressed his weight against the wall. He wouldn't get sick. Not now. Not when Brianna needed him most.

"How do you know these plans?"

"George came here last night," Jonathan said. "His mother overheard two of Lindsay's guards at the tavern."

Colin cursed between clamped teeth. While he appreciated the lad's information, he didn't want George involved.

He split his thumb and forefinger over his chin and

scratched the week's worth of beard growth.

If Brianna went to Edinburgh, there would be no returning, there would be no escape.

He would never see her again.

His stomach roiled at the thought. Rescuing her from Lindsay's manor would be difficult. Difficult, but not impossible.

The risk was worth her life.

"We go to the manor at sunset to rescue her." Colin straightened and gave Jonathan a hard look.

The soldier rubbed the back of his neck. "We cannot, laird."

"Ye've considered her rescue, but no attempted it. I will be damned if I let her go to Edinburgh and be tried for a murder she dinna commit."

Jonathan's shoulders tightened visibly. "There was more discussed at the tavern. Lindsay plans to attack Edzell tonight. If you are not here to defend the castle, she will fall."

Colin's head ached like a battle axe wound. "Alec," he ground out. "Has Alec returned yet?"

The defeated look in Jonathan's eyes answered Colin's question before the guard was able to. "No, laird. Still nothing."

What was taking Alec so damn long?

"Is there anything else ye wish to tell me about the overheard conversation that ye may have left out?" Colin asked.

"No. From what George's mother said, they were bragging about their employer's impending wealth and how much coin they would receive for their services."

The searing pain in Colin's head ebbed. The men were bragging. They were overconfident. Based on their words in the tavern, they already considered the battle won.

But it was not.

The battle was only beginning.

Chapter Forty-Six

Brianna paced the narrow space of her room, not that it did her any good. She stopped abruptly and laid her fingertips to the warm base of her belly. The flesh there was puffy, the way it often was just before her courses started.

But she hadn't had her courses in over five weeks.

In light of her concern for Colin, she had not realized the time gap until now. She'd read enough books to know what the delay meant.

Marie had been right.

Brianna's knees brushed the side of the mattress, and her fingers latched around the carved grooves in the bedpost, seeking its immobile strength.

Her stomach would swell with Colin's baby. It did not yet quicken in her womb, but it would.

Despair grew where elation may have once taken root. She had naught to offer the child. There was nothing left but cruelty, chaos, and hopelessness.

Her uncle would take Edzell tonight and either kill or enslave all her people. The weight in her chest compressed. If Colin still lived, her uncle would see to his death. The threat of tears washed the room in a smear of dismal grays. Even her own life would soon fall forfeit. Perhaps she would be allowed to birth the babe prior to being executed, but then the child would be raised in an orphanage.

"Forgive me." She cupped the tender swell of her belly.

Guilt rode her conscience.

She had never wanted this baby. She had taken measures to ensure this would never happen.

And now it had.

Another life would be implicated in her tangled, short-lived world, protected within the fragile shell of her body.

Her fingertips absently stroked the filthy dress over her womb, as if the caress could somehow make everything better.

No matter how she rolled the thoughts through her head, they never polished to a positive outcome. Yet still, she could not give up. She needed to fight, no longer for herself, but for her unborn child. For Colin's child.

A quiet grating sounded within the lock of the door.

She released the bedpost and glanced at the narrow window. The sun rose high, brilliant with the glow of early afternoon.

Had they come to take her so early?

The door swung open and one of Lindsay's mercenaries stepped through, his movements confident, full of purpose. If she could evade him, perhaps she could run for safety. Energy raced through her veins, pounding, jolting, inciting.

Brianna turned from the man in an attempt to climb across the wide mattress. Her toe caught the edge of the bed and she pitched forward.

Strong arms locked around her torso, trapping her, pulling her back against a solid body.

Horror jolted through her, raw and ugly. Had her uncle sent his men here for entertainment before she was to be tried for her father's death?

"No." She writhed with futile effort and choked back a cry. "I'm with child. Please."

Firm hands caught her shoulders and spun her around to a face with eyes as green as sunlit grass.

Chapter Forty-Seven

Colin's handsome face broke through the dizzying whirl of Brianna's chaos. The weight of his hands pressed into her shoulders.

He was no random guard seeking to harm her. In the confines of her small prison, he was her beautiful promise of hope.

He was alive.

She would be saved.

He pulled off the helm he wore and let it roll to the floor. His trembling fingers reached for her face and trailed over her brow, her cheeks, her nose, her lips, and, finally, trapped her jaw in his large hand.

"Brianna." His voice was hoarse. "My Brianna." The sinewy lines of muscle showed against his clamped jaw. His gaze lowered to her abdomen. "Are ye—" His eyes widened and shot back to her face. "Ye're hurt."

She didn't have to look to know he referred to the blood staining her dress. Marie's blood.

"Marie. She's—" The words could not leave Brianna's lips. The horror of the memory was too great, the guilt too heavy. Marie had died for her.

Colin's face hardened. "There's no time to talk about this now."

He pulled a bag from behind him. She had not seen him bring it in and realized he must have dropped it when he caught her.

"Quickly, put these on." He drew out a set of men's pants and padded armor.

She rolled the dress off her body and punched her feet through the legs of the trews, all the while acutely aware of the way his gaze trailed over her body, like a starving man eyeing a meal.

His stare lingered over her flat stomach, and his expression softened.

The shirt slipped from her fingers and fluttered to the ground. She focused on its retrieval rather than watch him watching her. She was not yet ready to see his face, to understand how he felt about the child. Not until he knew about Edzell.

"You do not know everything." She quickly pulled the shirt on and followed it with the stiff padded vest. Her nostrils flared at the odor of stale sweat, and the skin of her neck chafed against the stiff, scratchy fabric.

Before she could wrench the vest down, Colin's gentle hands tugged it into place.

"What do ye mean I dinna know everything?" he asked from behind her.

"My uncle plans to attack Edzell tonight."

The upper portion of her vest went taut over her shoulders and jiggled slightly as Colin secured the final tie. "I already knew that."

She spun around and found herself standing breast to chest with him, the thick stinking padding of her armor touching the thick stinking padding of his armor. "You knew?"

He smoothed her hair behind her ear. "I knew."

Her breath caught beneath the rush of her pulse. "You'll lose Edzell."

"I dinna love Edzell." He stared down at her with a tenderness she couldn't allow herself to believe.

"What do you mean?"

He grasped her upper arms, his hold firm, possessive. "I fight for what I love." He searched her eyes. "I fight for ye, wife."

The brush of his freshly shaven chin teased her jaw. Before she could react, his mouth closed over her lips in a kiss that burned with the memory of what they once had. The passion. The companionship. The comfort.

"I love ye, Brianna MacKinnon."

His fingers threaded through hers, and together they cradled her stomach. "And I love ye, wee MacKinnon." A warm smile touched his lips. "I love both of ye."

Brianna closed her eyes and basked in the moment. She was loved, her child was loved, and they were both safe with Colin.

The affectionate reprieve was short-lived. Edzell's people were not safe. Colin had come to her aid, and now Edzell was vulnerable. Its people would be at the mercy of her uncle.

"What about the servants? My uncle will see them killed."

His eyes stayed trained on her stomach. "I came alone so Jonathan and the other men could see them to safety." He winked. "And move all yer books."

Brianna felt the smile return to her face. Not only did her husband love her, he understood her better than even she realized.

The cacophony of rallying soldiers clattered outside the window, and Colin's arms tensed around her. "We've lingered too long. Put on the helm and let us leave this foul place."

The metal headpiece was heavy on her head and dug into her brow. Uncomfortable though it was, it would shield her hair from view and block her face.

"Remember, ye're one of them." Colin secured his own helm beneath his chin. "Dinna flinch, dinna look suspicious, just walk with purpose." He winked down at her. "I'll no let anything happen to ye."

Hopeless desperation melted from her shoulders, warmed beneath the aura of confidence and power her husband exuded. Nothing could hurt her when they were together. Nothing could go wrong. All would be well with her husband who possessed no fear.

* * *

Colin had never been so damn scared in his life. Lindsay's guards were everywhere, and until he'd led Brianna out of the manor, she and their unborn child were not safe.

His heart swelled. Their unborn child.

He steeled himself against the emotion. There would be time to muse later, when they were free from the threat of danger.

Soldiers moved through the halls in staggered waves, their voices loud with excitement for the impending battle. The uneven pounding of footsteps and slamming of distant doors echoed around them.

Colin had never been so grateful for his ability to pick a lock. Stealing the key to Brianna's room would have been impossible. Almost as impossible as finding old soldier's clothing large enough for him and small enough for her.

Brianna strode ahead of Colin, against the stream of guards. Her shoulders squared and her head hung low in a way that shadowed her face beneath the helm, the way he'd seen so many young soldiers march prior to their first battle.

She had been brave thus far, yet every casual glance in her direction, every shoulder that bumped hers, sent a fresh jolt of caution raking his nerves.

If they were discovered, she would be attacked first, and he did not know if he could move quickly enough to save her. His gaze skimmed the sea of dirt-streaked, mismatched soldier's clothing. Even he could not fight an army on his own.

The realization of vulnerability sat in his gut like a rock and burned the back of his throat. He hated the lack of control, the uncertainty. His wife and child were surrounded by danger, and there was nothing more he could do.

"Where are you going?" a man's voice boomed in front of Brianna.

Colin's hand tightened beside the hilt of the plain soldier's sword he wore at his side. He wanted to grasp the cool metal, to feel its comfort caress his palm. But such an act would draw unwanted attention they could not afford.

The man grasped Brianna by the shoulders, and every muscle in Colin's body burned with tension. He would rip the man's head off with bare hands at the slightest show of a threat.

But the man turned Brianna around, so she faced Colin.

Her gaze was lowered, but her chest rose and fell with quickened breath.

"That way, boy," the man growled. "Pay more attention or you'll find yourself with a sword in your gullet." He nudged her forward with a solid push and stormed off down the hall, cursing his irritation of inexperienced men.

Brianna moved forward with the surge of guards and kept her eyes downcast.

Colin turned on his heel and followed close enough to protect her. The river of men swept down the hall before being spit out a door, into the brilliant glow of the sun.

Holes showed beneath the mismatched cobblestone in the courtyard, and a large crack ran through the whitewashed wall of a nearby stable. Lindsay had poured his gold into an army while his home sagged into neglect.

And a pathetic army it was. For those who wore padded armor, the vests were similar to the cheap, stained garments Colin and Brianna wore. There were even fewer helms. As evidenced by the courtyard full of men, Lindsay had created an army of numbers, not an army of skill or pride.

Brianna followed the men in a pace that did not falter, even as she broke away and shifted toward the side of the large manor walls, where the sun did not touch. She walked as if she knew where she was going, as if she belonged where she was going.

The gravel crunched loudly beneath Colin's feet, and the helm obscured his vision too damn much. But he could wait no longer.

Now.

With the same air of purpose Brianna had displayed, he followed the direct path she had taken and found her waiting in the embrace of the shadows. She looked small inside the weighty guard's clothing. Fragile, despite the fierce glint in her eye.

He was not the only one who had lost weight in the past few days.

His chest grew tight. No, not his chest. His heart. She pulled at his heart and made his body cry out for her. He would rather the pains she suffered be his own.

With a strength that contradicted her appearance, she turned from him and darted toward the forest behind the manor. This time Colin did not follow. This time he would wait to ensure she made it to safety.

Chapter Forty-Eight

An errant squirrel darted across Colin's path and scampered beneath a nearby bush. He glanced over his shoulder to the trees behind him. No guards crept through the crowded brush toward him and Brianna, no thundering of hooves or baying of dogs met his ears. The sun danced through the leaves overhead and flickered around them, like shards of light through an unseen crystal.

An hour of fast-paced walking stood between them and the manor.

The tightness in his back eased. They had been running for too long.

Brianna's scent pulled at him, delicate, light, still evident even against the stink of her borrowed armor. He sucked in a slow, deep breath through his nostrils and savored the rush of memories that had been too painful to recall before this moment. Before he had her safe. Alone.

It had been over a week since he'd sampled the lush sweetness of her lips.

Brianna trudged through the forest ahead of him, the masculine trews hanging from her waist and hinting at the roundness of her bottom beneath. Her glossy brown hair draped down her back, past her narrow waist, like a sable cape.

She was his wife, the mother of his child.

And never was there a woman more beautiful. Never was there a moment he longed to hold her more than he did now.

He caught her hand mid-swing.

Just one look.

She stopped, and her warm gaze rose to meet his.

Her face was flushed beneath fair skin, her lips pink.

Just one touch.

He brushed the curve of her cheek with his fingertips, down her jaw to the delicate line of her throat. She tilted her head back and her lashes fluttered closed.

Her lips were mere inches from his.

Just one kiss.

His heart slammed in his chest. His breath came fast.

He grasped the back of her neck and threaded his fingers through her silky hair. If he was going to allow himself only one kiss, he would relish it.

He let the heat of her mouth tease him, the tempting whisper of her breath mingle with his. Their chins brushed, and he heard the shuddering intake of her gasp.

Her mouth was supple, parted. Ready. He groaned and took what she offered. His mouth crushed against hers and found her lips soft, like the sun-warmed petals of a rose.

Colin's pulse staggered with an erratic rhythm.

He pulled her lower lip into his mouth and ran his tongue against it. A low, hungry moan purred from her throat.

His hardened cock raged with desire too long denied, and he no longer had control of his actions. He caught her against him and plunged his tongue deep into her tantalizing mouth. Her fingers slid under his padded vest, scalding him with the gentle scrape of her nails. Their breath came hard and fast as clothing was torn away with mindless need. The air of the shaded forest bathed their naked flesh.

Together they fell to the earth's soft embrace, hands gripping, caressing. Mouths tasting, coaxing.

Her slender thighs parted beneath his insistent pressure, and her hips rolled in graceful arches toward him, the movements sensual and rhythmic.

He planted his hands against the moist ground on either side of her and plunged into the warmth of her body. Her tight welcome damn near unmanned him.

Her soft cries, the whimpering of his name, all of it faded into the open forest around them. His fingers clasped against hers, their eyes locked, and the pace of their love pitched to a starved frenzy.

Brianna wrapped her legs around Colin's narrow hips and clutched him to her.

This was real.

Delicious tension built up where he joined with her.

His teeth tugged lightly at her earlobe, and his breath tickled the delicate skin of her neck. "Come for me, wife."

He swelled inside her, and she knew he was near his own release. His hand moved between them and applied a light pressure to her sensitive bud. That was all she needed. A wave of euphoria caught her in its decadent, pulsing grasp, and she flexed upward to capture its intoxicating force.

Colin's rhythm increased, pulling in shorter, quicker thrusts. His body arched into her, filling her completely. He buried his face against her neck and gave a hoarse cry as his body went taut with his own release. His lips dotted a trail of kisses along her neck, his breath so heavy in her ear, it rivaled the deafening thud of her own heart.

He leaned up on his elbow and stared down at her. His eyes were a brilliant, sparkling shade of green that put the surrounding fauna to shame. "Ye look so beautiful when ye do that."

Heat spread up her chest and over her cheeks. "When I do what?"

He leaned forward and nipped her lower lip. "When ye come." His mouth brushed over hers. "I love to watch ye."

She tilted her face to kiss him full on the lips when he pulled back and rested his forehead against hers. His gaze locked with hers, so she could see nothing but him.

"I love ye, Brianna."

She slid her hands over his smooth jaw and held him captive between her palms. "And I love you, Colin."

He grinned down at her, and that dimple she adored winked at her.

Would their child have that same dimple? His auburn hair? His beautiful green eyes?

"Ye're smiling," he said.

Her smile widened. "So are you."

"Ye make me happy."

The simple statement said so much. Her parents had never known happiness such as what she and Colin shared. There had been no tender moments. There had been no love.

Her marriage had never been like her parents', and it never would.

Colin pulled out of her with a low groan and sat upright, unabashedly nude. He scanned the surrounding area with a sharp glance. "We need to hurry, lass." His lips lifted in a show of sheepish guilt. "I had only meant to kiss ye."

A hard thought tumbled through the world of their intimacy and shattered her languid state. Where were they going if not to Edzell? Where could they go?

"We need to hurry where?" she asked.

Colin glanced once more behind him before tugging the shirt over his head. "To find Jonathan."

* * *

A mile and a half later, the shrill bark of a crow pierced the air, the signal Colin sought. He cupped his hands in a tunnel around his mouth and mimicked the call.

Jonathan emerged from behind a nearby tree, and his dark eyes swung to Brianna. "My lady." Even his excited grin did not mask his exhaustion. "I'm relieved to see you safe."

She stepped forward and placed a hand on his shoulder. "Thank you, Jonathan."

He looked up with a reverence that would have left Colin uncomfortable had he not understood the depth of the man's loyalty.

"Thank you for leading our people to safety," Brianna said. "Were it not for your brave efforts, many would have paid with their lives."

Jonathan nodded once and stepped back, away from her touch.

Good lad.

"Everyone has been removed from the castle, then?" Colin asked.

"Aye, they've all been relocated to the woods and are slowly making their way to Monsieur de Caritat's rented home, as you directed."

"Alec?"

Jonathan pursed his lips and shook his head.

The delicate thread of hope he'd placed on Alec's shoulders snapped. He would be too late.

Colin looked up as a bird soared overhead. "Then Lindsay can have the castle."

"What?" Brianna exclaimed. "Why?"

He tore his gaze from the brilliant blue sky and met her anxious stare.

Color rose high in her face. "Why can he have the castle? Why can we not fight?"

"Lass, they have over a hundred guards to the dozens we do. In no way would it be possible for us to defeat your uncle."

Her brow furrowed, and her fingers pinched her lower lip, the way she did when she concentrated.

Abruptly, her hand fell away and her mouth curved into a sly smile. "Then perhaps there is a way to defeat him."

Chapter Forty-Nine

Wind fluttered Colin's leine and pulled at the coarse black mane of his steed. Edzell Castle stood behind him, a powerful force in need of protection. His gaze scraped the large hill to the north. The enemy would show themselves at its peak. The uneven ground and dense forest wouldn't allow Lindsay's attack from any other location.

Naught met Colin's stare, save a red sky threaded with veins of brilliant gold. A violent sunset for a violent night.

The flag rippled above the castle, the fierce boar's head painted on its surface marking Edzell as his, and he would see it defended.

Two dozen guards stood immobile behind him, as were the ten archers who stood on the roof and ten more who hid in the forest behind enemy lines. Five additional soldiers waited in the distance at Edzell's back, ready to set Brianna's plan into action. All were prepared to take on the army outnumbering them at least two to one.

Everything was prepared. Gunpowder lay piled in neat stacks on the hill, obscured by leaves. The men hiding at Edzell had additional barrels of gunpowder that they would detonate.

The guards behind Colin were silent. They did not rock on their feet or fidget with their armor. The Edzell guards were now trained men. Warriors.

And they were ready.

Lindsay, however, had mercenaries. Men who accepted coin for their services. Loyalty easily bought could also be easily lost. And Colin would see them run like the cowards they were.

The sky began to darken.

No sooner had the sun hidden her face beneath the valley of the hills beyond than the slow, erratic march of an unorganized army appeared.

Darkness fell hard and fast over the surrounding area and shrouded evidence of Colin's deceit. His heart pounded, and power jolted through his body, the way it always did before battle.

Lindsay's men breached the hill at a speed that spoke of each individual man's pace rather than the precision of an army.

Colin glanced from one side of the hill to the other, following the crowded, disjointed lines.

What they lacked in order, they made up for in numbers.

Lindsay had hired more men than Colin assumed. Over two hundred were visible, and perhaps more he could not see.

He did not flinch beneath the realization. His heart still beat strong, his body fired with the urge to fight, to *win*.

The guards behind him remained still.

Lindsay rode his great, thundering horse toward Colin with the indiscretion of a man not bred for war. Leadership did not propel him forward, arrogance did. He assumed the battle was already won before the first blade could be drawn.

Colin flicked his wrist, and his men roared around him in a savage cry of resistance. Their swords slapped against their targes, and the reverberations carried until the sound echoed off the surrounding hills.

Lindsay's mercenaries followed their employer's lead down the hill, some staggering on foot as they ran too quickly, others leaning forward on the few horses dotting their ranks. Any attempt at a battle cry was lost beneath the shouts of Edzell's guards.

The air swirled with the sharp scent of battle.

Colin's steed pawed the ground with restless anticipation.

Arrows streaked from the tops of Edzell's turrets and sprang from the surrounding forest, whistling toward Lindsay's soldiers with lethal accuracy. There was nowhere to hide, no cover to shield them from the deadly waves.

Lindsay's men slowed.

The first flaming arrow was loosed. The blazing head sank into the ground near a pile of dried leaves.

Colin leaned forward in his saddle, his heart racing.

Lindsay's men drew closer.

Doubt flitted through Colin's mind for the briefest of moments.

Warmth washed behind him, and his peripheral vision caught the brilliant flare of light as one of the barrels exploded.

Boom! The pile of gunpowder on enemy lines burst into a ball of flames. His horse startled at the sound, but did not run.

Lindsay's mercenaries hesitated.

Lindsay did not.

The two explosions were the first of a series of the discharged gunpowder. The sky flashed and glowed. Black haze descended the battlefield and acrid smoke seared Colin's lungs.

The constant barrage of blasts behind him left his ears numb to any other sound.

If Brianna's plan did not work, he and his men had made themselves vulnerable to slaughter.

* * *

Brianna pushed her nose into the crook of her elbow in an effort to breathe through the singed air. She was safely out of sight behind the large bush, even though the dry, choking coughs around her were close enough to catch her nerves. She strained through the smoldering fog in an effort to see what transpired on the battlefield.

Were Lindsay's men retreating yet? Her ears throbbed from the explosions.

She'd counted four barrels that had discharged thus far, which meant only three remained. If the blasts weren't enough to make her uncle's men flee, all ran the risk of failure.

She could sit and idly watch no longer.

* * *

The battle cries of Lindsay's soldiers had fallen quiet. A vile black cloud surrounded Colin and his men. His body was tight, ready for attack. A breeze swept through the valley and ripped back the curtain of smoke.

Several of the men around the middle of Lindsay's hoard had turned and were running back up the hill.

They were fleeing.

Colin's heart pounded. Several fleeing men usually turned into an army of fleeing men. Fear was contagious. It was no victory, but it was a damn good start.

Lindsay veered off to the side of his men and thrust his sword into the air in an age-old display of the onset of war. A handful of Lindsay's guards charged toward Colin and his men.

Edzell's guards were ready.

They'd been ready.

Boom!

Another explosion showered Lindsay's soldiers with sprays of sparks and fire. More men in the back began to run.

A Lindsay mercenary leapt toward Colin's horse with his blade swiping, a blow easily blocked. Colin's sword slid into the soldier's chest with almost no effort, and the man staggered to the ground.

Boom!

A barrel behind Colin detonated at the same time as another gunpowder pile up the hill. Chunks of dirt and grass rained down upon them.

"I told you, they have cannons!" A Lindsay guard shouted in the distance. "Flee!"

A man in padded armor beside Colin dropped his blade and ran.

That was all it took.

The other men who fought with Edzell's men turned and sprinted from battle.

Boom!

An explosion followed them, and shouts of fear peppered the air. Lindsay's force rushed over the hill with more haste than they'd descended.

Brianna's plan had worked.

Colin turned to where Lindsay sat on his horse beside

the castle, shouting toward his fleeing army, jowls quivering with outrage.

Lindsay was the last to turn and run.

Colin snapped the reins, and his horse leapt into a powerful run. Lindsay would not be allowed to escape, not while he still had Magda's confession.

Brianna would never be safe until that parchment was destroyed.

* * *

Not a single enemy stood in sight as far as Brianna could see. Even her uncle raced for his own life.

But her joy at their victory was short-lived.

Colin streaked across the battlefield in determined pursuit of those who had fled.

What was he doing?

She ran from the cover of the surrounding forest, toward the cluster of Edzell guards. Their bodies were still locked in an open-stance battle position.

Jonathan's eyes went wide when he saw her. "My lady, you are not supposed to be here."

"Where is Colin going?" she asked. "He's running toward the mercenaries by himself. He can't—"

But Jonathan wasn't listening to her. His eyes were fixed on the hill, narrowed, determined. "Get in the castle now, my lady, and see the doors locked behind you."

Brianna jerked her head to where he stared, and her body went numb.

No longer did the crest of the hill stand empty. A procession of soldiers on horseback rode forward in an organized line, directly toward Colin.

Chapter Fifty

Colin flattened his body against his steed's muscular neck. The castle blurred past him, and the oncoming wind tore at his hair and clothes. Lindsay had gotten a head start, but he would not escape. He couldn't.

A warning triggered in the back of Colin's mind, but it was too late. Men on horseback rode over the top of the hill and descended toward Edzell. Toward him.

His body raged with power. He would kill every one of them before he allowed Lindsay to get away.

The flank of a large white horse blocked his path and forced his own steed to lurch to a stop. Colin's body continued its forward momentum and slammed hard against the thick black mane. Had he not been leaning forward, he would have surely toppled over.

The owner of the white horse would pay for the offense with his life.

Colin righted himself and glared into a face mirroring his own. Ian, his twin brother, stared back at him, his mouth locked in a hard line.

For the first time, Colin recognized the Highland attire of the men on the hill, the white leines wind-pressed against massive bodies, the plaids swathed around their waists, the family and friends he had not seen in years.

Finally they had come. Alec had done his duty.

A man with stark white hair and a golden-dyed leine sat on a powerful black horse behind Ian's white steed. Colin's stomach slammed to the ground.

When he'd sought Ian's help, he had not anticipated the

appearance of their father.

"I canna let that man escape, Ian." Colin pressed his knees into his horse's sides in an effort to go around his brother, but Ian headed him off once more.

"If you sought the man in fine clothes, he collapsed on the other side of the hill."

Colin paused. Surely Ian confused Lindsay with another man. Lindsay had never been wounded from what Colin had seen. "I must go see for myself."

The glowing remnants from the fires reflected off his brother's stern expression. "Aye, let's go then."

Ian clucked his tongue, and his horse cleared Colin's path for him to gallop up over the hill. Colin didn't wait to see if his brother followed, and he did not slow as he approached the dark-clad figure lying face up on the ground.

Lindsay's horse was no longer visible, nor were his hired guards.

Colin slid from his saddle and crouched near the bloated body. Lindsay's eyes stared at nothing. Though it was dark, no apparent wounds showed on the body, yet one of Lindsay's fists clutched the fabric of his jacket, just over his heart. The man was dead.

Colin slipped wide buttons free of their closures and heard a satisfying crinkle. He skimmed the silk lining of the jacket, the body still warm to the touch.

Colin found the folded edge of the parchment and plucked it free. Hands shaking with anticipation, he ripped it open and revealed Magda's scrolling handwriting.

Tension bled from his back, and his clenched jaw relaxed.

He had the confession.

Several piles of leaves around him still smoldered from the gunpowder explosions. Colin stalked to the nearest one. He would see himself forever rid of the letter.

He held the parchment to the embers of leaves and smoking earth. Flames snaked from the red glow and licked at the wrinkled page, devouring the offending material in a steady, golden-orange wave. He held on, watching its destruction until his fingertips blistered with heat. Only then did he set it to the ground and wait for the last corner to curl into a pile of useless ash.

The deed was done. Brianna was safe.

He turned to Ian and wrapped an arm around his brother's neck. "It took ye damn long enough to get here."

* * *

Distant shouts carried on the wind. Not frightened shouts, excited shouts. Brianna waited in the wide entrance of the castle, far enough away to fool Jonathan into thinking she was locked within the walls, but close enough to still hear what transpired.

Her palms were hot and slick against the cool stone wall behind her. The hollow thud of hooves trotting over soft ground became louder, closer.

There were no clashing swords, no oaths or angry words. No threat lingered from what she could hear or see.

Her pulse fluttered. She chanced a peek around the corner.

A group of men on horses stood beside Edzell's guards.

Highlanders.

Her chest swelled with the sight of an auburn-haired warrior astride a white steed.

Colin.

All the joy and elation slid from her swollen heart and pooled in her belly like ice. That was not Colin's horse.

She could no more stop her feet from flying over the grass toward her husband than she could stop the rapid beat of her heart. He sat too stiffly upon the saddle, his lips pursed to a sharp line. Something was wrong.

War was bitter and hard and uncertain. Men would not always return home. She knew that now.

Brianna's steps quickened with a rush of apprehension.

"Brianna." Colin's voice sounded behind her, hard and angry.

She spun around and found her husband marching toward her, streaked with filth and sweat. His copper hair had been pulled loose from the leather thong and hung around his face.

He swooped her in his arms, his expression fierce in the wavering light of distant flames. "Ye werena supposed to be here." Rage showed on his face, but it was desire that sparked in his gaze. His chest rose and fell with each deep breath hanging between them.

"My uncle, did he escape?" she asked.

"No, lass. I believe the excitement of battle was more than he could bear."

She hated the flicker of sadness that rose within her, yet she could not quell the emotion. For all his cruelty, the man had been her uncle. The last surviving member of her family.

She glanced around to ensure none listened. "What about the confession?"

The surrounding soldiers carried on around them with deep conversations and elbow-nudging boasts. For all the people surrounding her and Colin, they were invisible in light of the excitement of victory.

"I burned the letter myself." Colin cupped her jaw and tilted her head toward his. "It's over, my love. Ye are safe."

Warmth spread through her belly and pulsed low between her legs. She wanted to feel the softness of his lips and the rough scrape of his whiskers against her chin. Except…

She leaned back in his arms. "How can you be in two places?"

His teeth showed white against the soot staining his face. "I dinna think ye've met my twin brother, Ian."

Brianna turned back to where the man dismounted from his white horse in a smooth, graceful movement. This was the brother who inherited the land and was most likely only minutes younger than Colin. No wonder the slight had been so difficult for Colin to bear. No wonder he had sought land on his own.

"And dinna think we arena talking about ye sneaking onto the battlefield later, because we will, aye?" She looked up at Colin and found his brow lifted with the same stern reproach as the twin she'd mistaken for him.

He released his hold on her and kept one arm draped around her waist in a protective show of ownership and affection. "It's time for ye to meet my family."

Alec's light blue gaze caught her attention from several feet away. He gave a deep nod in greeting. If her eyes did not deceive her, he might have even offered a slight smile. She peered harder at him and found his scowl returned.

"Alec was sent for your brother?" she surmised.

"Aye, I knew when I was going to be arrested that I wouldna get a fair trial. I also realized that after yer uncle finished with me, he'd seek to harm ye and our people. I sent for Alec to get my brother." Colin's gaze caressed her face. "To protect ye."

Brianna's lips parted with words that would not form. She knew Colin's brother had been deemed more responsible. Having to seek Ian's aid must have been a difficult decision.

And Colin did it for her.

He nodded toward a man with snow white hair and shoulders so wide she idly wondered if he could fit through a doorway. "I dinna know my father would come too." The slight downward tug at his lips showed his displeasure. "It appears ye'll get to meet him as well."

Colin's brother strode toward them. "Lady MacKinnon, it's a pleasure to see ye finally." He shot Colin a hard look. "After all this time."

Colin nudged his brother. "I dinna want her seeing yer good looks and running off with ye."

Ian smirked. He didn't have Colin's dimple. Nor the slight lines around his mouth that showed when Colin grinned.

The man with white hair stepped between the brothers. He clasped Colin's arm with his own and gave an abrupt nod. "It's good to see ye, lad." He didn't smile at his son, but the glimmer in his eye showed an affection Colin most likely would never recognize.

Brianna craned her head up to see him. Laird MacKinnon regarded her with the same green eyes as both his sons. "Colin's done well to marry such a fine lass. I've heard many good things about ye, daughter."

Daughter. Her heart lifted with the endearment. She offered her greatest curtsy and regretted wearing the guard's clothes rather than a well-made gown. "It is a pleasure to finally meet you as well, Laird MacKinnon."

"The pleasure is all mine, lass. I look forward to getting to know ye more during our stay. For the time being, I'd like to speak with yer husband before I release him back to yer care." His unreadable gaze settled on Colin. "There is much that needs to be said."

Chapter Fifty-One

The great hall was silent. Too silent, too empty. Colin stood several paces away from where his father gazed out the window with one thumb thrust through the loop of his wide belt.

As a boy, Colin had never thought to find a man larger or more powerful than his father. Though the years had turned his father's blond hair to a clean white, Colin still held that belief.

How could an old man appear so imposing?

"Ye've no ever been good at making decisions." His father's booming voice echoed in the large room. The same volume Colin remembered, the same tone. The same words.

His father studied him with a stare that had not softened with age. If anything, his look had become sharper, more probing. "And I've no ever been good at admitting when I'm wrong." His head twisted to the side, and a deep, hollow pop sounded from within the back of his neck. "I was wrong about ye when I said ye wouldna be a good leader. Ye've proved that to me today."

Colin forced himself to keep his father's gaze, though the unruly adolescent in him wanted to glance away. "Ye dinna know what decisions I've made." A hot dagger of pain twisted in his chest. "Ye dinna know the people who have suffered for my actions."

"Ye have suffered more than they have."

Was his father not listening to what he said? "That's no true. If I hadna gone back into the manor, Brianna would never have been arrested." Regret scorched through him. "Marie would still be alive." He clenched his teeth, as if the force in his jaw could rip the pain from his words. "She is dead because of me."

His father's hands clamped onto Colin's shoulders, and his eyes lit with the fierce determination he was known for. "That her death weighs heavy on ye means ye understand yer wrong. Let it stain yer soul, let it burn into ye, lad, so ye learn from yer mistakes and prevent them from happening again, aye?" His grip eased. "Ye've been a good leader to yer people."

Colin opened his mouth to speak, but his father arched a brow and stopped the words from flowing before they could start.

"Alec told me everything ye've done, and I know he wouldna lie. He no ever has and he wouldna start now." He lowered his chin. "No even for ye."

His father released him and stepped toward the open window. He braced his weight against the frame overhead and nodded outside. "Ye've done well with this land and its people. Ye've grown up."

"Da, I dinna—"

His father grinned over at him. The rare smile softened his hard features, and the handsome man he had been in his youth shone through. "Who would have thought Colin MacKinnon would ever know humility?"

"And who would've thought my Da actually smiled?"

His father chuckled and pushed away from the window. He stared down at Colin and his mouth fell stern, but the sparkle in his eye remained. "I want ye to share the lairdship of the MacKinnons with yer brother. The way it should have been from the beginning."

Colin stared at his father, and the world around him stood still. Everything he had ever wanted was being given to him this very night.

And yet the price had been too high.

"Humility and speechlessness from my oldest. 'Tis a rare day indeed." His father clapped him on the back. "Though perhaps ye should discuss it with yer wife first, aye?" He nodded toward the open door behind Colin. "We'll talk in the morning. The choice is up to ye."

Colin turned and found Brianna standing in the doorway,

one slender hand resting against the painted wall. The pink gown she wore hugged her curves and made her skin glow like moonlit cream. Her hair was washed free of the effects of war and gleamed where it spilled down her shoulders.

His father's retreating footsteps echoed off the high ceiling. Only when they disappeared down the hall did Brianna make her way toward Colin, her smile hesitant.

His chest swelled with a joy he longed to share with the woman he loved. "Did ye hear?"

"I did." Her hands twisted against one another. "This is what you have always wanted."

Indeed it was. If the servants rushed, they could have Edzell packed in two weeks' time, and they could be back on the Isle of Skye while the weather was still warm. Back to the land of his birth, the castle he grew up in and the people who lived there.

Colin paused. The people he hadn't known for almost ten years.

Would his boyhood home feel as foreign to his memory as did the people?

He took Brianna's hands in both of his. So soft, so delicate.

Yet those hands had battled with the force of a warrior for Edzell's people.

Fulfilling his dream would force her to give up everything she'd fought for. And everything he had fought for alongside her.

"Are you not happy, husband?" she asked.

He glanced up and found her concerned gaze on him. "Ye dinna want to leave Edzell, do ye?"

"I don't understand what you mean," she said. Did he intend to leave for Skye without her?

"Ye've worked too hard to leave, Brianna. Ye love it here." His eyes filled with something somber. "Edzell is yer home." He rubbed a hand over his tired face and left a trail of black grit behind.

Brianna tried to swallow the thick lump of emotion in her throat. "And where is your home, husband?"

He caught a lock of her hair in the hook of his forefinger and let it slide through his grasp. "Wherever ye are."

She hesitated, uncertain what his words meant.

"Being laird of Dunakin Castle was a dream in my youth, a desire to possess what I felt belonged to me. Yet here, I've come to know the people, I've tended the castle, I've trained the soldiers." He stroked the back of his hand down her neck, and a wave of goosebumps raced across her skin. "I fell in love." He looked down at their clasped hands. "It took me getting what I want to realize it's no what I want at all. No anymore. No since ye." He pulled her toward him and pressed a kiss to the top of her head.

Hope quickened her pulse. "I don't want you to sacrifice something so important. Not for me."

"It's no sacrifice when I think what I gain from this decision. A loving home with a bonny wife." He watched her carefully at he spoke. "One who wouldna mind helping to keep the accounts again so her husband can train with the guards more often."

A giddy bubble rose in Brianna. "Truly?"

"If ye dinna mind."

Brianna shook her head vigorously. "Of course not."

"That isna all I gain in staying here." His hand moved between their bodies to cradle the gentle swell of her stomach. "I'll soon be a proud father." He brushed his lips over hers. "What will ye do if ye bear twins?"

A shy blush warmed Brianna's cheeks. "If they are girls, I have already selected their names."

"Oh?" He leaned back and his brows lifted.

She placed her hand on top of his. "Elizabeth and Marie."

His sharp inhale was slow to ease from his chest. "I dinna think finer names have ever been selected."

She rose on her tiptoes and planted a kiss on his lips. A soft, sweet kiss that simmered with a desire she could not ignore.

"I think we'll both need to bathe before bed." His grin displayed the dimple she loved so. "Preferably together."

Brianna tilted her head in a coy gesture. "I've already bathed, husband."

"Aye, but ye're all dirty again."

A glance at her clothes confirmed she was indeed grimy.

Black smudges showed on the light fabric where his hands had caressed her body. "It would appear that I am. Fortunately for us, a bath awaits us already."

He swept a kiss to her lips and nudged her toward the door. "We should hurry so it doesna get cold."

She nipped his lower lip, and the swell of longing deepened to a sharp tug. Her feet scuffed across the floor in hurried distraction before Colin lifted her into the soot-stained cradle of his arms.

His lips nudged hers. "I love ye, wife."

She arched her neck, straining toward the warmth of his mouth. "I love you, husband."

And she did, with all the heart-swelling affection any one person could possess, with no dread for the future, only eager anticipation of a life enlightened by love.

Acknowledgments

Once again, there are so many amazing people to thank for the creation of this book. Thank you to Laura for being steadfast and supportive of me during a harrowing life event that transpired during this book. Thank you to the incredible staff (Randall Klein, Sarah Masterson Hally, Brielle Benton, and anyone else I may have missed) at Diversion Books for their hard work and for taking the time to answer all my questions (Hannah Black, I miss you already!) and help me through marketing.

Thank you so much to the incredible groups who support me—my loving Lalalas, the inspiring Fire Breathing Flamingos and the fabulous First Coast Romance Writers. The Romance Writers of America is filled with authors who give selflessly and are always there to back a new author; I truly consider myself fortunate to be involved in such an amazing network of women.

Thank you to Margie Lawson for the invaluable knowledge I gained in the Immersion in 2014 (Jolaj and the Gang forever!)—I was able to apply some of that newfound knowledge in the revisions of this manuscript and feel it's stronger because of you.

Thank you to my beta readers who amaze me with their speed reading and whose honesty and opinion I value: Alli Searle who I think loves Highlanders as much as I do (and that's saying something!), Katie Couch who also acts as final editor on final reviews—I could never ask for a better Madikat than you. Thank you to my amazing critique partner, Hillary Raymer, who inspires me, encourages me and keeps my butt in line—I don't know what I'd do without you.

Thank you to my minions, parents and brother & sister-in-law for their amazing support. They completely blew me away with everything they did to help me market *Deception of a Highlander* and never stop telling me and everyone else how proud they are of me.

I'm so, so very fortunate to have so many wonderful people in my life.

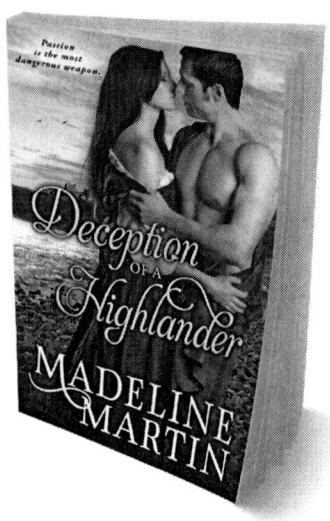

Available Now!

Scottish Romance doesn't get much steamier—or more dangerous—than a spy hunting her quarry, and losing her heart to him instead.

To pay a seemingly impossible debt, Mariel Brandon has become a spy for Aaron, one of England's deadliest minds. Aaron's latest mission for the sharp-witted and daring Mariel is to find two people in a heavily fortified castle on the Isle of Skye, a castle headed by the clan MacDonald and the powerful Kieran. Mariel is to seduce Kieran and get him to take her to Skye. If she succeeds, Aaron promises to let Mariel's young brother go, and to free both of them from their debt. If she fails, her brother will die.

What she doesn't count on is craving Kieran MacDonald almost immediately upon meeting him. Now Mariel must keep a secret from Kieran—one that could get them both killed—as she tries to form a plan that will save her brother, get her out from under Aaron's thumb once and for all, and keep her in Kieran's strong arms forever.

Madeline Martin lives in Jacksonville, Florida, with her two daughters and a menagerie of pets. She graduated from Flagler College with a degree in Business Administration and works for corporate America. Her hobbies include rock climbing, running, doing Mud Runs and just about anything exciting she can do without getting nauseous. She grew up in Europe and still enjoys traveling overseas whenever she can find the time to get away. Her favorite place to visit thus far: Scotland.

CPSIA information can be obtained at www.ICGtesting.com
Printed in the USA
BVOW04s1528011115

425147BV00004B/124/P